. . . er was born to an Am͟
͟ mother, and educated in the US, the UK, China
͟ Italy. She spent twenty-five years working, writing
͟ and raising her children in Japan and Singapore before
relocating to the UK in 2016. She is the author of the
novel *Lillian on Life* and has had short stories published
in *Ecotone, Good Housekeeping, Synaesthesia* and
Barrelhouse.

Praise for *Yuki Means Happiness*

'The theme of Alison Jean Lester's novel is the maternal
instinct, movingly evoked here in various guises. It's funny,
warm, scary – and thoroughly recommended' *Daily Mail*

'Beautifully rendered . . . Lester has the most wonderful
eye, capturing the little details of Diana's alien new life
with such simplicity and precision as to capture a rare
beauty in the everyday . . . Lester has constructed her
novel like an elegant piece of origami, every element deftly
arranged into something as close to perfection as I can
imagine' *National*

'With Alison Jean Lester's beautiful prose, the simplicity
of the narrative, and the uneasy complexities of her
characters bubbling to the surface, the plot is much more
than *what the nanny saw* . . . she has the Midas touch'
Mitford Society

Also by Alison Jean Lester

Lillian on Life

Yuki Means Happiness

Alison Jean Lester

JOHN MURRAY

First published in Great Britain in 2017 by John Murray (Publishers)
An Hachette UK Company

First published in paperback in 2018

1

A CIP catalogue record for this title is
available from the British Library

ISBN 978-1-84854-961-6
Ebook ISBN 978-1-84854-964-7

Typeset in Sabon MT by Hewer Text UK Ltd, Edinburgh
Printed and bound by Clays Ltd, St Ives plc

John Murray policy is to use papers that are natural, renewable
and recyclable products and made from wood grown in sustainable
forests. The logging and manufacturing processes are expected to
conform to the environmental regulations of the country of origin.

John Murray (Publishers)
Carmelite House
50 Victoria Embankment
London EC4Y 0DZ

www.johnmurray.co.uk

For Kiri-chan

I

When Naoki Yoshimura walked into Au Bon Pain on 14 July 1996, it led to the worst thing that has ever happened in my life. And also the best. At the time, I merely found it strange to see him again. It had been two and a half years. Still fine-featured and clean-cut, he had aged more than I'd expected.

It would be the second time I'd sat across from him with a job offer between us. The first had been in the autumn of 1993, when he and his wife, Emi, had travelled to Boston from Tokyo so that Emi could give birth in the States and get citizenship for their baby. The West Coast or Hawaii would have been a shorter flight for someone from Japan, but Naoki had done a master's degree in political science at Harvard, and still had friends in the area.

Back then, I'd been working at Mass General for the eighteen months since finishing my nursing degree, and I was on the fence about my job. Apparently I was quite good at caring for geriatric patients. The fretting and cantankerousness of the terminally aged didn't bother me in the way it did some of the other nurses, maybe because I dealt with it by not allowing them into the depths of my mind. I nodded and said, 'I know, I know,' stroking their filo pastry forearms. I took the best care I could of their bodies, and I stayed calm when they were anxious. I suppose that's something to be proud of, but I wasn't one of the ones who found satisfaction there. The elderly patients' conversation was often extremely funny, when they weren't depressed after surgery, and sometimes I could make them feel a bit more confident, a bit less lonely, but I never really connected with them. When I had the chance to be with children, by contrast, I was aware that it brought me right up out of my often withdrawn self. I asked repeatedly for the chance to try out paediatric nursing, but all the noises I made were deflected and ignored by the hospital.

Naoki's strange little advertisement somehow found its way onto the bulletin board in the nurse's lounge: 'Nurse needed for one month with newborn, Japanese family, excellent wages. Must be native English speaker. Must be very clean.' I can't imagine that many people responded to it, given the very short-term engagement, but I called right away, and was invited to visit Naoki and Emi for an interview.

Naoki (pronounced NAH-oh-kee) was probably five foot six to my five foot eight – not a huge difference – but when he opened the door to welcome me into the apartment I suddenly felt different in my body. Outside in the hallway I had walked, but following him into the sunny living room I galumphed. The feeling intensified when his wife got up off the couch to greet me. Nearly eight months pregnant, she was still the subtle one in the room. Maybe five foot one, with a long torso and slightly bowed legs, she possessed the porcelain beauty of an expensive doll. I know that sounds outmoded and idealistic, but it's still the truth as it appeared to me. Her eyebrows curved in identical arcs above her almond eyes and were so fine that I could imagine someone with a one-haired paintbrush applying them. Her nose was very straight, above lips whose defined Cupid's bow lifted the centre of the upper one into view in a way that implied sensuality, no matter what she was like inside.

Naoki sat down next to Emi on the couch, indicating a chair for me, and the early October sun shone on their hair. Before they asked me anything about myself, Naoki showed me a scar on his right forearm.

'I got this in Boston,' he said.

'Oh?'

'A souvenir.'

'A good one?'

'Yes, actually! That's funny, right? I fell on the ice, tried to hold on to a bicycle that was locked up to a lamppost, but the pedal, it was a dangerous pedal. It tore my coat and my skin.'

'That's a good memory?'

'No, no, it was the doctor. I went to Mass General for the stitches, and when the doctor was finished I was very impressed, so I said, "Very tidy stitches," and she said, "I used to be a tailor at Saks." I can't imagine a Japanese doctor ever making a joke like that!' He laughed with his mouth open.

I wasn't sure the doctor had necessarily been joking. It was possible that what Naoki couldn't imagine was a tailor becoming a doctor. Either way, though, I could see why she had made a good impression.

They didn't seem bothered by the fact that most of my experience was with the elderly – I sensed that they approved of it, possibly morally – and when I described my education, playing up how in-depth the paediatric courses had been and how recently I'd been registered (so I remembered that part of my education very well) they nodded as they listened. Emi's English was quite good – she'd been a Japan Airlines flight attendant before her marriage – so when Naoki spoke Japanese to her it never appeared to be in order to explain what I had said, but rather to comment on it. After one of these discussions Naoki asked me the one question in the interview I hadn't anticipated.

'What do you like to read?'

'Oh. You mean—'

'Books. Novels? History? What do you like?'

'Oh, well, at the moment it's spy novels.'

'I see. Who?'

'John le Carré?'

His face didn't indicate either approval or disapproval. He just said, 'What else? Music? You like music?'

'I do.'

He nodded. 'Classical music is important.'

That sounded final, so I nodded too, and so did Emi.

'We play classical music now, and we will continue when the baby is born. For the brain.'

'OK. That's nice.'

Naoki looked at Emi and asked a subtle question with his face, and she must have answered with hers, although I couldn't track it, and when he turned back to look at me it was a surprise when he said, 'So, we are happy. You can have this job.'

Yuki Yoshimura was born at 2.27 a.m. on 16 November 1993. When I visited the maternity ward at ten that same morning I was a bit bleary from having been woken up by

4

the excited call from Naoki, and from spending a fair amount of time wondering why he thought calling at three was appropriate.

I found Emi in her bed and Yuki in her clear plastic bassinet, both sleeping. The hair on that baby! Her face was so round and small but her hair was full of spring. I'd never seen a newborn with hair so lively. It looked like a bumper crop, entirely ready for the world, unlike Caucasian newborn hair, which in my experience seldom offered any protection at all. I wanted to pick Yuki up and feel her tender scalp for the fontanelle I couldn't see, but I didn't want Emi to find me handling her baby without permission, so I just stared at them. I wondered about the internal workings of Emi's body, the shape of her pelvis, which way her daughter had faced when her head emerged, whether Emi had needed stitches. I also wondered if they'd keep on sleeping and I'd end up leaving without having said a word to Emi, but then she stirred, and stretched, and winced. I said a quiet hello.

'Oh!' she said, and smiled as she tried to push herself up to sit. I stepped over to the bed and pressed the button to raise her upper body, and with that action I stepped into my job. That was the agreement. Naoki had paid me a sum to give Mass General one month's notice, and then once I was out of that job it was just under two weeks of waiting before Yuki was born. Now the waiting was over.

'How are you feeling?'

She smiled wanly. 'How to say? I think . . . like a shark attack.'

I had to cover my mouth not to bark with laughter, and it was a moment before I could speak. 'Oh dear. Here, let me get the shark for you.' I brought the bassinet closer to the bed. 'Very dangerous-looking, I agree.'

We both looked at Yuki for a moment, and then I asked if I could hold her. 'Of course,' Emi said, but when I reached for the baby she said, 'Wait a moment please,' and pulled a pair of surgical gloves out of a box on her bedside table, handing them to me as if I had simply forgotten that I'd need to cover my hands. If she had been a friend rather than an employer I might have questioned her, but she was the boss, and I pulled on the gloves before lifting her tightly swaddled infant into my arms.

'Oh! You are so good at picking her up!' Emi exclaimed. 'I do not know how to do it yet.'

'It's early,' I said. 'You'll learn today I'm sure.'

'I don't know. I think my hands are too small.'

It was true that mine looked Amazonian cradling Yuki's Christmas ornament of a skull, but the idea that any mother's hand could be too small was silly. 'You'll be fine,' I said, and unclipped the ID at the end of the bassinet so that I could read the details.

'One hand!' Emi exclaimed, as if I was doing acrobatics rather than holding a newborn.

I looked at her admiring face, and then at the ID. 'It says here that she only weighs about six pounds, so she's going to be very easy for you to hold. Please stop worrying, Emi, you're going to be fine.' Then Yuki began wiggling and arching and fretting. I waited through a few of the amusing grimaces that chased each other across her reddening face.

'She is hungry?' asked Emi.

'I'd say so,' I told her.

'OK,' she said. 'Wait a moment.' She undid the top two buttons of her pyjama top, then reached out her hands. I passed Yuki down to her and she settled the baby's head in the crook of her elbow, awkwardly, but that didn't matter to Yuki, who turned her face to the flannel-covered breast. The large, mahogany-purple nipple Emi opened her top to offer was exceedingly easy for Yuki to locate, but difficult to get her tiny mouth around. I wasn't aware of having a lot of preconceptions with regard to Japanese people, as I'd had no real contact beyond dinners in a few Japanese restaurants − polite? precise? − but clearly they existed in me, because I was deeply shocked that a Japanese nipple could be so large.

The month I spent attending to Yuki and her mother in their serviced apartment overlooking the Charles River, and keeping the frequently absent Naoki happy with a notebook full of eating and sleeping data, was both simpler and more complicated than I had expected. I was with Yuki from nine until noon every day, and again from five until after her bedtime feed at around eight. No one needed an IV or catheter, no one developed an infection, no bones were broken, no arteries fountained. I had to keep Yuki clean and warm, and to pay attention to the desiccation of her umbilical cord. I had to source the right sort of dough-nut cushion for Emi to sit on, as she had undergone an episiotomy, and each day I had to help her wind a thirty-two-foot piece of white cloth around her belly to support the tightening of her uterus. Easy. The difficult part was accepting that neither Emi nor Naoki wanted to learn how to do what I was doing. Paediatric nursing had always looked a lot like teaching to me – an effort to help both children and parents understand how to take care – but Naoki just wanted Emi to rest and to eat special foods to help her to recover and to keep her milk supply plentiful. Emi seemed to be just fine with that. Everything else was up to me.

Emi's industrious mother arrived two days after the birth, and stayed in the apartment with her for a week, which was as long as she thought Emi's father could survive without her. I didn't see any real need for my presence while she was in Boston – one extra pair of hands in surgical gloves seemed like enough to me – but it became clear that Emi's mother's role was to take care of Emi, and I was to keep Yuki happy. She had arrived lugging an entire suitcase full of dried foods, powders and pastes that I was told were the keys to postnatal recovery. Most of them were derived from rice, seaweed, fish and red beans, and she cooked them in combination with fresh fish, dark green vegetables and squash. For the week she was in Boston I arrived in the morning to delicious smells. Soy sauce, sugar and sesame oil. Miso and sweet rice wine. Fresh ginger and spring onions. And rice. There was always a rice cooker steaming in the corner. I learned that the smell of rice could be just as comforting as the smell of mashed potatoes or fresh bread.

One of my favourite memories of that time was when Emi's mother taught me how to make miso soup, and I actually started making it for Emi in the morning once she had left, partly because it felt a little bit like nursing – food is medicine; I wish more people understood that – and partly because I missed the smell of it. Cooking wasn't part of the arrangement, of course, but the job was pretty boring most of the time. I got really good at judging when the kelp and the bonito flakes had been simmering long enough before adding the miso, and at cutting the silken tofu into perfect little cubes.

My other happy memory of that month is the moment I recognised the transformation of Yuki's desperate, papery red legs and arms into pinker, fleshier, satisfied limbs. Of course it was Emi's milk that was nourishing her, but once Emi's mother had left I was the one doing the grocery shopping, so I took some credit in a trickle-down sort of way. Naoki expected the food I bought to be as fresh as possible, and this meant that the break between noon and five wasn't entirely time to myself, as I had to shop frequently. It also meant that I wasn't so much a nurse as a nursemaid. I never resisted these responsibilities, though, and not only because the pay was so good. It was only for a month, after all, and when it wasn't deadly dull, it was interesting to watch a new mother from another culture doing what was expected of her. She stood at the kitchen counter in her robe and slippers expertly wielding a cleaver I would have been afraid to handle. Her tiny hands were as deft with that heavy knife as they were at sprinkling the perfect number of sesame seeds on stewed vegetables, and it was so hard to believe she still didn't feel fully confident holding her baby, but in a way it makes sense. Practice is everything. Emi knew how to cook, so she was the one cooking. I was the one holding Yuki.

Emi didn't talk very much. We had conversations, of course, particularly if she was awake when I arrived in the morning and checked on how the night had been. But it

9

didn't always feel like we had to talk. She didn't show much interest in me, and I didn't mind that. The fact that Mozart piano concertos and Bach cello concertos were playing for most of the day meant there were few awkward silences.

When Naoki was in Boston rather than New York, where he was involved in the production of some sort of movie, I'd sometimes find him in the kitchen having coffee in the morning, and his face never failed to startle me. He was disarmingly cute when he smiled, but the folds of his upper lids came fully halfway down over his irises. To my untrained eye this meant his face always looked sad at rest, and it was always at rest when I walked into the kitchen in the morning. He looked tired, but he always told me that he'd slept well.

I don't know where he went after he finished his coffee. He'd place his mug in the sink and leave the room with a sweep of energy that I interpreted to mean I was expected to put his mug in the dishwasher. It bugged me that he clearly never considered doing it himself, but I also realised that if I didn't do it, Emi would have to. So I did it.

My unhappiest memory of that month came at the beginning of the third week, when Emi finally took a shower. Until then it had been sponge baths only, and she hadn't washed her hair at all.

'Actually,' she said at the door to the en suite bathroom, 'we are not supposed to wash our hair for thirty days.'

'Wow. You rebel.'

She laughed. 'We're not supposed to shower yet either.'

'Why not?'

'I think maybe so we don't get cold?'

'Oh. Don't showers warm you up?'

'We believe in baths.'

'You could have a bath.'

She glanced in the bathroom, and shook her head. 'This bath isn't deep enough.' She smiled at me, and shrugged, and closed the door.

While Emi was in the shower, Yuki did the explosive sort of poo that goes right up a baby's back, so I took her to the guest room and unwrapped her from her clothes and diaper on her changing pad on the double bed. As I did, the crisp little stump of her umbilical cord dropped off onto the pad. I decided to leave it there while I cleaned her with baby wipes; I'd pick it up when I came back from washing her. It had been sponge baths for Yuki as well since the birth, as I needed to keep the cord dry, but now that it was off I could give her a good soak in the baby bath in the kitchen.

I remembered the stump when I was about to lay Yuki down again to dress her, but I couldn't see it anywhere. I felt around for it on the patterned bedspread and on the floor, but the surgical gloves gave me limited sensation. I knew I had to get Yuki dressed quickly so Emi wouldn't think I'd left her naked for too long, despite the central heating, so I stopped looking. I heard Emi return to her bedroom as I was snapping Yuki into a tiny cardigan over her winter onesie, and I called out to her. 'Yuki's cord fell off!'

I heard her slippers slap into the room.

'How is she?'

'Fine! It's a lovely little belly button.'

I started unsnapping Yuki's clothes again to show her, and she said, 'Where is it?'

'It's here somewhere,' I said. 'I think maybe it fell off the bed.' I leaned back so that Emi could have a view of her daughter's tummy, but she gave it only a glance before scanning the wood floor. A worry line had appeared between her eyebrows. 'Or maybe it's on the bed?' I said, and did Yuki's clothes up again.

'We must find it,' Emi said.

'OK,' I said, and picked Yuki up so I could lift the changing pad away and feel for the stump there. Then I put her down on the far side of the bed, and took off the dry set of gloves I had put on after bathing her. 'You feel on the bed, Emi,' I said. 'You've just had a shower. I'll feel on the floor.'

We couldn't find it. Maybe it had attached itself to the arm of my sweater, or to my sock, and had then fallen off somewhere else in the apartment. Maybe I had wrapped it up with the wipes and the diaper and thrown it away. Whatever had happened to it, the disappearance caused Emi enough distress for her to go to the telephone in her bedroom. I sat on the far side of the guest bed next to the very relaxed Yuki and the extremely irritating gloves, and waited. Yuki's head had lolled to the side but her eyes were looking up towards me in that hilarious 'You have *got* to be fucking kidding me' way newborns have.

'Tell me about it,' I thought back at her.

Her eyes looked like they might resemble her father's. The little nursing blister on her top lip certainly made her mouth look like her mother's.

Emi appeared in the doorway looking even paler than usual. 'We must try to find it some more.'

'Really?'

'I have a box for it. We keep it.'

'Oh. I see.'

'Naoki said he told you to take care of it.'

'He did, yes.' We looked at each other while I did some thinking. 'He said, "Take care of the umbilical cord." I thought he meant I needed to make sure there was no infection there. I didn't realise that he meant "*Keep* the umbilical cord".'

She nodded, the worry line still a fixture on her face.

'I'm very sorry, Emi.'

She nodded again, looking very small and sad. I pulled on my gloves to pick Yuki up and brought her to Emi. 'Have a rest with Yuki,' I said. 'I'll look everywhere.'

I felt every inch of the apartment floor with my hands, and got the dirty diaper and wipes out of the trash to check there as well (for once I was grateful for the latex glove supply) but I couldn't find Yuki's cord stump anywhere. My unhappiest memory of that month is of Emi's face when she showed me the little box it was to be kept in, and having to accept that I had caused her such distress.

'Why do you keep the cord?' I asked her quietly, as if we were standing in a sacred place.

It was a long moment before she spoke.

'It is my connection to my baby.'

When I walked to the subway that evening, I felt awful. I did spend a moment thinking that forging more of an emotional connection with Yuki would have been a better use of Emi's energy than worrying about the dried-up remains of the physical connection, but I now think it's possible that Emi was less concerned about the loss than she was about Naoki's reaction to the loss. She was cheerful when I returned the following morning, though, and when

Naoki reappeared a few days later he made no mention of the misunderstanding.

On the day the family left Boston, I picked them up to take them to Logan Airport. Once the suitcases were in the trunk and Naoki and Emi were standing by the car, I finally saw the opportunity to touch Yuki with my bare hands. I opened the back door and lifted her out of Emi's arms to put her in the car seat I had borrowed, but first I held her against my chest. Naoki flinched a little and reached out a hand to stop me, but I already had her in the crook of my arm. I stroked her face with the skin of my fingers. A soft breeze lifted her copious hair, and when I touched that too it was so silky I could barely feel it. She stared at me, and I stared back. I wanted to take her back upstairs and watch her grow some more, but Naoki looked at his watch and said, 'Shall we go?'

At first-class check-in I shook Naoki's hand. I hugged Emi, probably for longer than she was comfortable with, and kissed Yuki's forehead. I doubted I'd ever see them again.

2

'Emi has left us,' Naoki told me in Au Bon Pain two and a half years later, with such disgust that I could only assume infidelity.

'Is she with someone else now?'

'Of course not.'

The only other reason I could come up with on the spot for a woman to leave her husband and young daughter was abuse, but if Naoki had maltreated her, why didn't he just say that they had separated? Clearly, in his mind at least, Emi was to blame for something. I didn't know what to say, so I switched to practicalities. 'Who's taking care of Yuki?'

'I am,' he said defiantly, tearing the end off his croissant.

'Oh! Did you bring her on this trip?'

He looked irritated at having to admit the truth. 'No. She is with my mother.' When I didn't say anything right away he told me, 'This is normal. My parents' house is next to my house. Yuki is happy. But my mother can't help all the time. And I want Yuki to speak English.'

I processed this. 'I see. So it's even less of a nursing job than last time.'

'Yes, but of course, if she gets sick . . .'

He didn't finish the sentence. Again, he offered me a generous wage.

'I don't know, Naoki,' I said. 'I'm sure I'd be advised against leaving nursing for babysitting.'

He made the offer more generous.

We agreed that we'd meet in the same place early the following morning, before I had to be at work, and parted.

I thought that I needed to think, but I doubt I'd walked even two blocks before I was seeing myself on my way to Tokyo to take care of a little girl who needed me. I had a job in a paediatrician's office by then, and there I'd taken care of other babies since the Yoshimuras had left Boston, but those babies were never handed over to me to care for so much as to get data about, or to vaccinate. Whenever I handled a wriggling infant I remembered holding Yuki so soon after she was born, and I always imagined the struggles of a butterfly before it burst from its cocoon. I wanted to see what Yuki had become.

Also, I'd lived in only one town and one city in my life, and they were thirty miles apart. Suddenly I saw an opportunity for an adventure. Not a physically strenuous adventure, or even an emotionally risky one, but a new and challenging experience. I was young (I'm still young, only thirty-four, but I know that back then I was even younger than my years), and I felt no hurry to solidify a career track given the steady demand for nurses and my good contacts in Boston. I also believed I had a sufficient picture (hard-working, quirky, precise) of the man who would be my employer.

The only danger I could imagine as I walked away from Au Bon Pain that Sunday afternoon was that of losing Porter, and I wasn't sure how much I minded that.

I'd met Porter at a cocktail party in the home of my mother's best friend, Clare, six weeks before. I usually turned Clare's frequent invitations down, but I hadn't seen my parents in a few weeks and I knew I'd see them there. We all lived in Boston, but we were all busy, so attending would be an easy way to kill a few birds.

Porter was the only other young person at the party. I was twenty-four; he was twenty-six. He was fine-haired and lanky, and when he talked he needed space, so we retreated through the open double doors to the butter-yellow foyer. He paced, and he wheeled his arms, but it didn't make him seem crazy, only unconventional. He told me about the job he'd just returned from: managing a Yemeni construction team in Abu Dhabi. He had names for all the guys – the 'little guys', he said, because Yemenis were small. 'There was one I called Clouseau, not just for his moustache but also his walk.' He smiled at something I couldn't see, striding two or three paces and turning around, swinging his arms, gathering steam as he talked, looking like an improviser coming up with a story on the spot. I felt silly standing there listening to him lie to me.

'I don't believe you,' I told him, and he stopped striding across the shiny parquet and pivoted on his heel.

'What?'

'I don't believe you worked with those people.'

'But . . . I did.'

'Things like that don't happen,' I said.

I was fully aware that Clare had invited this friendly, clean-cut young man so that we could chat and perhaps flirt, and now we were standing in plain view looking as if we were fighting. He even had his hands on his hips.

'How can you say that?' he said. 'This is my life I'm telling you about.'

I'd grown up in the small town of Patuxet, halfway along the coast between Boston and Cape Cod, and I'd been to nursing school in Boston. My father was a biologist; my mother was a career counsellor. The father of one of my friends was a professional cartoonist but beyond that I had no conception of careers other than what was conventional in the people around me. I couldn't bring myself to apologise because absolutely no part of me believed him. I'd never heard of Abu Dhabi, much less Yemen, and I'd never heard anything so far-fetched. I felt stubborn and embarrassed at the same time, so I started to giggle. His face relaxed, and I'm sure Clare's and my mother's did too.

Porter and I stayed in the foyer until my parents wanted to leave. I realised when they came out to get me that I'd started pacing when I talked too. Not as much as Porter, but some.

When he called to invite me to lunch a few days later, I said yes mostly because I felt bad for making him feel so dismayed at the party.

We sat at a table on the sidewalk. He ate a burger and I ate an interesting salad, and wasps buzzed around our plates, finding mine much more attractive than his. Porter ate with one hand and gesticulated with the other, expressing with his body as much as with his words that he was a man at loose ends. I had to concentrate so hard on getting wasps out from between the tines of my fork that I didn't say much. It was extremely hot, my dress was too heavy, and my hair was coming out of my ponytail. I was flushed and uncomfortable, and every time I looked up at Porter through my curtain of insects I saw a man from another world. He started talking about Hawaii. Nobody in Boston talked about Hawaii. Why was he talking about Hawaii?

'I've been thinking about going to check it out,' he said. 'What do you think?'

'I've never considered it.'

When he didn't say anything, I realised he had stopped moving. He was looking off to his left, out across the street, out across the world. It was disconcerting. 'Why Hawaii?' I asked, and put my knife and fork down for good.

That perked him up. He shrugged his shoulders happily. 'Seems like it would be weird. Exotic enough, but you could still get stuff. It wouldn't be quite here, and it *totally* wouldn't be there.'

'Where?'

'The Middle East.'

Porter had had to leave Abu Dhabi in a hurry (if you believed his story) because of a dispute with his employer. He was worried about his Yemenis under a less benevolent supervisor.

'Hawaiians seem nice,' he went on. 'Do you think you might like it? Do you like swimming?'

'I love swimming.'

'Great,' he said. 'Come with me.'

I didn't imagine he was serious, so I ignored him, but it came up again, every time we went out.

I liked him a lot. A *lot*. He told me stories that made me laugh, and I worked on suspending my disbelief, but I wasn't finding it easy to trust him. I felt like we were paddling at the edge of a lagoon, and the water was clear and fresh, but we'd begun moving away from shore and I knew I would lose my footing. I hated that feeling, and I avoided real intimacy, which is to say, sex.

What's the percentage of women who regularly climax during intercourse? Thirty? I get the impression that we're supposed to be sad about that, but I wonder how many women have felt like orgasm in company could actually send them around the bend, and are part of the seventy per cent because they *want* to be. How many have felt, as I have, that solitary orgasm is a simple, sweet, necessary thing, and that one in company is another animal entirely? A beast, in fact: something to be approached with caution, or avoided entirely, with no more sadness about it than one would feel on not being able to get out of the Land Rover on an African safari. I raise my hand. Am I alone?

I wasn't a virgin when I met Porter. I came to sex a bit late, I guess, always shying well before the final hurdle, but when a very magnetic, very persistent colleague finally proved irresistible, I enjoyed it. I enjoyed what I suppose I'd call the real weight of it – the way his hand descending to press my breast in bed was heavier than the same hand rising to cup my breast outside my apartment; the way a recumbent embrace forced air out of my lungs, making me hold my breath in an artificial sort of anticipation. I was anxious, absolutely, but I also didn't want him to let me go, and once the sharp snap of penetration was past, intercourse turned out to be a long, rhythmic hug I could find no fault with.

I went to bed quite happily with a more melancholic man after that first experience didn't become a relationship.

20

During one of his spells of depression and withdrawal I taught myself to climax. While people who climax easily during intercourse would no doubt assume that I would have desired sex more often after that, I actually desired it less. I made the mistake of telling that boyfriend what I'd learned in his absence, and he asked me to teach him. I didn't want to, but I knew I should. And then I wished I hadn't. Trying to show him how I did it myself made me feel confused and panicky, out of control, vulnerable and ashamed in a way I hadn't felt since childhood. Sex was suddenly much more complicated: layered, and frightening. A bed with a man in it came to look like a whirlpool to me. I thought I might drown.

As a result, when I told Porter I was going to take a job in Tokyo, wanting to get on a plane was sixty per cent desire to be useful and adventuresome and forty per cent desire to delay the decision regarding letting him get his hands on me. It's clear to me now that I was opting for a new and challenging experience abroad in part to avoid accepting the one – romantic love and its many terrors – that was developing for me at home.

'How long will you be gone?' he asked.

'Oh,' I said. 'What a good question. I didn't actually ask that.'

Porter nodded sadly. 'I see.'

'You do?'

'The duration of the job isn't important to you. Just the job is.'

Looking at his face – his already dear face – gave me a lump in my throat that felt like I'd swallowed tiny sparklers. I said something stupid about him not having to wait for me to decide about Hawaii any more, so he could just go ahead.

Consternation crinkled along his brow line. 'But you love how I smell.'

I nodded. He smelled like fresh hay.

'Do you know anyone else who smells like hay?'

'No,' I said thickly, and tried to clear the sparkler from my throat. Now it felt like it was oozing warm water as well as sparkling. 'I'm sorry,' I whispered.

Then he snapped his fingers as he always did when he'd just had an exciting idea. When I looked up at his face he was smiling.

'What?'

'We're not done,' he said, 'even though you're crying. Actually, because you're crying.'

'I'm not crying.'

'Sure.'

'I'm not,' I said, and pushed him playfully, released from my suffering by his cocky kindness.

'Mark my words,' he said, practically dancing, and tapping me on the nose. 'We're. Not. Done.'

Those three words rang in my ears as I prepared to move to Tokyo, and depending on my mood they were either threatening or thrilling. It was both a wrench, and a relief, to leave him.

3

Naoki met me at the airport. It was August, which is typhoon season, so the descent into Narita Airport was bumpy. After about half an hour on the road, the already dark sky turned charcoal, and the clouds fire-hosed rain at the windscreen. The traffic on the crowded expressway slowed to a crawl, and I had no view at all of the landscape we were driving through. All I could see was water. All I could hear was water. Our general chit-chat stalled, and I just observed Naoki as he tried to perceive the cars around us through the deluge. Every once in a while a gust of wind slapped the car and rocked it. Naoki had both hands on the steering wheel and his eyes on the two disembodied red lights in front of us.

'How will I see the exit?' he asked, and I tried to put my mind to the question, but of course I couldn't help. I looked at my watch, but could barely see the hands, and in any case, I wasn't sure whether I had changed it to Japan time on the plane or not. The humidity in the car was so oppressive I imagined I was having difficulty breathing, so I shouted to Naoki, 'Can you please turn up the air conditioning?' He looked annoyed at having to sort out better air for me, but once it started flowing I'm sure both of us started feeling less helpless.

Naoki took an exit – I don't know if it was the exit he had intended to take, but he made it work – and after a while there was more space between the raindrops and a little more light to see by, and we were driving along an elevated road between huge flat buildings. Then we drove under another elevated road, and the sudden protection from the rain, the relative quiet, made me feel like we were floating. Finally, after a whole Etch A Sketch of severe corners, Naoki brought the car to a stop on a narrow two-way street, next to some cement steps bisecting a short, steep slope of low shrubs.

It was still raining quite heavily but the wind had died down. I took off my seat belt but Naoki didn't move to get out of the car right away so I turned to him for a cue. He was looking down at his hands. He flicked me a smile before looking down again and saying, 'Yuki is looking forward to meeting you.'

'That's great.'

'There's just one thing, though.'

'OK.'

'It is better if you don't talk to her about Emi.'

'Oh. It is?'

'Yes.'

'But—'

'It is. It is better. Emi left Yuki, and it is better.'

Before I could think of what to say he slid an umbrella up from between his seat and the door with a 'Wait here'. He opened the door a crack to unfurl the umbrella and got out. He took my suitcase from the trunk and up the steps, leaving it inside the front door, then came back down to escort me up to the house. We jostled together as we climbed the narrow steps, and then I was inside the dark entry hallway without him for a moment while he shook and furled the umbrella. The floor was stone and the beige walls looked like stucco, but I smelled wood, and salty meat.

Naoki called out when we were both inside and the door was closed behind us. A woman's voice sang out in response, and Naoki gestured me forward about ten feet to where the stone hallway ended and the floor rose a step and became wood. 'This is where we take off our shoes,' he told me. I put my wet sneakers next to his wet loafers on the floor in front of a shoe cabinet, and followed him past a closed door (toilet) and a staircase on the right, into a dining area with a kitchen to the right and a straw-mat-floored room to the left. He stepped aside, and there was Yuki sitting in a high chair at a wooden table.

'Hello, Yuki! I am Diana!' I blurted, which was probably rude. I should have waited to be introduced to her grandmother first, but it was so amazing to see that child, all filled out and with a shiny bob of fine hair, sitting up, holding a spoon!

'Harro,' she said, unprompted, and returned her attention to the cut-up sausages dotting the rice in her bowl.

'Please correct her pronunciation,' said Naoki before introducing me to his mother. He was her spitting image, minus the chignon, and she smiled and bowed, and I smiled and bowed and thought how different meeting her was from meeting my own mother, who pumped your hand when she met you, shoulder and elbow way up high. No one pumped my hand on the day I arrived in Tokyo. Or on any other day I spent there.

'You can call her Yoshimura-san,' Naoki told me. Yoshimura-san said something and Naoki told me she had asked whether my flights hadn't been too tiring. He interpreted my answer – that the drive from the airport had been the most stressful part of the journey – and we all laughed politely. Then there was talk of the weather. I wanted to stay with Yuki but Naoki encouraged me through open paper-covered sliding doors into the straw-mat-floored room – the tatami room. The floor gave a little underfoot. Shelves and boxes of toys lined the wall on the right. The wall on the left had a recessed area which looked to me like a better place for storage but which contained instead a hanging scroll painting of nothing more than three small dragonflies, above a rough brown vase holding a single branch, with a single flower. I remember thinking the vase ugly. We looked out the floor-to-ceiling sliding glass windows at the rain. Less than ten yards away stood his parents' traditional, dark wood house. From a corner of the eaves hung a chain, all the way to the ground, and down the chain poured the powerful but obedient rain. Where I came from, rain from a gutter was encased in metal, and the metal was ugly. There, though, the rain did the encasing, and the effect was mesmerisingly lovely.

When we returned to the dining area I noticed a dish cabinet with a large stuffed red fox standing guard on top of it. The fox's body was parallel to the wall and its head was turned as if it had just heard something dangerous, or perhaps delicious, off in the distance. Seeing it gave me a shift in my sense of place. The fox's regard was so intense and its body so energetic that for a moment I believed that it was the one standing on the crust of the earth, and we were functioning beneath it. Yoshimura-san noticed me staring at it, and Naoki noticed her notice me.

'Bancooba,' he said.

'Sorry?'

'I bought the fox in Bancooba.'

'Oh. Sorry, I don't know—'

'Bancooba. Canada. My honeymoon was in Bancooba.'

'Oh! How nice. I hear Vancouver's a great city.'

'Yes.'

'You'd recommend it for a honeymoon?'

'Many Japanese go there for their honeymoon.'

'I see.'

'Shall we go upstairs?'

'Could I go to the bathroom first?'

'Of course.'

'Diana,' Yuki said, clear as a bell, and my heart jumped.

'Yes, honey?'

She grinned. 'Diana.'

'Yuki.'

'Diana.'

'Yuki.'

'The door is after the stairs,' said Naoki.

The toilet was mystifying, more like Captain Kirk's chair on the *Starship Enterprise* than any WC I'd ever visited. A Washlet, it was called, and it had a panel of electronic controls for a range of bidet functions just where Kirk's controls appeared, but I couldn't read any of them that first day. Even a stylised water spray under a stylised bum escaped my understanding. Not that I wanted to use any of them. I just wanted to pee and then to make the pee go

27

away. I didn't dare press anything, so in the end I had to go out to the kitchen to ask Naoki how to flush.

I'd thought he would just explain to me but he walked me back into the toilet. My face burned red as we leaned over the yellow water together and he showed me that there was a very discreet square button in the usual place on the side. I'd been so dazzled by the technology that I hadn't even thought to look there.

Naoki retrieved my suitcase and took me upstairs to show me my room. He also showed me his bedroom on the left of the short hallway, the toilet and bathroom opposite the stairs, and Yuki's room next to the bathroom and opposite mine.

'She sleeps in my room, though,' he said.

'Oh.'

I knew some people whose children joined them in the night sometimes, but no one who slept with their kids the whole night through. I remembered that Yuki hadn't had a crib in Boston, but I hadn't imagined that she might still be sleeping in her parents' bed at two years old. I was even more surprised that she slept with her father now her mother was gone. The double bed was low and covered in stylish grey sheets, and didn't broadcast 'family' at all. It was so much a bachelor's bed that if there hadn't been the arm of what appeared to be a stuffed monkey poking out from between the pillows, I might not have believed him.

Naoki didn't seem to think I'd find it at all strange. 'All her clothes are in her room,' he continued, and then encouraged me to unpack while Yuki finished her lunch.

Was I hungry? I didn't know. My head was spinning. Naoki thought I should eat something, and said he'd ask his mother to prepare a small meal for me while I put my things away. He returned downstairs and I blinked at my room – wooden floor, single bed, two-door wardrobe, desk; above the desk, a sliding window, open. I stepped across the small square of floor and looked out the window. It gave me a view of the narrow street to the side of the house – even narrower than the one in front – and the three-storey apartment building opposite. That was all. I listened to the rain, and to a ringing in my ears that sounded like the engines of the jumbo jets I'd flown over on, as if I hadn't landed yet.

Yoshimura-san had prepared something she called 'pizza toast' for me. 'She wasn't sure if you like Japanese food,' Naoki told me, and I tried not to look disappointed, thanking her as I sat down. I thought I'd hate the pizza toast for not starting my adventure with a sharp local flavour, but it was absolutely delicious and I wished she'd made twice as much.

Yuki, still in her high chair, watched me eat. I must have been curved uncouthly over my plate, because she tipped her head sideways and leaned forward to get me to look at her. She said something.

'She's asking you if it is delicious,' Naoki told me.

'Mmmm, yes!' I told her. 'It's yummy!'

'Delicious,' Naoki said.

'That's right. It's really yummy!' I didn't know if Yuki had understood me, but she was smiling from ear to ear, so we laughed together.

'Delicious,' said Naoki. 'Teach her "delicious".'

4

My body thought morning was night when I woke up in Naoki's house the first time. Naoki was standing in my bedroom doorway, repeating my name to drag me into day.

'I know jet lag,' he said when I finally opened my eyes and tried to blink the sand away. 'You will not get up if I don't wait here.' He disappeared from the doorway only when I was standing unsteadily by the bed in the big Red Sox T-shirt I slept in. Once he was gone I turned back towards the bed but he said my name sharply from the doorway again. He did know jet lag. I would have climbed right back in. I had to stand under the shower for a long time, turning the water from warm to cool and then even colder, before I started feeling less like a torture victim, more like a person who had travelled willingly to that house.

Downstairs, the sun was streaming in through the glass doors of the tatami room, highlighting the colours of the toys and the absence of any child playing with them. 'Where is Yuki?' I asked.

'I took her to my mother. I am going to show you the supermarket.'

'She could have come with us,' I said.

'Next time,' he said. 'You need to concentrate.'

He showed me where everything was in the kitchen, and sat with me while I had instant coffee and a piece of toast.

'Can you show me where a pharmacy is as well?' I asked.

'Are you sick?'

'No. I'm a nurse. I need to know where to get medicine.'

It was as if he'd forgotten why we'd met, why he'd employed me the first time around. 'Oh! Yes. There is one. I don't know how you will understand yet, though. Everything is in Japanese.'

'I'm sure I can find a common language with the pharmacist,' I told him, and he looked at me blankly.

'They'll recognise the name when I tell them what medicine I want.'

He nodded. 'Good. That's good.'

Outside the weather was hotter than it had been in Boston forty-eight hours before, and upsettingly humid. I'd never seen a photo of a sweating Japanese, and hadn't imagined sweating there myself. Mentally foggy, dazzled by the sun, disconcerted by the wet air, I made my way carefully down the stairs to join Naoki on the street.

'Is this humidity normal?' I asked him.

'Yes.'

We walked past boxy houses, low-rise apartment buildings and a playground on our way along his street. Above us electric power lines gathered in huge knots around concrete poles standing closer together than any I had ever seen. We came to a small intersection and Naoki stopped next to a utility pole at the corner. 'This is our address,' he said, pointing to a sign attached to the pole, a line of Japanese characters above a hyphenated pair of numbers.

'What's the street called?'

'Nothing,' he said. 'These little streets don't have names. But the blocks have numbers. This says *"Nishi Azabu"*. That is the part of the town.'

'What does it mean?'

'*Nishi* is west. *Azabu* is, well, it is a type of cloth.' He pointed at the sign again. 'This is the *choume* number and this is the block number.'

'Chomay?'

'Yes. So you just remember this sign, and turn right here when you are coming home.' He started walking again, turning left.

After about fifty yards the street we were on met a much bigger road.

'This is Roppongi Dori.'

'Big enough to have a name,' I said.

Black cars, grey cars, white cars, bright green taxis and cute snub-nosed trucks flowed steadily past us on either side of the massive superstructure of a raised highway. We turned left and were mercifully on the side of the road in the highway's shade. The buildings shot up, and suddenly there were words everywhere, but nothing I could read right away, which gave me the same sensation that comes from rolling a rubber band between finger and thumb, only in my eyeballs. Somewhere along the way to the supermarket I saw a large sign outside what might have been a restaurant. At the top of the sign it said 'MONTHLY EVENT', but everything listed underneath was in Japanese. I put my hand on Naoki's arm to stop him walking, and pointed to the sign.

'Can everyone read that?'

'What?'

'The English words. Does everyone they want to attract know how to read English?'

'Probably.'

'Wow.'

'Not speak, maybe, but we all know the alphabet.'

He looked at the sign some more. 'And a lot of the Japanese here is actually English.'

'You're kidding.'

'No.' He stepped up to the sign. 'This one says *kurouzudo paatii.*'

'That's not English.'

'Closed party. *Kurouzudo paatii.*'

'Then why not put the English?'

'No. They wouldn't do that.'

'Then why put the English at the top?'

'I think, to be attractive. To seem modern. It's decoration.'

'That's interesting.'

'Like Americans get Japanese tattoos.'

I laughed. We started walking again.

'I want Yuki to speak better than that,' he said.

Like all the supermarkets in my experience, the one Naoki took me to that day offered vegetables and fruit at the front, and meat and dairy products were in refrigerated displays at the back. Otherwise I was lost as to how the items were organised because I didn't understand what they were.

'Here is soy sauce,' Naoki said, leading me into a central aisle and gesturing at a section of shelves at least five feet tall and easily eight feet long.

'Which one do you use?'

Naoki reached out and chose a tall bottle. 'Kikkoman.'

'It doesn't say Kikkoman.'

'Yes it does.'

Of course it did. I told myself to remember the hexagon with the little insect thing inside it on the label. Naoki took me around the rest of the store pointing out his preferred rice, his preferred miso paste, his preferred brand of kelp. When we arrived in front of bonito flakes he said, 'Any of these types is OK,' and started walking off again.

'Wait!' I said. 'So how do I choose?'

He thought that was funny. 'It doesn't matter.'

'Price?'

Finally he seemed to take pity on me, and walked back to where I was still standing. 'Yes, price is fine. Choose by price. Sometimes I will bring back the dried fish, and you can make the flakes yourself. That is better.'

Before we left, he bought some sashimi for lunch. 'I will teach you how to use the rice cooker,' he said.

I had expected to feel more at home in the pharmacy, so I was completely unprepared for the riot of firetruck red, royal blue, lime green, fluorescent yellow and hot pink that spilled out onto the sidewalk in bins of bottles, cans and canisters, and racks of make-up sponges and tooth-brushes. The large signs advertising the prices were covered in exclamation marks and starbursts. Inside it was the same, even back by the pharmacist himself, where I was accustomed to things being a bit more sedate, a bit more earnest, a bit more white and clean and antiseptic. Sure, he was wearing a white coat, but the drugs on the shelves behind him were much more colourful than the ones we dispensed in the States, and the whole establishment gave the impression that, of all the shops on the street, the pharmacy was really the place to be, and taking medicine was wonderful fun.

We retraced our steps along Roppongi Dori, and after a couple of long blocks Naoki said, 'Where do we turn?'

My stomach dropped. Pop quiz.

'I don't remember. You didn't tell me how to remember.' That came out whiny.

'You are right. We turn right after this building.'

There wasn't a shop at street level, so it looked like an apartment building, or maybe an office building. The second floor had two-toned stripes of stone. 'Turn right at the striped building,' I said out loud, making Naoki look back over his shoulder, scrutinising it as we turned.

'Now you find the sign I showed you,' he said, and I was so rattled that I felt like crying with relief when I did.

Leaving the sound of the cars and all the visual stimulation behind, closing the door on it and stepping into the cool dimness of Naoki's entry hallway, I felt a relief that I would come to look forward to every time I went out. Back out of my shoes and standing on the gently yielding tatami under the humming air conditioner, I was no longer aware of the cars and the concrete and the millions and millions of people around me. The only sound I could discern from outside the house was the *zinggg-zinggg-zinggg* of cicadas calling for mates.

'Hemp,' Naoki said from the dining area, holding a small dictionary.

'Sorry?'

'*Azabu* means hemp cloth.'

Naoki's mother had always been a housewife. His father, the CEO of a major conglomerate, had a puffy rectangular head on top of a heavy body, and wore thick glasses over his baggy eyes. It was hard to discern his genes in Naoki, who didn't seem to share his father's empire-building inclinations either. Naoki went to his movie-production office in the morning, but never wore a dark suit like his father did. He left the house in slacks and a shirt when the weather was fine, and added a sweater, and then an overcoat, as it grew colder. He often stayed out late, though, like his father did. More and more often, in fact. I mainly interacted with him on the weekends. And I hardly interacted with his parents at all. That gave me hours and hours of not mentioning Emi to Yuki, wondering if I'd ever understand what had happened to make her abandon her child. I thought back to my time with her in Boston, wondering if I had seen but not recognised the seeds of post-partum depression, but I didn't have any experience to help me decide one way or the other.

I didn't like pretending Yuki had no mother, but just as with the surgical gloves, I agreed to it to keep the job. It wasn't too difficult to steer clear of the subject with Yuki about ninety per cent of the time, but it came up when I was reading to her. Naoki had a selection of children's books in English, including *The Very Hungry Caterpillar* and *Dear Zoo*, which were no trouble because they only involved creatures and fruits and vegetables. I hadn't had *The Cat in the Hat* in my hands and a child on my lap since babysitting in high school, so I'd forgotten about the mother in that one. ' "I know some new tricks," said the Cat in the Hat. "A lot of good tricks. I will show them to you. Your mother will not mind at all if I do." ' Reading that, I stopped and shifted my focus to the top of Yuki's head to see if I could divine any emotion there. Eventually she looked up at me to see why I wasn't reading any more, so I carried on, realising that Yuki didn't know what the word 'mother' meant, any more than she knew what 'tricks' meant, or 'mind'. It was at the end, when the mother came home, that Yuki pointed and said something. I didn't understand enough Japanese at that point to know what it was.

I retired *The Cat in the Hat* just to be safe, and went out on my second Sunday to the bookstore I'd read about in my copy of *Gateway to Japan*. I hadn't felt brave enough to venture outside Naoki's neighbourhood on my first Sunday off, and I'd stayed in on the Saturday evening as well. I told myself I liked spending my evenings at home with a book, and it was true. But I was hiding. Having been so intent on adventure when leaving for Tokyo, my feet were suddenly cold. Now that I had a compelling reason to go out, though, I pulled myself together.

I turned left at the striped building and walked along Roppongi Dori, noting the pharmacy with fondness simply because I recognised it, and descended into the subway for the first time. I bought the right ticket. Mental pat on the back. The trains weren't crowded in the late morning on a Sunday, so I had a seat for the three stops until I had to change to the above-ground Yamanote Line at Meguro

Station. There, I exited with most of the people in my carriage. At the ticket machines I watched a few people buy their Yamanote Line tickets before buying my own (pat on back), and climbed the stairs to wait for the train that would take me north to Ebisu, Shibuya, Harajuku, Yoyogi and then Shinjuku.

All the seats were full but there was room to stand without feeling crowded. I reached up to hold one of the hanging handles, considered how the bottle in the advertisement for something called iichiko looked a lot like the bottle for Calvin Klein One perfume, and then looked down at a head of shining sprayed curls cascading from either side of a very straight, very white parting. The curls descended towards a skirt of many-layered black lace above narrow black lace-up boots. The hands on the lap were in short black gloves, despite the heat. Maybe a lot of Japanese people actually didn't sweat. I looked out the window at the flat buildings we were passing, hearing numbers in my head because those were the only symbols on the advertising that I could read, other than the McDonald's sign. I looked down at the seated young woman's head again. There was black glitter in her hair. As we approached Harajuku she seemed to be getting ready to get up, so I stepped back out of her way, and she made eye contact and smiled at me. The black crack she had painted down the left side of her ghostly face swayed out and back, and I registered the care she had taken in making a very slight seepage of painted blood look real. Her eyes were pink, either from the face paint, I imagined, or from how early she'd had to get up to dress and apply the make up, or both. No one was staring at her but me.

It seems like most people now know about the tribes of extravagantly dressed young women and men who gather to see and be seen on the bridge at Harajuku, but I didn't. I also didn't know the size of Shinjuku Station, and the resilience required to find your way to your exit when there were over a hundred to choose from. Over a *hundred*. Standing at the bottom of the stairs with so many people moving around and past me, not one of them unsure of their direction, it was impossible not to feel like I'd rung the wrong doorbell, showed up at the wrong party. It would have been a relief to turn around and go back to Naoki's, but enough of me wanted to be able to pat myself on the back again. If I couldn't find the bookstore, I decided, the two pats on the back I'd already given myself didn't count. That got me moving forward, and I found my way to the ticket gate and a man in a black uniform and a hat very like the one worn by the police in Boston. He didn't smile, but he didn't look afraid of what might come out of my mouth either, so I said, 'Books Kinokuniya?'

'Yes,' he said, and came out of his glass box by a door on the other side of the ticket gate and encouraged me to come through to join him. Then he took me by the elbow to the centre of the area and indicated with a slow cutting motion just how straight I needed to walk, and with a slight crinkling of his eyes, a slight sharpening of his focus, just how far. 'Easto exito,' he said, and went through the motions again.

'Oh, OK, thank you!' I said, and started walking in the direction he had indicated, hoping that the fingers of his firm hand had cast a spell that would lead me straight to the exit. They hadn't, but they got me going one more time, and even when I was lost again I didn't want to go back home so much because I was closer to my goal. People were nice to me when I walked up to them wearing my sweetest face and said 'Books Kinokuniya?' I mirrored the way they bowed when I thanked them, and after twenty minutes of effort I made it, sweating, onto the escalator of the store.

I wasn't alone in the international children's book section, as it was a perfect destination for a family outing on a hot weekend. Non-Japanese and partly Japanese children of all sizes sat on the floor to read or look at pictures, and parents browsed and chatted. I wondered if I looked like a parent to them. Maybe they'd imagine that I'd left the kids at home with their dad, or maybe that he'd taken them to a swimming lesson, or for a bike ride. Part of me wanted to join the chat, but I didn't want to admit to being a nanny. I knew that when I returned to the States, telling people I had left my nursing job for a stint as a nanny in Japan would sound exotic rather than idiotic, but I couldn't be sure that foreigners in Japan would see it that way. Anyway, hanging out with other foreigners wasn't part of the adventure I'd imagined for myself, and now that I'd made it to the bookstore, I was back to patting myself on the back for my audacity.

I bought *Opposites* by Sandra Boynton (animals only, and the grown-up dinosaur next to the hatching dinosaur looked as if it could be any passing dinosaur). The store also had *We're Going on a Bear Hunt*, and I bought that because the children go out and have an exciting adventure with their dad and there's no obvious mother at home when they rush back into the house and hide under the bed covers.

I wished that Yuki were home when I got back to the quiet house on that Sunday, and that I could have been tasked with putting her to bed. The house was cold without her. But Naoki was out, and when Naoki was out on my days off she slept at her grandparents' house. I had to wait until Monday morning to see her again.

Receiving the huge smile she gave me when I went next door to get her was like eating honey off a spoon. I picked her up and squeezed her close to me as I crossed the stepping stones in the garden between Naoki's parents' house and ours, counting them off, making sure even coming home was a learning experience.

Straight after breakfast I sat cross-legged on the tatami and sat Yuki in the well between my thighs, opening *We're Going on a Bear Hunt* in front of us. When we came to the drawing on the last page, Yuki said, '*Mama wa?*' I didn't know what to say, so I didn't say anything right away, and she repeated the question. '*Mama wa? Mama wa?*' She waited again, so I asked the question in English, 'What about the mama?' Now that I'd asked the question she waited for me to answer it, but I didn't. 'What about the mama?' I asked her again, hoping she'd try and imagine an answer herself, but of course she was much too little for that. Even if she'd tried, she would have tried in Japanese, and I probably wouldn't have understood. She asked me again, '*Mama wa?*' and I asked her again, 'What about the mama?' I smiled and raised my shoulders as if we were playing a fun little game, but she began to repeat the question over and over, rocking back and forth on my lap. I was tempted to tell her I didn't know, but I stopped myself. 'Where's the papa?' I asked her instead. '*Mama,*' she said.

'Papa,' I said. 'Where's the papa? Is the papa in bed?' Her clever young brain couldn't reject the question, and her body grew still. Energetic, but still. She looked at the book again and pointed a tiny finger at the dad.

I retired that book too, and on subsequent days off I brought home everything by Sandra Boynton I could find.

5

Yuki was physically robust despite being so petite. She did indeed have her mother's Cupid's bow, and her father's narrow eyes. The fold of her eyelids had her viewing the world through down-pointing lashes, which made her look very modest, as if she were always standing behind a fine beaded curtain, but she seemed to be able to see perfectly well. Her lids closed almost entirely when she was happy, retracting her eyelashes and giving her eyes the upside-down U look of a happy cartoon character. She was one of those children who could take the heart right out of your chest.

She enjoyed acquiring language, and I was touched by her willingness to learn and her efforts to please me as we struggled with each other's languages and made each other giggle. She loved to draw, and the only time that I had trouble handling her, other than when she was extremely tired, was when she couldn't get me to understand what her squiggles were. Not understanding each other was a serious challenge, but I read to her several times a day, and we watched Japanese kiddy TV each afternoon for at least an hour. Within the first week I learned to understand when she was saying 'One more time', and she learned to understand when I was saying 'Wait, please'. Soon after that I picked up the words for delicious, happy, tired, difficult and ouch, while Yuki worked on please and thank you, and on foods and colours.

'What colour is that?' I'd ask every time we passed a big plastic bin outside the neighbourhood dry cleaner ('Fashion Cleaner Paris' – the only sign on our street in English).

'Bahliew,' Yuki would answer proudly. It also sounded a bit like 'Bahdiew'.

'Blue. That's right!'

Blue in Japanese is *ao*, pronounced sort of like 'ow', which was how I remembered it: When you're black and blue you say 'Ow'. I didn't know how Yuki remembered blue.

She took ballet classes on Wednesday afternoons, and that was a great place for me to learn vocabulary. I sat with the other little girls' mothers on chairs along one wall of the studio, so we could hear everything. The teacher was unusually tall and lanky, with remarkable confidence and an unremarkable face. She spoke quite slowly for the little children, and repeated herself a lot, so I had time to catch individual words. Sometimes she was actually speaking English – she said *ahppu* (up) and *dahn* (down) a lot – and of course she used French words too (*purieh* for plié and *guran purieh* for grand plié), but she used a lot of useful Japanese, and I was learning all the body parts from her.

One day she had been saying *oshiri no ana* a lot while leading the little girls in their matching pink leotards through their grand pliés. She had her left hand on the barre and her right one pointing first straight up above her head and then straight down at the ground. I looked it up in my pocket dictionary.

Oshiri turned out to mean butt. Actually, *shiri* meant butt. O gave the word that followed it some respect. Sometimes it was translated as 'honourable'. *Ana* meant hole.

Butthole. Honourable butthole.

Ha.

I was very happy I hadn't turned to ask the mother sitting next to me to translate.

I remembered a long-ago ballet teacher talking about imagining a string coming out of my head and attached to the ceiling, keeping my neck long and my spine straight, but I'd never heard a ballet teacher encouraging children to keep their buttholes directly above the floor. I was so impressed that the important thing was to get the position right, no matter what you had to say to achieve it. I wondered if children could really identify where their bones were, the spine above all. I thought about all the ways you could tell a child how to keep her spine straight and concluded that telling her how to position her butthole was probably the most effective. I usually thought of Americans as so much more open than the Japanese, but I was pretty sure most of us would hesitate to say butthole to a small child in public, no matter how good the reason.

At bath time that night I turned on the tap in the tub upstairs. The bathroom and the toilet were separate, and the bathroom was basically a big walk-in shower with a deep bath and a sink. While the tub filled I helped

47

Yuki undress and then she sat on a tiny Hello Kitty stool and I sat on a bigger stool and guided her through washing herself. We named her body parts in Japanese for me and in English for her. I tested her to see if she remembered a relatively new one: 'How about your belly button?'

She scrubbed back and forth across her tummy while I reached over and turned off the tap in the bath.

Finally, I brought out my newest bit of vocabulary: '*Oshiri no ana wa?*' (What about your honourable butthole?)

Yuki stood up, squatted a little and leaned over. She was still small enough for her head to be quite heavy for her, and she nearly toppled forward as she scrubbed between her legs. I caught her by her slippery little arms. 'Woah!' I said, and she laughed.

'*Muzukashii ne!*' she said, her eyes twinkling in her shining wet face.

'Yes,' I agreed. 'That bit's difficult.' Then I rinsed her off and lifted her into the bath to soak and play. As it often did, the broad Mongolian spot at the top of her buttocks disturbed me. I knew it was normal, I knew it didn't hurt one bit, but it looked too much like a bruise.

I didn't drain the bath when she was done. The bath had a built-in system that reheated the water when Naoki wanted to bathe before bed. Sometimes I fell asleep to the sound of his splashing. If I was fully awake, the sound forced me to imagine Naoki naked, which was unwelcome, but if I was half-asleep it made me feel a little bit like family. In Patuxet the bathroom had been next to my bedroom, and I had always woken up to the sound of my father shaving, splashing his razor in the basin.

When I bathe my children (Hadley, six; PJ, three) or take them outside to play in the kiddy pool, I'm frequently reminded of bathing Yuki, and of taking her to swimming lessons. PJ's now the age Yuki was when I had to leave Japan in a hurry. He's bigger than she was, by a lot, but when I've got my hands on his wet body I feel the same zing that used to come off her, the same intense combination of concentration and recklessness.

At the first swimming lesson I took Yuki to, I was surprised by the number of flotation devices Yuki's swimming instructors strapped to all the little children once they were in their matching navy blue and red swimsuits and their matching red bathing caps. Each child had a few moments one-on-one with an instructor during the lessons, either agreeing to or avoiding putting their faces in the water, but mostly they floated around in gangs attached to colourful foam noodles, or played with toys on the edge of the pool. I shouldn't have been so surprised that there wasn't much actual swimming taking place, given that there were nine little kids in the class and only two teachers. I reveal my preconceptions again when I say I thought they'd have something like the Suzuki method for swimming, and that they'd be turning out little Mark Spitzes in the same way we imagined they turned out tiny violinists.

I always wanted to stuff Yuki's clothes into her locker and hurry up to the viewing gallery to watch the class – playwear doesn't really wrinkle, after all – but watching the mothers fold their children's clothes so carefully, I felt the pressure to start taking care with Yuki's as well. I held her tights up with one hand and pulled the toes down so they were even, then I folded them over and rolled them tightly, tucking them in between her shoes. Doing so made me feel less of a clumsy giant, and strangely pretty. I stole glimpses at the ways the other mothers were arranging their little stacks of clothes in the lockers, and pretended to be an old hand at it myself. In the company of those women, all of us straightening and folding and tidying away, I felt like I'd pledged to a sorority and we were all following the rules that we knew would keep us clean and beautiful and safe.

Some of the mothers smiled at me each time we arrived in the locker room before the lesson, but then dropped their eyes. It felt strange, since we saw each other every week, but I can't say I was too disappointed, because I knew how to greet people, but after that I could only ask questions like 'How much is it?' and 'Does it taste good?' and 'Where is the subway station?' If they'd told me they were hungry or needed to go to the bathroom I would have understood too, but it didn't add up to a conversation.

Up in the viewing gallery I sat alone while they chatted, and waved vigorously at Yuki when she looked for me. She seldom did, but I watched her like a hawk just in case. When you're the nanny, you don't take risks with the child's feelings. If I'd been her mother, and had been chatting instead, she probably would still have known I loved her even though I was turned away. As the nanny, I felt I had to offer double the attention to make her feel secure.

50

Looking back, I recognise that I also gave Yuki double the attention because I had as much of a need of a safe repository for love as she did. But even if I hadn't, and even if I hadn't loved Yuki so much, I still would have done what I did.

6

'Nobody has volunteered what happened between Naoki and Emi,' I wrote to Porter, 'and I'm not comfortable asking.'

He was working his way across the continental states before flying from LA to Honolulu. I'd had a letter from him from Chicago, postcards from Lincoln, Nebraska; Eldorado Springs, Colorado; Zion National Park, Utah; and Carson City, Nevada, and another letter from San Francisco, but as he hadn't made it to Hawaii yet I still didn't have an address for him. So I just wrote an instalment, every few days. I told him about how comfortable it seemed Japanese people were not to talk when they were together. I told him about learning when to bow. 'I feel like in the States, the default position is "I'm going to stick my nose in your business until you tell me not to". In Japan it's "I'm going to keep my distance until you reach out in an unmistakable way". I feel like bowing is everyone's promise of that.' I wrote how Naoki might be an exception to this, given how blunt he was with me. I didn't yet understand that the combination of seniority and hierarchy added to my being foreign and female meant that those rules didn't apply to us. I was way down the ladder, and he could behave however he liked.

While I didn't know what had happened between Emi and Naoki, I did know that Emi was living with her parents, and wasn't dating, because we bumped into each other in early October in the subway station near Naoki's house. Well, I say 'bumped', but there was no physical contact. I was about to buy a ticket, I heard someone say my name, and I turned to see her walking over to me in a very nice black coat and boots.

'What a good surprise,' she said.

'Wow. What are you doing here?'

'This is a good station for me, if I want to go to Roppongi.'

'I see. How are you?'

She shrugged in a way I remembered. 'I am fine. How is Yuki?'

'Yuki's great!' I said, and then wondered if I should have sounded a bit less enthusiastic. Maybe Emi would feel hurt that her daughter wasn't pining for her. Then again, Emi had left Yuki, so maybe knowing that she was fine was welcome because it made her feel less guilty, if she felt guilty. As usual when I was unsure, I stopped talking.

'Where are you going?' she asked.

'Omotesando.'

'Oh! So am I! I could join you? Would you like tea?'

I wasn't sure it was a good idea, but I didn't have any concrete hard feelings of my own about Emi. Also, I hadn't made any friends in Tokyo yet, and my Sundays off were normally solitary excursions punctuated by short, transactional conversations with waiters and shopkeepers and museum ticket-sellers. I said yes to the opportunity to sit and talk with someone for a while, in the hopes of gaining

54

a better understanding of the situation, and we both bought a ticket.

She didn't ask me more about Yuki on the subway, only about how I was adjusting, how I liked the food. 'It is *matsutake* season,' she told me. 'Has Naoki bought some?'

'I don't know. What are they?'

'They are mushrooms. I think he should buy you some to try.'

'I usually do the shopping, like in Boston.'

'That must be difficult.'

'Not just difficult. Ridiculous.'

'Can you read the ingredients?'

'About one per cent of the time. Fortunately I can tell if something is chicken or fish. And beef is redder than pork, but I can also tell the difference between the kanji now.'

'Oh?'

'The character for pork looks like a little insect next to a window. Beef looks like an old-fashioned American telephone pole.'

I enjoyed seeing Emi laugh. Laughing lightened her up.

We walked up the broad sidewalk from the station. Usually when I walked through that part of town I looked for the young people who dressed up to show off on the bridge over the railroad tracks. The girls stood out more than the boys because of their brightly dyed, teased-up hair, and the petticoats that filled out their costumes: schoolgirl, tartan schoolgirl, goth, tartan goth, Lolita, gothic Lolita, tartan punk, gothic Lolita punk. They wore black lipstick, white lipstick, huge false eyelashes, platform shoes. They carried parasols and furry purses and disturbing plush toys, and they travelled in pairs and trios and packs. Walking through the area with Emi, though, sort of happy to see her, sort of unsure of myself, I kept my head down and kicked through the fallen yellow leaves. Both their shape and their colour were so regular, and they weren't browning or becoming crisp. They looked, and felt underfoot, as if they'd been cut out and scattered on the ground especially for our delight.

Emi pulled me gently across the sidewalk by the elbow of my jacket.

'This is my favourite place,' she said, opening the door to a tea shop on a corner of the broad Omotesando boulevard. All the clientele were women, and it looked to me as if all of them had just had their hair cut, or at least washed and styled. I had my own favourite café a few blocks further along, and it was still my favourite after visiting Emi's preference, as hers was more expensive, and I had trouble fitting my fingers into the handle of the dainty cup my Earl Grey arrived in.

When Emi tipped her head up to the waiter to order for us, I looked at her prettily pointed chin, wondering if that was the way Yuki's chin was going, or if it would square off like Naoki's. Once the waiter was gone Emi looked at me and then away, fiddling with a bracelet. We'd already talked more in about twenty minutes than we had in most of the days we had spent together in Boston. I was assessing whether I felt I could ask Emi about her break-up with Naoki when she looked back at me and asked if I would let her see Yuki.

'See her? Do you mean meet her?'

'Yes.' Her cheeks were suddenly flushed, and I felt mine do the same. I was already on edge about being out with Emi when her name wasn't allowed in Naoki's house, and now I was being asked to divide my loyalty even further. My real loyalty was to Yuki, of course, and I could probably have been convinced that letting her meet her mother might have been good for her, but above all I didn't want to lose my job. So I said, 'I don't think I can do that, Emi,' and then our tea arrived. We sat back. Emi cleared her throat. I looked at the roses painted on the porcelain cups and saucers.

'I understand,' she said, and looked out the window.

'Can I ask . . . Why aren't you allowed to see her?'

'You have to ask Naoki that question.'

'It's up to Naoki?'

'Yes.'

'He can stop you?'

'Yes.'

'So, you don't have joint custody?'

'No. Not in Japan.'

'Wait, it doesn't exist?'

'I think . . . only if the parents decide, their own way. But they don't usually do that.'

She let that hang, and I started again, trying to churn up some idea of what she could have done to be denied visits with Yuki, and then she sighed. It looked like she was trying to gather strength.

'The parent with custody decides everything,' she said. 'The other parent . . . it's like . . . they die.'

I didn't know how to make sense of that. 'Can't you complain to the court?'

She shook her head, not looking at me. I was clearly making her uncomfortable. 'The court doesn't care.'

'The family court?'

'Yes.'

'Doesn't care.'

'Yes.'

'But . . . *family*.'

'*They* are the family now. I am outside.'

She looked desolated. It was awful to observe. Her aloneness, her separateness, created an atmosphere around her I wished I could dispel.

'And if you go to Naoki's house?'

'No.'

We both looked out the window, until I said, 'Emi, if you could tell me about what happened—'

She shook her head again, very firmly, and bit her lip.

'OK,' I said. 'Sorry.'

We drank our tea.

'Are you dating?' I ventured.

'No.'

'No, or not yet?'

She smiled a little, but didn't speak. We drank some more. When I was finished I went to the bathroom, and when I walked back through the tea shop to Emi sitting all alone at our table, I tried to imagine what it would be like for her to leave that tea shop and go home to her parents and to an evening, and a new week, and a whole future that didn't include her little girl. I was encouraged by knowing that she wasn't happy-go-lucky, that she seemed to be hurting, that she couldn't make herself talk about what had happened. I decided there was something I could do for her.

'How about this, Emi?' I said when I was seated again. 'You don't meet Yuki but you meet *me* sometimes, and I tell you how Yuki is?'

The look she gave me showed not only gratitude but also the sort of calculation that I'm sure I would have made in her position – one that added up to my offer being the first step in regaining access to her daughter. I did feel some danger in what I was proposing – I remember how breathless I felt – but Emi wasn't aggressive, and she had taken no for an answer without a fuss when I had refused to let her meet Yuki. I was reasonably sure I could keep things under control.

On my way home I did something I had wanted to do for a while: I pulled a fat weekly men's magazine out of the recycling bin in the subway. I'd often seen men reading such magazines on the train, and I knew from looking over their shoulders that one of them featured a cartoon of the adventures of a very game but usually confused penis, which had the look of a young seal, with arms. It was clear there were sections designed to titillate, but these appeared adolescent compared to the magazines I'd been shocked to discover when babysitting for the one divorced man with kids in Patuxet. The men on the Tokyo subway trains usually flipped the pages very fast, and I needed time to study one. I thought it would be funny.

I'd been making an effort to study how to read Japanese a few nights a week, at the desk in my room. I'd bought a book of fundamental kanji ideograms, but I loved the tables for learning the Japanese phonetic symbols the best – *hiragana* for Japanese words, *katakana* for foreign words. They reminded me of times tables, and I was determined to be able to read *hiragana* as easily as I could calculate numbers. I put the symbols together so that they added up to people's names and places I'd visited. It focused and calmed my mind, and relaxed me. I opened the magazine and looked for words I could sound out.

After the first few pages of what seemed like token articles on politicians (identifiable by their clothes and haircuts) and celebrities (ditto), we were into young women and their breasts. Young women and girls and their breasts, actually. I stopped at a page of somebody's best ten adult videos (*adaruto bideo*), and that meant I was now working on *katakana*, the phonetic system for foreign words, because so many of the words for describing those videos were English words. I panned through the kanji next to the photos for whatever nuggets of *katakana* I could find. There was F *kappu* (F cup), and *rezu* (lesbian). There was *toire* (toilet) and *baibu* (vibrator). Next to a photo of a topless girl with bangs and a headband it said something about *rorita* (Lolita), and seven times on the page, as stark as an erect penis among the tangle of kanji, it simply said FUCK in my own alphabet.

I hadn't expected to be aroused, and when I realised I was I wondered if I was ashamed, but I decided it made sense. Unlike the women in American magazines, these ones didn't look strong. They weren't showing off their muscles. They didn't glisten. The American ones made you feel like it was OK if you didn't know what you were doing because they were superhuman. They'd take care of everything. The Japanese ones didn't look like they had ideas for you. You were the boss, and they'd do whatever you had in mind. They were at your service, and they made *you* feel

60

strong. You wanted to bite them because it felt as though you'd be making the first mark. You'd be in control. Nothing you didn't want to happen would happen.

I cut that page out of the magazine and put it in my drawer next to everything I was saving to send to Porter once I had an address. I didn't think I'd actually send it, but it was part of the interesting story I was living – a story that someone at a cocktail party might find hard to believe – and I liked the thought of that.

After studying that magazine I sometimes put a hand on my chest for a few steps when I walked, to feel the gentle movement of my breasts. I didn't dress provocatively – I still don't – so I never saw much of my shape reflected in windows or shiny buildings as I walked around the city, but when I laid a hand across my breasts to feel the rise and fall of their weight, and therefore their power, I knew they were attractive, and that started to be OK with me. The young women in that magazine looked so untroubled, so receptive to whatever you might have in mind, and I liked the idea of feeling that way. I *wanted* to feel that way. I started picturing myself as perfectly comfortable with the fire of desire my body might light, and I started imagining going to bed with Porter more. I had been imagining it all along, but what I imagined had always been the old type of sex. Manageable, climax-less sex; the kind where I hadn't done anything to create desire. After three months away from him, and after postcard after letter after postcard saying 'Wish you were here', swimming out into deeper water together began to feel less dangerous.

And then I got molested on the subway.

*

I might have been able to make it all the way through my Tokyo experience without being groped, because I didn't have to commute to work on trains so crowded that station attendants pushed bodies inside to help the doors close. Yoshimura-san wanted to take Yuki out with her one morning, though, and I saw the opportunity to fulfil a promise I'd made to my mother.

We'd had a particularly dramatic earthquake a few days before. Dramatic to me, anyway. The house had rattled in a way that felt like a drum roll, and I took Yuki to stand in a door frame with me as I had been instructed, holding my breath for whatever it was building up to, but no climax came, no damage was done, and no one was hurt. It wouldn't have been dramatic at all to anyone accustomed to rumbles like that. I told my mother about it on the phone. Neither of us had really considered the possibility of a natural disaster when I left for Japan, but now we had to.

'Come home,' she said.

'No, Mom. I think I'll be OK.'

'When's the next one due?'

'Due?'

'When was the last big one in Tokyo?'

'I'm not sure.'

She called out to my father. 'Len, when was the last really big earthquake in Tokyo?'

His distant voice called back. 'Nineteen twenty-three.'

'Nineteen twenty-three. I think one must be due.'

'What, like a comet?'

'No, but—'

'I think that these rumbles release pressure, actually.'

'Is that how it works?'

'Feels like it.'

'Do me a favour, whatever it feels like. Go down to the embassy and register, so that the government will look for you if the city collapses.'

I could have walked to the embassy in about thirty minutes, but I had to try to be home within two hours and I didn't know how long I'd have to wait in Citizen Services, so the train made sense.

I took my place at the end of a long line of commuters in dark coats on the platform. When a train arrived, double the number of people who got off wanted to get on, so the line moved forward by only a few bodies per car. It was three trains before I was second in line and likely to make it onto the next arrival. I'd been on moderately crowded trains before, and I knew it was normal for the last people on to turn their backs to the interior of the train and face the doors, pushing backwards against the people inside in order not to get squashed between the doors. On trains this crowded they didn't turn around, leaving their backs facing out for the white-gloved pushers to shove.

My group's train arrived. The people inside it who stood in the way of the alighting commuters stepped out in front of us to let them off before moving back inside, and then it was our turn to find a way in. In the crush my shoulder bag was shifted from my side to around behind me, and was sandwiched between my butt and one of the men submitting to the shoving required to get the doors closed. Once they did close I felt the collective exhalation we were allowed between stations, and smelled onions and smoker's breath, and marvelled at the fact that no one was talking.

I needed to go two stops. The repositioning that took place at the first stop meant I ended up uncomfortably face-to-face with a pudgy man until the next one. It didn't work to turn my head right or left rather than face him – I would have been breathing into an ear – so I looked down, at my coat, at his coat. I thought about my bag, which I still couldn't see, and decided there was no way anyone would be able to bend their elbow far enough to slip a hand into it, so I didn't have to worry about being robbed, and in any case, Japan was one of the safest countries in the world. And then I felt the knuckles of a fist pressing against my crotch. The hand had found its way into the flap of my coat and the knuckles were kneading my pubis. It could have been attached to quite a few of the arms that surrounded me, but I looked back up into the eyes of the man I was facing and they were saying, 'Please let me stay here. Please don't tell.' I tried to lift my arms to push him away from me but I couldn't bend them, and I ended up looking into his eyes again, trying to broadcast my revulsion in a way that would shame him into stopping. But of course he was the one shaming me into stopping, freezing me like a threatened rabbit, until the train doors opened and I was carried out on the tide of commuters getting off and buffeted on the platform by the commuters getting on, turning like a leaf in a whirlpool, horribly disappointed in myself for not having shouted at him. I knew how to say 'Stop' in Japanese – Yuki said it when Naoki tickled her – but I hadn't been able to make a sound. He'd known I wouldn't.

Walking along the approach to the embassy I felt externally taller and broader than the people I passed, but I felt much, much smaller than my ideal interior self. Once I was through security, the confident voices of a pair of blue-eyed giants in grey suits striding through the lobby hit my ears like clappers. Inside Citizens Services my body settled into feeling like more of an M again, less of a triple L – the size I'd had to choose when I needed new tights in Japan. I'd never seen a quadruple L on offer, so I guessed the two women ahead of me in the waiting area had to get their tights via mail order. They looked like they would have made a fuss on the subway. No. They looked too powerful to be targeted in the first place.

When Yoshimura-san brought Yuki back home that day, I squatted to help Yuki off with her shoes and coat and picked her up in a bear hug to bring her into the tatami room, spinning around a few times before reluctantly putting her down and asking her what she'd like to play. She went straight to the dressing-up box and started pulling out hats and lengths of deconstructed kimonos, and I kept my eyes on her, only on her, because when I was looking at her I didn't hate myself.

That night I sat down to write to Porter. He was loving Honolulu, his apartment in Moiliili, and his job as a construction project manager. There would have been some sort of relief in writing down what I had suffered on the train and sending it away, knowing that it would be several weeks before I'd have a response, by which time I'd probably be feeling better. But I couldn't imagine writing that story down without writing down all the other times I'd been invaded. It didn't seem right to describe just the one incident, just as it wouldn't be right to draw someone a

65

map with only one landmine on it when there were in fact others to watch out for. There had been two other times. Possibly three. I'm not sure if the second time counts. I don't want it to count, but I think it does.

The first time was in the Patuxet Public Library, when I was ten. A man appeared at the end of the row of stacks I was in, vigorously rubbing the placket of his faded corduroy pants. I quick-marched to another part of the large reference room, where he found me a second time. I was too young to be able to put words to the look he gave me, but I can describe it now as if it happened yesterday. Under the thinnest veneer of defiance he was asking me to pity him. 'Let me stay here,' his look said. 'Please let me stay here.' I don't know what shape his eyes normally were, but at that moment they were practically square with the effort of broadcasting his message. 'Please don't tell. Please don't move. I need to do this. Please let me do this.' I pulled down a book, any book, and went to find my mother so that he couldn't get me alone a third time.

I didn't talk about it until we were back at home, and when I did my normally interruptive mother just listened gravely. I was pretty sure that I was supposed to receive some sort of reassurance right away, but when she finally spoke she said, 'I think you should talk to your father about this.' I went and found my father watching TV in the den. Talking about it a second time was harder than the first. 'I'm so sorry to hear that,' he said. It felt like reassurance was coming, and I started to relax, but, ever the scientist, he continued instead with a lesson. 'Some men can't help themselves,' he told me. 'They just feel the compulsion and have to act on it. Some men even whip it out.'

I think that was supposed to be helpful, but it felt like lemon juice on a paper cut. I walked out of the den into a world where there wasn't just one masturbator in one library; where it was a fact, stated without any obvious judgement for or against, that some men couldn't help themselves.

The second time came at the beginning of the next summer, when I was eleven, and ready for the beach. My father wasn't coming along, so I showed him my new bathing suit before my mother and I left. He held me out at arm's length to get a look at the whole picture. 'Oh!' he said, suddenly rubbing his fingers against my tender nipples, the way you might if you were checking whether the paintwork on your car had a scratch. 'I believe you're beginning to get breasts!'

'Shut up!' I said, grabbing him around the waist, face aflame. I hugged him with my eyes closed, hiding my body from his eyes and wishing the moment away. I'd like to have been the type of child who could storm out when offended, but are there many girls who know how to do that rather than choosing a gesture of forgiveness? Hugging my father after that made me aware of pressing my growing breasts against him, hoping I was the only one who thought about them. The sense that he was marking the stages of my sexual development never left me. And of course he was, as any parent would be. The hardship came in being forced to *know* that he was.

So that second time does count.

The third time, I had just turned thirteen. We'd all been at the beach this time. I was cold from swimming too long, and hungry, and in order to hurry my parents up I'd put on my shorts and T-shirt and scrambled up the steps to the sidewalk overlooking the sand. I was watching my parents chatting and laughing as they folded up the towels and packed away the cups and drinks when a young man appeared in my peripheral vision and slipped his hand between my legs as he passed behind me. 'Well, hello,' he said in my ear, with none of the plea for pity of the library masturbator. I'd like to say he said it provocatively, but the way he said it sounded more like I was supposed to think I'd done the provoking, and that he'd merely responded with warmth. I don't know that there's an accurate way to describe the aftermath of that moment. Familiar with the usual types at our beach, I'd never seen a man with that sort of rolling walk before. I'd never heard such a voice. I felt like I'd met an alien, but the end result was that I suddenly felt like an alien myself. I stood on the same sidewalk by the same beach I'd visited all my life, and I no longer knew the world I was in. My hands shook. My thighs jumped. My parents hoisted the tote bags onto their shoulders. I needed a disguise. I raised my chin and cocked my hip like a much older girl. I watched my parents climb the steps to join me and I didn't say a thing.

I sat for a long time over that letter to Porter, fiddling with my pen. I was tempted to risk letting him know more about me, but I'd never taken that risk with anyone. I didn't know how he'd respond, and I didn't want to know. Sometimes what felt like an attack to me the world considered a mere indiscretion, and it was easier not to insist on my version of events.

Eventually I wrote that I'd been to the embassy, since he might have been glad to know that I'd registered. I described the pushers who packed us all into the train, and I told him I could have lifted my feet off the train floor without consequence if I'd wanted to.

Then I pulled the page I'd been saving from the men's magazine out of the drawer and balled it up, dropping it in the wastepaper basket by my desk. It still bugged me from there. I took it downstairs to the quiet kitchen and stuffed it in with the burnable garbage.

7

The feeling of wanting to steer well clear of sexual thoughts stayed with me for weeks. I concentrated on Yuki, on innocence, on nature, on the changing of the leaves from yellow to red, the need for tights under our pants, the roasted sweet potato seller who drove his truck around the neighbourhood at a crawl in the dark evenings playing a recording of himself singing, 'Baked potato, baked potato, stone-baked potato.' I hadn't known what the sound was until Yoshimura-san appeared at the front door with a sweet potato in a little brown paper bag for each of us. Naoki was out, and I supposed his father must have been as well, so she was at a loose end. 'Baked potato?' she said very deliberately, and I invited her in. We hadn't finished our dinner and Yuki was in her high chair. I saw Yoshimura-san look appraisingly at our bowls of spaghetti Bolognese before putting the potatoes on the table. She handed one to me before getting a spoon to help Yuki eat hers. She sat down and pulled away some of the skin, releasing sweet steam from the soft yellow insides. I put my teeth against the charred and papery pinkish skin, and then my tongue, testing the heat, tasting the smoked-earthiness, and then bit into it. We think our sweet potatoes are sweet, but the taste of the potatoes Yoshimura-san bought from that truck was an extreme of sweetness I'd never experienced in a vegetable. It was unbelievable. It felt like we were sharing a secret, a midnight feast of things children shouldn't eat, when it was actually just a potato. We hardly spoke. I said, 'So sweet!' and Yoshimura-san smiled and nodded, satisfied that I was enjoying myself, and then she taught me '*amai*', and we took turns asking Yuki if it was sweet in our languages. Naoki's mother seemed like such a nice lady, and I felt like I was in the right place.

I had that feeling again one Saturday morning when Naoki arrived downstairs tousled and smiling. Yuki and I had already eaten breakfast and were sitting on the floor of the tatami room looking at a Japanese book about the seasons. Because it was for children it was written in the phonetic *hiragana* I'd been memorising rather than in kanji, so I could manage to read it to her. Well, I could pronounce it to her. I didn't always know what I was saying, since I often recognised only the symbols, not the meanings of the words. She couldn't read it, but she knew what I was saying. When Naoki came in and said '*Ohayou gozaimasu*', we both said good morning back and then I asked him, '*Yuki* means snow?'

'Yes.'

'So is that what Yuki's name means?'

'No, no. Her *yuki* means happiness.' He sat on the floor with us. 'Yuki-chan brings me happiness,' he said, attaching the honorific suffix used for children and other cute people. He pinched her cheek, and she smiled at him because she could tell that whatever he'd just said was good.

'Does your name mean something?' I asked him.

'Of course. It's *nao*, and then *ki*, which is . . . something like honest, and then tree.'

'Honest tree?'

'Yes.'

I started to laugh.

'What is funny?'

'Sorry. Sorry. It just sounds like how some Japanese people say "honestly".'

'Honest tree. Honestly. Oh. Yes. You are right.' He smiled faintly. 'That is funny.'

'*Kore nani?*' Yuki asked, pointing to a snowball in the book to get our attention back. She wanted to know what it was called. Naoki told her in Japanese and I said, 'That's a snowball.' He and I looked at each other and smiled, and it was a nice moment, but also weird, because I knew that Naoki didn't care who I actually was, he just knew we both loved Yuki.

'How about my name?' I asked him.

Naoki thought. 'Diana. *Dai*, and *ana*.' Now it was his turn to laugh. '*Dai* means big. And *ana*—'

I remembered what *ana* meant. 'Oh my God.'

'*Ana* means hole!'

Naoki started to choke with laughter and got up, sliding like a teenager across the tatami and through to the kitchen to get himself a glass of water. The giddiness was contagious, and Yuki got up too and pretended to be off balance as she crossed the slippery kitchen floor, ending up with her arms around one of Naoki's legs.

That was a fun moment. But it was a little bit uncomfortable as well. He didn't look like a father. He would have if there had been a wife in the kitchen with them, but alone with Yuki he looked more like a bachelor friend of the family. When she stepped up onto his foot, he didn't know it was a signal to try to walk around with her attached like a bush baby. I'd thought that was something every father knew, as if by instinct. So while I did feel that I was in the right place at that moment too, it wasn't because we were sharing something special any more. It was because I was beginning to think he wasn't a very good father. I had tried to see him as devoted. You'd have to be, I thought, if you were willing to raise your child without her mother. But I did wonder, more and more often, if he wasn't just selfish, and if Yuki wasn't like a trophy he took out of the cabinet to look at when he felt like it.

I was still downstairs after eleven that same night because Yuki was sleeping in the tatami room rather than upstairs. Naoki asked me to put her to bed in the tatami room if he went out in the evening. It seemed to make him feel like she was waiting up for him. Even though I knew Tokyo was safe, I didn't like the idea of her being downstairs on her own while I went up to bed. The kids you babysat were supposed to be upstairs, and you the babysitter were supposed to be downstairs, not the other way around. Also, I wanted to waylay Naoki if he came home drunk. It was hard to predict whether he would be drunk or not after an evening out, but I always prepared for it. People talk about how Japanese businessmen do their real negotiating when they loosen up in bars after hours, and I'd seen the blooms of unchewed, undigested noodles on the sidewalk in the mornings. Waiting up made me very uncomfortable, but at the same time I knew that on any given night, innumerable women all over Tokyo were doing the same. It was normal. I wasn't alone.

Naoki did come home drunk that night, and I couldn't stop him from going into the tatami room. I didn't seem to exist for him at all when he was drunk until he had gone in to see Yuki. Standing behind him I saw his usual shudder of joy as he slid the doors fully open. He kneeled down by the futon and took her in his arms. Her head lolled back and he kissed her neck and inhaled deeply to breathe her in. I waited a little while, and then I put a hand on his shoulder to get him to stop, and he stood over me while I settled her again.

His face was flushed and the cold air he'd brought in on his camelhair jacket dissipated as he asked for green tea. I made it for him and we sat opposite each other at the kitchen table, where he looked past me towards the tatami room, over Yuki on her little futon, out at the dark garden that separated his house from his parents'.

'Yuki is my angel,' he said.

He could seem harmless enough when he was sober, but when he'd been drinking the selfishness turned into melodrama. I just nodded.

'She is *pure* good,' he said, and drank some tea. He stared into his cup for a little while, and then he said, 'When I was bad, my mother made me stand in the garden until she wasn't angry any more.'

If he'd been sober I might have shown my surprise, and maybe we would have talked about it some more, but when he looked at me I could tell he wanted to see the effect his statement had had, and I kept my face smooth. I wasn't in the mood for his sloppy emotions.

'I think I'll take Yuki upstairs now,' I said, pushing away from the table.

His unguarded face opened completely to try to understand why I hadn't engaged. It was as if he believed that because I was American I'd want to hear all about his psychology.

Eventually he nodded.

I went to the tatami room and gathered Yuki into my arms. As I walked to the stairs I said, 'Get some sleep now, OK?'

'Sure,' he said, trying to sound American, but he said it with two syllables – shu-ah – rather than the one syllable he should have been going for, the one that rhymed with fir. That would have made him sound Californian. He'd told me early on that he felt sure he'd make it to Hollywood. But 'Shu-ah' just made him sound like someone from Patuxet.

Putting Yuki to bed in Naoki's room had become a bit less strange to me since becoming friendly with Michiko, who lived with her husband and their toddling son, Atsushi, in the building I could see from my bedroom window. I could see their building from Naoki's kitchen window as well, and often when I was making breakfast or at the sink I saw her come out onto the balcony to hang up Atsushi's clothes. She patted the wrinkles out and pulled the seams straight, and when it was breezy Atsushi's colourful little shirts and pants danced. I felt like they waved at me, particularly after we'd met at the neighbourhood garbage collection location. Tuesdays were for recyclable plastics, Wednesdays and Saturdays were for burnable waste, Thursdays were for incombustible waste, and Fridays were for other recyclables. I'd met quite a few friendly people there, since we had to bring our garbage down so frequently, but Michiko was the first person who had said more than good morning to me, and she had said it in English. She had spent four years as the PA to the CEO of a big cosmetics company, focusing on his international correspondence, which was always done in English, but since she'd had the baby, 'Well, you know.'

Michiko was prettily plump, and her rosy-cheeked face was flawless. She wore dresses with sweetheart collars, and cardigans with lace trim. Once we'd chatted several times standing next to our garbage, we started taking the kids together to the little playground a couple of blocks away, usually after their naps, and sometimes we ventured out with picnics to parks on sunny days, and to music programmes at the National Children's Castle when it was wet and we knew we'd all get headaches at home. At first I made peanut butter and jam sandwiches for these expeditions, but Michiko made seaweed-wrapped rice balls with tuna inside, and little portions of fried chicken or stewed carrots and lotus root, so I started making tuna sandwiches sometimes too, with lots of celery inside to prove I knew something about nutrition.

Michiko taught me that futons only came singly in Japan, and that there were no double futons on folding frames like the ones that were becoming popular as guest beds in Boston before I left. There was only one bedroom in her apartment, a tatami room where, like other couples who slept on futons rather than in a double bed, she and her husband slept singly, and brought Atsushi in with them.

'Who does he sleep with, usually?'

'Usually me.'

Michiko was making green tea to warm us up after the playground. The kids were watching TV.

'And you'll do this even when he's out of diapers?'

'Yes.'

'Once he goes to school, even?'

'Yes.'

'So, Japanese children sleep with their parents for years, and then are expected to sleep by themselves as adults? Even as married adults?'

She nodded as she placed our cups on a tray.

'Meanwhile, in the US, we force our children to sleep alone when they need us most, and then expect them to sleep comfortably with someone else when they are grown up.'

She brought the tray to the table, smiling at the comparison, and I smiled too, but I was truly confounded by the difference, and I couldn't get either approach to sound right when I went over them again in my mind. I tried to imagine having spent the nights of my childhood in my parents' bed. The effort didn't produce a warm fuzzy feeling at all. But being at Michiko's apartment always did. As far as I could understand what passed for normal in housewives' magazines in Japan, Michiko and her little family were it. All her gestures, all her statements, all the little details, from the very rounded toes of her flat shoes to the teddy on the terry-cloth toilet-paper holder, were designed to create comfort and stability, and an entirely family-centric atmosphere. So I tried to transfer some of the positive feelings I had about Atsushi sleeping with his parents to Yuki sleeping with Naoki, and I put her to bed between his slate-grey sheets.

Once I had tucked Yuki in to her father's bed and was in my pyjamas and brushing my teeth, I was thinking less about the way Naoki was with Yuki, and more about how Yoshimura-san had been with Naoki. I felt for that child left out in the garden. Both Naoki and I were only children, and we both knew what it was like to be alone in the parental high beams with no siblings to share the burden. I'd never been forced to stand outside the house until my mother was no longer angry, and I didn't know what that sort of shaming felt like. But when my mother announced to me when I was sixteen that she'd been having an affair, she pushed me through the door into her own personal secret garden and left me there to fend for myself.

The crazy thing was, I'd been worried that my father was conducting an affair, given the way I'd seen him kissing my mother's friend Clare at midnight on New Year's Eve a few months before. It was such a long kiss. One Mississippi, two Mississippi, three Mississippi, four Mississippi, five Mississippi. All the hubbub of the party went silent as I took them in, connected at the mouth, framed by our dining room window. Clare's eyes were behind my father's profile, and all these years later I can still see the smile at the visible corner of his mouth and feel the champagne bubbles in his heart. Normally self-effacing, even a little weedy, he was completely unabashed, and I couldn't even begin to understand it as an act sanctioned by the countdown to the beginning of the new year, not to be considered an indiscretion. I felt terrible for my mother, and I started looking for

Clare-coloured lipstick on his collar and Clare-coloured hair on his coat.

The day of my mother's announcement three months later was a boring wet Sunday, more end of winter than beginning of spring. My father had been to pick my mother up at the bus station. I was lying on my bed doing nothing when I heard our car crunch up the driveway. I didn't go downstairs to meet them, and it wasn't too long before my mother was at my door.

I said hi and she came over to the bed, lying down right next to me, making me scoot over closer to the window.

'You've probably been wondering where I've been lately,' she said.

I hadn't, actually. I was about to say so when she continued. 'Staying later at work, going up to town on Saturdays sometimes, and now this whole weekend away in New York.'

It honestly hadn't occurred to me to ask myself or anyone else why she was at work longer or away for the weekend. I was sixteen. There were TV dinners and I didn't have to cook. That was all that mattered. But I didn't want to hurt her feelings, so I just shrugged.

'Well,' she said, 'taking the social psychology class at night has been really interesting for me.'

'That's good.'

'And the people, well, some of them, the conversation has been really exciting.'

She stopped there, so I said, 'Uh-huh.'

'Anyway,' she said, putting one hand over her eyes, 'I found myself falling in love.'

I didn't want to turn towards her; she was too close. I didn't want to touch her either, but I was trapped. I just stared up at the ceiling with my heart in revolt, thinking, *This is not supposed to happen.*

Eventually I said, 'Who with?'

'My professor.'

'The one who came to New Year's?'

She nodded. 'I've been having an affair.'

'*You?*' I said.

She misunderstood me completely. 'Why the hell *not* me?'

'No, no. I just . . .' I reached out and touched the cool glossy paint on the window frame.

'Never mind,' I said. 'That's not what I thought.'

We both stared at the ceiling. Then she continued with what she had come upstairs to say. 'I went down to New York to attend a conference. With, um, the professor. And it was very interesting. Friday afternoon was fascinating, and some of Saturday morning. I spent most of Saturday afternoon running, up and down the sidewalks of Manhattan. Up and down, up and down. There was a reception Saturday night. I felt great for a while, but I also felt out of place. And I decided not to stay any longer, and to keep away from the professor. So I'm back. Really back. No more late nights. No more weekends away.' She patted my thigh. 'And your dad's been wonderful.'

Now I looked at her. 'Dad knows?'

'I told him before I went.'

I thought of the way he'd joked through our TV dinners when he must have been lacerated inside. 'And he's OK?'

'Yes, he's OK. So don't worry.' She patted my thigh again, as if we'd been having a nice little pep talk, and then pushed against me to get up off the bed.

'Wait,' I said, sitting up.

She stopped by the door and turned around. I rubbed my face. It felt like she had just woken me up and the light was too bright for my eyes. 'Why did you tell me all that?'

'Well, I thought you deserved to know.'

'Why?'

'Things have been weird,' she said. 'And now they're not going to be weird any more. I thought you'd be glad.'

'Oh,' I said.

'Now what's that face for?'

'Nothing.'

'What I told you is a *good* thing, Diana, not a bad thing. It's a good thing. Everything's fine now. The air is clear. Come down to set the table at six thirty.'

She closed the door behind her.

I sat where I was on the edge of the bed and listened to the echo of the conversation. If I had been worried about whether or not she was having an affair, maybe her announcement would have been some sort of reassurance, but as I hadn't, the information was just shocking. The air wasn't clear at all, it was suddenly full of sharp new smoke. The conversation rang in my head like a bell buoy in a storm, DANGER DANGER DANGER, but I was expected to accept it, not just by my mother, but by my father as well. He must have guessed that she had come upstairs to confess to me. Given the mood she was in, she might even have told him that was what she was going to do. And he hadn't stopped her. I'd been feeling revulsion for her and pity for him, but resentment joined the mix. Where was the parent who was supposed to protect me from such horrible intimacy?

Somehow I had to go down to dinner. I didn't see any other feasible option for myself. I turned my brain off, and ordered my legs to take me downstairs.

You don't know when a parent is going to snap. They may crackle and pop a bit, but you don't expect them to snap and suddenly think that something insane is appropriate. Now that I'm a parent myself, I know that I'm most likely to say or do something I'll regret when I'm tired or stressed, not by the kids, but by something else. Normally manageable small-children behaviour becomes infuriating and impossible, and I want to blame them for making me want to spank them when I don't believe in corporal punishment. So what was going on for Yoshimura-san that caused her to think that taking her silent fury out on her one precious son, leaving him stranded in the garden, standing stock still and waiting to be forgiven, would be the solution to her troubles? What had been going on for my own mother? I couldn't know. But I did know I was too young and too sensitive to be told what she told me.

I went to bed that night feeling sorry for the child Naoki, and a bit more willing to tolerate the troubling adult he had become.

8

The sleeping arrangement in Naoki's house changed abruptly one Saturday night at the end of November, when the phone rang as I sat watching the little television in the dining area. It rang so seldom, and never that late.

'OK,' Naoki said, by way of hello, and then, 'Yuki can go to her own bed now.'

The way he said it sounded as if we'd been arguing over the subject and he was calling to tell me that he had decided to give in, but I had only ever argued with him in my head.

'Right now?'

'Yes, tonight, please . . . I will have a guest.'

I put sheets on Yuki's bed and shook some fresh air into the quilt that had always been on it. I turned out the overhead light and clicked on the elephant-shaped night light plugged into the socket next to the bed, then transferred Yuki to her room. She looked just right to me among the cheery butterflies on her bedding, but I wondered if she'd be happy to find herself there in the morning. I was tempted to leave her door and mine open in case she woke in the night in distress, but I didn't want either of us to hear whatever Naoki and his guest got up to. I decided that closing the doors would be better, banking on Yuki not waking up in the wee hours, since she never had before.

She was still sleeping when I checked on her in the morning. I opened our doors so that I would know when she woke up, and also so that I could hear Naoki's movements, and I lay back down. It was a workday, and I saw both Naoki and his ladyfriend quickly pass my room on their way to and from the toilet, around eight.

Yuki woke up when they were downstairs. When I got to her she was sitting up, clearly surprised to be in her own bedroom, but not obviously distressed.

'You're in Yuki's bed!' I said.

She looked down at a big butterfly on the quilt and laid her hands on its green and yellow wings.

'*Papa wa?*'

'Papa's downstairs.'

She clambered out from under the covers and slid off the bed, taking my hand and heading for the door, but I delayed our descent by taking her to the toilet and getting us both dressed first. Even so, Naoki and his guest still hadn't left, and when I walked into the kitchen with Yuki on my hip they were standing by the sink dressed for business. The woman was drinking the dregs of her coffee. I felt like I'd stumbled into the final moments of a successful meeting, and wondered what sort of contract had been agreed.

'*Ohayou gozaimasu, Yuki-chan*,' said Naoki happily. The woman put her cup in the sink and turned towards us. Yuki straightened her legs so that I would know to put her down, and went to Naoki with her arms raised. He picked her up and introduced her to the woman, whose name was

Akemi. Akemi asked Yuki a question, and, because every adult we ever met asked Yuki how old she was, I understood her. There was a conversation among the three of them for a little while after that, with Yuki shrugging sometimes and nodding sometimes, staring at Akemi and trying to get her measure. Like I was.

Akemi was a few inches shorter than Naoki, but definitely taller than Emi, longer in the leg. She wore her hair in shoulder-length layers, and she dyed it brown. Her breasts looked fuller than Emi's, but her lips were thinner, meeting in a flat line. Her eyes were the appraisal tools of a confident – even intimidating – decision-maker. I was very impressed by the strength she exuded. I couldn't imagine her leaving her own home to avoid a fight like Emi, or giving up her job to have children like Michiko. I wanted to like her for it. I certainly appreciated her swift, firm handshake when we were finally introduced. But when it was time to go, she walked away from the sink just like Naoki did, leaving her dirty cup for me.

I didn't tell Emi about Akemi right away, in case it wasn't serious, but eventually I thought she had a right to know. It was the third or fourth time she and I had met for tea. Of course I told her Yuki was fine first, and I gave her some details of the new English words Yuki was using regularly. I told her about how she had walked up to a little boy in the supermarket who was picking his nose and said, 'Zat's gross!'

Emi's hand flew up to cover her mouth as she laughed. 'How embarrassing!' she said. Above her hand her eyes were happy-sad.

'Well, it would have been if the little boy had understood, but he didn't. He just kept picking his nose with Yuki staring at him.'

Emi laughed harder, doubling over, and took a tissue packet out of her bag to wipe her eyes. I drank my tea. The porcelain cups were so delicate they didn't insulate the tea at all, and mine was cold and bitter. As I put down my cup I said, 'Naoki seems to have a girlfriend,' very casually, even though Akemi had stayed overnight three times already.

Emi dropped the last of her smile and pulled on the corners of her tissue packet before putting it back in her bag. When she looked up again she asked, 'Is she nice to Yuki?'

'They haven't really spent any time together yet. I imagine she will be if they do.'

She nodded, and looked out the window for a while. 'Maybe this is a good thing,' she said. 'Maybe she will want time alone with Naoki, and he will let Yuki come to me.'

'That would be good,' I said, and we both thought about that for a while. There was no worry line between Emi's eyebrows until I said, 'But he's got me.'

'What?'

'If I didn't live there, he'd have to find someone else to take care of Yuki when he and his girlfriend wanted to be alone, right? But I'm there six days a week, and on Saturday evenings and Sundays he's got his mother right next door if he needs her.'

Emi took a deep breath in, and exhaled at length. 'How is Yuki with his mother?'

'She seems happy,' I said. 'I find her a bit intimidating, but Yuki always looks glad to see her.'

'She is very tight,' Emi said, describing Yoshimura-san perfectly. There was something about Yoshimura-san's tidy, smiling exterior that went well beyond tidy. I'd seen no signs of the sort of anger Naoki described, but there was the day she stared at the garden.

I was folding clothes on the floor of the tatami room while Yuki took her nap upstairs. I was pleased with how long I was able to kneel without getting pins and needles in my ankles and feet, and I had good feelings about how I did the laundry as well. Folding was like playing with tangrams, and I did it more and more efficiently as I judged and rejudged my fold placements. Laundry is not normally a nanny's duty, of course, and I hadn't thought to discuss it with Naoki at the beginning. Neither had he. The laundry had just piled up during my first week there, and when I needed to do some for myself I realised the majority of the clothes were Yuki's and mine because Naoki took his shirts and trousers to Fashion Cleaner Paris, but there was still his underwear to be done. I remember shrugging as I looked down into the basket before taking it all downstairs. I did a colour load and a white load, and only felt strange the first time I laid Naoki's briefs on my thighs to fold them. They were so much smaller than my dad's billowy boxers, and his undershirts were narrow and short. It was hard to see them as men's things, so it didn't really bother me.

I faced the window as the bright winter blue was starting to fade out of the sky. As usual I did the shirts first, concentrating on getting the arms lined up correctly, but when I started on the many socks I had to match, I could look out the glass doors from time to time. That's when I saw Naoki's mother in her own tatami room, eight stepping stones away.

89

Her sliding glass doors were closed, but the internal rice-paper doors were open. She was sitting on a chair, which was odd, but she had put a little carpet under it so that the feet wouldn't damage the tatami. She wore a grey kimono, and as usual her hair was neatly arranged behind her head. She stared out at the garden, so I had her right profile to me. It wasn't a peaceful profile. It also wasn't an inscrutable profile. I'd say she was grinding her teeth. If I was anywhere inside her peripheral vision, it wasn't evident.

'Diana-chan!' crackled over the baby monitor, and I was relieved by the break in the tension. I went upstairs to find Yuki bright-eyed and ready for whatever we did next. 'Hello, Yuki-chan,' I said. 'It's time to put away the laundry.' She crawled out from under the covers and climbed down to join me in front of her chest of drawers. Laundry is a very hard word for any little child to say, let alone a Japanese one, so I always had her put it away with me for the practice.

Back downstairs Yuki went straight into our tatami room to decide what to play with, so I followed her and said, 'Look at *obaa-chan*.' Yuki located her grandmother, still in her tatami room, now in the half dark. '*Baa-chan!*' Yuki sang, waving and then jumping up and down, but failing to get any attention. The intensity of the way Yoshimura-san ignored us made me wonder if, when she punished young Naoki by making him stand in the garden, she had sat in the tatami room and refused to give him her attention in this same way. Had she sat guard, to make sure that he didn't move, or had she turned her back on him completely, sure of having shamed him into obedience? I didn't know which was more chilling.

'Come,' I said to Yuki, turning on the light so that Yoshimura-san disappeared and the windows reflected us alone. 'Let's make some pictures.'

After Yuki's bath that night I read to her in English, and Naoki read to her in Japanese. He came back downstairs when I was tidying the tatami room, and he stood looking out the window. He was still there when I finished, and I turned off the light so he could see outside. The street light on the corner glowed over the garden wall, showing his parents' house completely shuttered for the night. I joined him by the window, wanting to ask him why his mother might have been staring out at the garden for so long. I tried to open the subject with, 'Does your mother love this garden?'

'I think so.'

'Uh-huh. How about you? You don't go out there much.'

'I will,' he said, looking out the window again, 'in the spring. Sometimes. You too. You go out. But never let Yuki go out alone.'

'Of course.'

After a pause, Naoki said, 'I don't love this garden.'

'Uh-huh.'

'When I was young, and I made my mother angry, she made me take off my clothes, except my underpants, and stand in the garden until she wasn't angry any more.'

Maybe he had no memory of telling me when drunk. Since that first time I had often pictured him standing silent and ashamed in the garden, but I hadn't known he'd had to strip. Now I took the clothes off the image in my head, so he was shivering. I pitied him so much I had to distract myself by imagining Yuki safely tucked up and warm in her bed.

Sitting across from Emi on the day I told her about Akemi, I realised that although I didn't want to leave Yuki, my presence also made up part of the wall that Naoki had built to keep Yuki and her mother apart. So far I'd been willing to maintain the status quo Naoki insisted on, but the more I got to know both Naoki and Emi, the more I wondered if the status quo was healthy. I thought perhaps that Emi could start repaying me for keeping her up to date on Yuki with some answers.

'What did you *do*, Emi?' I asked without preamble.

'When?'

'What did you do to make it possible for Naoki to keep you away from Yuki?'

'What did *I* do?'

'Yes. Why can he legally keep you away?'

'I told you.'

'You mean, because he was given custody?'

'Yes.'

'It can't be that simple.'

'Why can it not be?'

'Did you put her in danger?'

'No!'

'Then why is the law behind him, and not you?'

'Because he has custody. Like I told you.'

'I don't get it. You're still her mother. I would have thought that joint custody would—'

'There is no joint custody in Japan.'

'What?'

'Yes.'

'That can't be.'

'Why not?'

'Because it's, well, I just can't believe it. It's wrong!'

'Japan is different.'

That sat in the air between us for a while.

'OK,' I finally said, 'but what about visitation rights?'

'Visitation rights.' She considered the two words. 'No, we don't have that.'

'Shouldn't you be able to see her?'

'That is supposed to be decided outside the courts.'

'Supposed to be?'

'Naoki would not talk about it.'

'Not even to your lawyer?'

'My lawyer wouldn't talk about it. Because the courts don't talk about it.' She clasped and unclasped, clasped and unclasped her hands.

'The courts don't talk about visitation?'

'Custody goes to one parent.'

'But—'

'Custody is total.'

I sat back in my chair to show that I was finished pressing her, although everything she said engendered more questions in my mind. I now knew a little bit more about Japanese divorce law, but that was all. I was no closer to understanding what had gone wrong in her marriage.

9

Maybe Porter called the next day because in one of my recent letters I had written, 'I've started to love Washlets. Do they have Washlets in Honolulu? I'm not sure I can come if they don't.' I was joking, of course, both about going to Honolulu and about Washlets, but it was true that I was a real convert to the bidet toilet.

He called in the morning, after breakfast. I was about to put some laundry in the machine. Yuki was in the tatami room, looking through a magazine. We were going to cut pictures out and then decide what we wanted to do with them. Maybe make a collage. The phone rang and I picked it up and said, '*Moshi moshi*,' and when no one said anything I caught the sound of birdsong, and a distant radio. 'Hello?' I said, but there was still nothing but birdsong and radio. I knew it was Porter, though. Only Porter would be cocky enough not to worry that I'd hang up right away if he didn't say anything. Eventually he said, 'Diana,' and whipped the breath from my lungs.

'What's that bird?' I said, to avoid sounding too delighted.

'A Japanese white-eye. Want to hear it again?'

I said, 'Yes please,' just to stay in the feeling of being suspended somewhere outside myself.

'OK.'

There was a lull in the sound, and I couldn't hear a bird, only a change of song on the radio, and then the bird started making its music again, burbling roughly in a lower register at the same time as it piped a whistling tune above. I didn't want the moment to end, and then Porter's voice said, 'I want you to picture the scene. I'm sitting inside my ground-floor bedroom with the sun coming in the open window. I'm reading a book. I haven't finished my coffee but it hasn't cooled off yet. There's a breeze. Someone else in the building isn't working this afternoon either, and they have their radio on. Just when I think the moment couldn't be more perfect, this birdie starts singing. I don't want to disturb it so I dial your number and slowly, slowly extend my arm out the window so that you hear it when you answer.'

'What if Naoki had answered?'

'Then he would have hung up, and the moment would have gone back to normal perfect, rather than extraordinary perfect.'

Porter's voice sounded just like the voice in his letters, and his *joie de vivre* had me seeing colours I hadn't even considered for a long time. 'Tell me you're wearing a Hawaiian shirt,' I said.

'I'm wearing a Hawaiian shirt.'

'Are you really, though?'

'I am, actually. They look good on me.'

'I bet they don't.'

'No, they do.'

'Wait. How long have you had this number?'

'Six days.'

I thought for a moment. 'You asked Clare, who asked my mother?'

'Yep.'

'And then you waited six days.'

'Ooh, you sound peeved. I like it.'

I didn't know what to say, and he jumped back in. 'It's hard to find the right moment with this nineteen-hour time difference. I couldn't imagine what would be a good time, and I didn't want to wait three weeks to write to you and get an answer. So I just took the afternoon off, and waited for the right time to present itself to me.'

That was the nicest thing anyone had ever said to me, and I didn't know what to say in response. I heard 'How's life as a project manager?' come out of my mouth, immediately regretting how mundane it sounded.

'It's fine,' he said. 'Good enough. What's happening with you?'

I knew Yuki couldn't understand me, but I hesitated to go into detail about the revelations of the previous day. 'Well,' I said, 'I'm learning.'

'Good things?'

'I'm not sure.'

'Huh. You're learning about Japan?'

'Yes, sure, but I'm also learning about this family. Well, wait. I'm seeing things about this family, and I'm being told things by this family, but I shouldn't say I'm learning. I don't know what it means.'

'Things like what?'

Before I could decide how to answer, Yuki called over to me, '*Hasami wa doko?*' and I called back, 'Aren't they with the crayons?'

'You understood her?' Porter said.

'Yeah.'

'Do you always understand her?'

'Nope. And I'm supposed to use English with her anyway. She's not supposed to speak Japanese to me so much.'

'What did she want?'

'Her scissors.'

'Wonderful.'

Neither of us said anything for a moment, and we might both have been smiling. Then he said, 'Lots of people here speak Japanese.'

'Uh-huh.'

'Look out the window. Are there flowers?'

'It's winter.'

'I win! There are flowers outside my window all the time!'

'What a concept.'

'It's the Garden of Eden, Diana. None of the fruit is forbidden, and God's smiling. Oh, and I'm taking a judo class at the community centre.'

'Ha!'

'Can you teach me how to say "Ouch!"?'

'Sure.' I laughed. 'It's "*itai*".' Yuki looked over at me to see if I was OK, so I smiled and shook my head.

'*Itai*,' Porter said.

'Very good.'

'Can I say "*Itaaaaaaaaaai!*"?'

'If it's appropriate.'

'Oh, it's always appropriate. I get my ass kicked every class.'

'You could take judo here, you know.' It was out before I realised what I was saying.

Porter went quiet. Then he said, 'But I couldn't get a job like this, could I?'

'No, I guess not.'

'Listen,' he said. 'I better go. It's not because calling you is expensive, even though it is, and it's not because I have something else to do. It's because I want to remember every word of this call, and if there are a lot more words I'll forget some.'

I wanted to kiss him so much I pressed the handset hard against my face and it depressed one of the number buttons and the phone squawked.

'*Itaaaaai!*'

'Sorry sorry sorry sorry!'

'Tell me that's not what passes for birdsong in Japan.'

'It's not. I'll find a way to call you when there's singing in the garden. Send me your number in your next letter, OK?'

'I could just tell it to you over the phone.'

'No. I want to have to wait.'

'I'll write to you right now.'

'I'll write to you tonight.'

'Go and cut some stuff up.'

10

Akemi was a real fixture by December.

On the Sunday before Christmas I showered and dressed and headed downstairs for breakfast. I didn't have any fixed plans, but I thought I might see if there was somewhere I could skate. The smell of miso was trapped in the stairwell. I heard silverware clinking on porcelain, and a woman's voice, so I knew she was with us.

Yuki was in her high chair, across from Naoki, who had bed head. Akemi was crowding the table with small bowls of all the leftovers from the fridge, plus rice, plus soup.

I stared at the spread of food. Akemi said, 'I know. We're hungry,' and I caught a whiff of sex. Yuki wanted an apple, and there was an interesting moment while Akemi had trouble deciding whether she should be the one to get it. I said I would, because I needed to get my own breakfast anyway. Akemi ceded the kitchen and sat down. She and Naoki dug into bowls of sticky fermented soybeans to get their strength back.

'Are you busy today?' Akemi asked me when I sat down.

'Not really.'

'We were wondering if you would like to come shopping with us.'

For a millisecond I received the question as a social invitation, but when I sensed a bit of nervousness in Akemi as they waited for my answer, I knew what they were after. They couldn't reasonably ask me to take care of Yuki on my day off, but they could pretend to want to be with me in order have an extra pair of hands on the excursion.

'We can have tea together,' she added, confirming my assessment.

'Sure,' I said, choosing not to stir things up by asking for overtime. I could pretend we were out together just for the enjoyment of it too. I was curious about Akemi, and I had never seen her in action for very long, and never outside Naoki's house. It was time I did.

Naoki loved to buy foreign food, so after breakfast was cleared away we drove to the most expensive supermarket in Tokyo. Naoki and Akemi discussed the relative merits of various sauces and pâtés and I played Name That Fruit or Vegetable with Yuki, holding up the produce they had chosen. Price was clearly no object. Three narrow cucumbers laid out on a Styrofoam tray and wrapped in cling wrap went for nearly four dollars. A plastic box of strawberries that would last barely one meal went for twelve. Something to write to Porter about, I thought, but then I remembered how, at the end of a lunch with Emi (I'd asked not to have to meet for tea for once), we were each served one perfect strawberry on a small, rough, dark brown plate. The strawberry was sliced in half almost to the stem and artfully separated, served with a little kiss of whipped cream. Next to each plate the waitress placed a small, two-tined fork. Once she had left I laughed, and Emi saw the strawberry through my eyes and laughed too. But that one bite was fantastic, and sufficient. It came to me that maybe the normal rules of supply and demand didn't apply. Maybe the twelve dollars of strawberries we were buying would last a long time, and maybe each strawberry would be valued so much that twelve dollars would be money well spent. A bargain, even.

'Strawberry,' I said, and Yuki said, 'Sutorawbeddy,' and we did that a few times until I broke the word down. 'Straw,' I said, and she said 'Sutoraw' a couple of times until I started saying it really fast and the speed smoothed out her pronunciation and finally she was able to imitate me perfectly. Naoki and Akemi came and went and the food started to really pile up around Yuki. The music in the store changed to 'Jingle Bells' and as we'd been practising that song, Yuki tipped her head back to sing it, like a little bird in a nest of luxury foods. 'Jingoodeebeh, jingoodeebeh, jingoo ooooo deebehhhh.' Naoki approached us holding a baguette from the bakery, and he laughed, and Akemi joined us from the other end of the aisle with a small can of smoked oysters, and she smiled as she listened, and her eyes twinkled. I'd never seen her eyes twinkle before. I was surprised she didn't say anything, though. Neither of them reached out to touch Yuki, or squeeze her, when that's all I wanted to do.

We left the groceries in the car and headed across the street to a big, bright coffee shop. It was warm inside, and Yuki and I had staticky hair when we took off our coats and scarves because our hair was thinner than Naoki's and Akemi's. They sat opposite Yuki and me at a table right by the window, talking quietly together in Japanese while I tried to keep orange juice off Yuki's clothes. I looked out the big window, in plain view of the coffee shop crowd and the shoppers on the street, realising with a start that I was on display as a status symbol. Naoki could have put Yuki into daycare. He could have hired a maid from the Philippines. Sure, he wanted Yuki to learn English well, but at the same time, everywhere I went – to ballet, to swimming lessons, to the sandbox in the neighborhood playground – I advertised Naoki's wealth and position. I went with the smoked oysters and the strawberries. Although he never really made me feel that way. Akemi did.

Yuki was bored because no one was talking to her. I asked her to look out the window with me, and we took turns pointing to all the red things we could see. I listened to Naoki and Akemi's conversation, though. Akemi poured them both a second cup from their individual teapots. I now understood enough Japanese to know that she said she was going to have to stop drinking coffee entirely.

I wondered what that meant, and turned my head to gauge her expression. Her eyes flitted over to mine, and she wasn't able to disguise all of her alarm that she had misjudged my Japanese ability. In that glance I understood that Akemi was pregnant.

I looked down at the skin revealed by the parting in Yuki's hair, at her hands tracing the lines on the place mat. Akemi would be moving in completely, then. I tried to picture the four of us, and then the five of us, in Naoki's house. I saw us all jostling around in the small upstairs hallway. I imagined Akemi's mother coming to stay when the baby was born, and wondered where she'd sleep – in the tatami room? – before remembering that Japanese women usually went to their mothers when they gave birth. It was

Emi's choice to give birth in Boston that had forced her mother to come to her instead. But what about when Akemi came back? What would she and Naoki expect from me? Surely they wouldn't ask me to take care of the new baby like I'd cared for the newborn Yuki. Who would take care of Yuki in that case?

I tried to imagine a situation I'd be comfortable with and failed. And yet I couldn't stomach the idea of leaving Yuki yet either. When would I, actually? I fell into bed each night, exhausted by both the physical and the emotional act of caring for her – the long flights of stairs into and out of the extremely deep subway whenever we went into town; the constant requests to sing 'Puff the Magic Dragon'; the way she would never, ever, put her coat on without my help; the effort required to fade away when Naoki wanted to spend time with her but she wanted to stay with me – but I woke up excited to see her in the morning, every morning.

How was I going to make the decision about when to give up that job, then? Why didn't nursing *feel* like the better career choice I knew it was? When was the welfare of lots of people I hadn't yet met going to speak to me more than the three-year-old holding my hand? (Looking back, I doubt I'm the first woman to have mistaken a desire for her own children as a desire to work with other people's children.)

I wrote all my questions down and sent them to Porter, adding a PS: 'I keep forgetting to tell you about the unwillingness of Japanese women to be heard when they go to the toilet. In some public bathroom stalls there are little gadgets on the wall with a button you can press for a recording of the sound of a flushing toilet, and flashing red lights to show you how long your sound cover will last. I asked Michiko if there had been one in her office toilet, and she said yes. It stopped women from flushing the toilet repeatedly when they were in there, and wasting a lot of water. That was interesting. I'd thought it was such a nice thing to do for women, to recognise their sensibilities like that, but it turns out that it's just more economical. Or it's both. I haven't yet pressed the button myself, as there's usually someone else in the toilet pressing like crazy, keeping the wall of sound cover intact. I bet I'll get used to it, though. I bet it will be one of the things I miss about Japan when I leave.'

I I

When Emi finally told me the story of the end of her marriage, on the Sunday after the holiday, it felt like a belated Christmas gift.

We had agreed to meet in Omotesando, as usual, but for lunch rather than tea. We always decided when our next meeting would be before saying goodbye to each other, so that she didn't need to call the house. If for some reason I couldn't make it, I would call her when Yuki was napping or distracted.

In the subway on my way there I looked up at the promotions for all the important basics hanging above our heads: rice, tea, beer, whisky, travel and men's magazines whose young cover girls' barely covered, creamy breasts swung gently forward and back with the movement of the carriage. I'd seen a Shinto purification ritual where a priest waved a rod adorned with rustling, zigzag-shaped white paper streamers over people's heads. What if it were fantasy breasts being waved over your head instead? I wondered. Old ladies, women with little children and spotty schoolgirls got on with their lives under those waving breasts. So did Emi; so did I. What kind of ritual was that?

We sat side by side at a popular revolving sushi bar. I chose some tuna and took off its plastic cover. I'd learned to use chopsticks well enough to dip the fish rather than the rice in the soy sauce, most of the time. The waitress brought us each a tea bag and Emi put hers in her cup and filled it with hot water from the spigot in front of us. I followed suit. She looked so miserable staring into her cup that I wondered why she had come out at all.

'Is everything OK?' I asked when I'd finished chewing my tuna.

'No,' she said.

'What happened?'

'Nothing. Everything is the same.'

'So . . . oh. Yes, I see.'

'It's terrible.'

'I bet. Yes. It's such a difficult situation.'

A pair of blond models sat down on the other side of Emi and asked the chef to make them some asparagus sushi, and some corn sushi. Emi picked up her chopsticks, looking reluctant, merely resigned to eating. The models talked loudly about how someone had only been paid the equivalent of about two thousand dollars for a commercial. Things settled down again when their food arrived, and Emi lined her chopsticks up next to her plate. I drew in a breath to ask her how she was coping, and she said, 'I think I will tell you what happened.'

'Oh! OK. Thank you.' I put my chopsticks down too.

'You won't believe me.'

'Yes I will.'

She shook her head. 'You won't, but I will tell you, so that you know him.'

108

'OK.'

'I made soba noodles for lunch, and we were eating it together. Yuki loved soba, and she had learned to suck the noodles into her mouth. I was feeding her, one noodle at a time, and I realised she was not chewing, not at all. I tried to make her chew, but she already had the habit, so she couldn't stop just sucking the noodle. So I started cutting them smaller before I put them in her mouth, but then Naoki told me to leave them because he wanted to see how long a noodle she could eat. I told him I did not want to, and he said he would do it, and he took the chopsticks, so I stood up and moved away. He also cut the noodles, but longer and longer, and he laughed and said to Yuki how clever she was when she sucked the whole noodle. They got longer and longer, and she was so happy pleasing him, but then the noodle was so long and she, um . . . What is the word?'

'Choked?'

'She choked. No. It's like this.' Emi stuck her tongue out a little and expanded her throat.

'Gagged?'

'Yes. Gagged. And Naoki laughed again. I didn't know how he could laugh at that, so I said that.'

She didn't say anything else.

'And then what? He asked for a divorce?'

Her look said, *I knew you wouldn't believe me.*

'Sorry,' I said. 'I'm listening.'

'First he shouted at me that he is a good father, and then he picked Yuki up and took her to his parents' house. Then he came home and made me pack.'

'How? How could he force you to leave?'

She didn't say anything, so I apologised again.

'No,' she said. 'Don't be sorry. It is unbelievable. I know. I thought it was just temporary. I thought he would calm down. I wanted him to stop shouting. But I made a mistake. I didn't take everything, just clothes. He had my *hanko* and he used it to file for divorce.'

'Sorry, he had your what?'

Emi picked up her bag and slid her fingers into a small pocket on the lining, pulling out a small black case, sort of like a single lipstick case but flatter. She clicked it open to reveal an ivory-coloured plastic cylinder nestled in red felt, and took it out to show me the kanji carved into the end. 'This is my name,' she said.

We both looked at it.

'Yoshimura.' She pronounced it very deliberately. 'He didn't want me to keep his name, but I did.'

'He took your . . . this thing . . . Seal. I think it's called a seal. He took your seal and pretended to be you?'

'Yes.' She put the seal back in its indentation and clicked the case closed, slipping it back into the dark of her bag.

'Now you know him,' she said. 'He can't be criticised.'

She picked up her chopsticks, putting some salmon in her mouth in a definitive way I'd never seen her use before. I took some salmon off the conveyor belt for myself and ate too. After a while I said, 'I think Akemi criticises him sometimes, actually.'

Emi looked at me, and then shrugged with her eyebrows. 'Maybe he actually loves her.'

I tried to imagine if he did, testing his behaviour against the benchmarks I'd been taught for judging affection. He went out with her, and they slept and ate together. They talked, not so much at the table, but I did hear them chatting in the bedroom at times. He didn't talk to me about her when she wasn't there, though, and when she was I never saw him reach for her, never once. No, I didn't perceive love, from either of them towards the other. I couldn't say it didn't exist, though. Theirs could have been a great passion. It was possible my benchmarks were inappropriate.

Emi started stacking our used plates for the waiter to tally when we were done. We both watched the sushi passing on the revolving bar in front of us for a while, and we both chose another plate. While I chewed my eel I wondered if I dared ask another question, and discovered that I did.

'Did you ever go back to the house to try and talk to Naoki, or to his parents?'

'Yes.'

'But it didn't go well, I guess.'

'No. Of course not.' She drank some tea. 'There is another thing for you to know. Naoki's mother is very tight, very intimidating like you said. But Naoki's father, he is very powerful.'

I thought about what she must have meant – how the Yoshimura family overreacted to things in a big way, and had big guns in their armoury if you didn't like it – and felt the injustice of her situation like a flash fever. I cleared my throat.

'Would you like to see Yuki?'

Emi's eyes widened, and the strength of her reaction made her look frightened.

'Not *meet* her,' I blurted. 'She would tell Naoki about that. But I can help you just to see her.'

'You mean from a distance?'

I nodded.

So that was my belated Christmas present to Emi.

12

I'm not going to say that I have ever regretted inviting Emi to see Yuki. The way everything turned out, I know it was the right decision. But on New Year's Day I was invited, for once, to have dinner with Naoki and Yuki at his parents' house (Akemi was with her own parents), and I felt happy among them. I now knew that Naoki had been an uncompromising and manipulative husband – a wicked one, in fact – and I was no longer able to smile with any genuine feeling when I saw him in the mornings and evenings. I eyed him for signs of viciousness like you would a dog you didn't know. He was surprisingly tender with his parents, though, despite the bitter feelings that surfaced when he was drunk, and on that evening everyone was cheerful, including me.

Yoshimura-san served us a feast of the foods traditionally eaten at the New Year, and we sat on big flat cushions around the low table in the tatami room eating sweet, shining black beans, chestnut and sweet potato paste, bamboo shoots, big stewed mushrooms with lotus root and carrots, shrimp, rolls of thick stewed seaweed, and heavy, gooey glutinous rice cake in a citrus-flavoured broth. Naoki told his father to be careful, explaining to me that several old people died every year from choking on the rice cake. He laughed. His father laughed. I felt a momentary echo of the story Emi had told me of Naoki feeding Yuki noodles till she gagged, but we were drinking sake. A sake buzz isn't like a beer or wine buzz. It's pure liquid warmth, amazing in a drink that looks just like water. Naoki's father leaned back to undo the top of his trousers and then, after some more sake, the zip as well. Yuki clearly enjoyed the atmosphere in the room, and stood by her grandfather pretending a pair of chopsticks was a violin and bow. Yoshimura-san hummed a quiet tune for her, and Yuki lifted her little feet in a dance.

I asked Naoki if his parents had any photos of what the neighbourhood had been like when Naoki was young, or even earlier, before they'd built the second house, before the war. His mother left the room for a little while, and came back with a large photo album. The black and white photos on its faded black pages showed the larger garden. A few photos were professional shots taken when Naoki turned a month old. Yoshimura-san was seated in a kimono on a bench by the pond – there was no bench there now – with tiny Naoki in her arms. His father, somewhat of a dandy it appeared, stood proudly by. The next photo showed Yoshimura-san nursing her son. I'd heard from Michiko how awkward kimonos were when you needed the toilet, but they looked ideal for nursing. Yoshimura-san's breast lifted out of the loosened neckline like newly risen bread. She tutted. 'I was fat then,' she said in Japanese, and turned the page. Naoki tapped a photo of a persimmon tree against a wall. 'We used to dry the persimmons,' he told me.

'I've never had a persimmon,' I told him, a little mechanically because I was still amazed and thinking about the intimate photo of Naoki and his mother.

'What?' he said in surprise.

'We don't have persimmon trees in Massachusetts.'

'I love persimmons.' He tapped the photo again and told me, 'That's the kitchen now.' A little while later he said, 'You should buy some persimmons.'

'OK. I don't know how to choose them, though.'

'It's OK. I will show you.'

He never did. But the next morning he did take me with him, along with Yuki and Akemi, to see the emperor greet his people.

'It is good you are here,' he told me as we parked as close to the Imperial Palace as we could. 'I've never done this.'

'Neither have I,' Akemi said.

'Yuki will see the emperor,' Naoki said. 'I have never thought about that before.'

The sky was bright and the cold air was still as we walked beside the moat, whose gently puckered water was like an antique mirror reflecting the massive stone wall and the grey and white keep on the corner. When we came to one of the open gates of the palace we joined a flow of people that had no visible beginning and no visible end. Naoki put Yuki on his shoulders and I folded up the stroller and carried it over my shoulder by its strap, and we moved along at a slow but steady pace between rows of police and plainclothes security officers. I had no idea how far we'd be walking, and withdrew a bit into myself in case we'd be trapped inside the throng for a long time. I don't know how long we walked, I can't remember, but I remember Naoki saying, 'There!' and suddenly we were standing outside a modern palace building looking up at the balcony where not just the emperor but the whole royal family would appear to address us. The hair of thousands of loyal Japanese gleamed in the bright sunshine – I was reminded of the sweet black beans we'd eaten the night before – and then the family appeared, the men in waistcoats and tails, the women in pastels, and thousands of red and white flags were waving and hundreds of children were hoisted onto shoulders and tiny irascible old women were viciously elbowing their way nowhere in particular. The hubbub didn't die down during the short, indistinct message from the emperor, but an eerie silence followed it. Then the people waved their flags again, and some male voices shouted '*Banzai!*' A teenager to my right had his camera up but the royal family disappeared. 'Oh! They're gone!' he said in Japanese to what looked to be his mother. 'That was quick!'

'But it was great,' she said.

He seemed to recognise his mistake. 'Yes, yes,' he said, 'it was great.'

Then it was time to leave, to make room for the next ocean of visitors, as the emperor would be back out on the half-hour like the politest, most powerful cuckoo in the world.

On the following Saturday, 4 January, when the city came back to life again, Emi sat down next to me on the bench by the window in the swimming pool viewing gallery. She didn't say anything, and I only glanced at her. I didn't think anyone could have recognised her, because Yuki hadn't started taking swimming lessons until after Naoki made Emi move out. It wouldn't have mattered if we had talked, but I think both of us were afraid of treating the situation casually. After a few minutes of watching Yuki I turned my head a little towards Emi again, as if I were looking somewhere else in the pool, and she nodded slowly to let me know that she had identified her daughter. When I turned back, I could see Emi's reflection in the glass. The teachers cajoled the children to the far side of the pool, and for a little while I watched Yuki splash around in Emi's face.

The mothers and I knew when to leave the gallery in order to be in time to see the kids return to the locker room for their showers. Emi stayed where she was, continuing to pretend that she was watching a child in another class.

Downstairs, the children came squealing into the locker room doing that tight, heel-heavy speed walk that everyone does if they want to hurry on a wet floor, and were herded by a teacher into the shower for a rinse. The mothers and I were ready for them by the lockers when they were finished. The really excited ones shouted '*Okaasan!*' like little crows when they identified their mothers. Yuki found me and I crouched to peel her bathing suit down. It was a bit harder to do, suddenly. She was growing, and I felt great, since I took credit for getting food into her. When I held the bathing suit against the floor for her to step out of, she put her hands on my face rather than my shoulders, and when she was free of the suit she didn't take them away. I looked into her face to ascertain why, and she gently patted my cheeks. '*Diana-chan wa Yuki-chan no okaasan desu ka?*' she asked.

Are you my mother?

I had wondered if that would ever happen, but I wasn't prepared. I pulled the towel off my shoulder and wrapped Yuki in it, squeezing her hard. 'No,' I said gently, right by her ear, my heart pounding with the importance of saying the right thing, then I moved her so she was facing me. 'I am

117

your friend,' I told her, and repeated it in Japanese to make sure she understood. As if she possibly could. And as if that's what I was. I couldn't imagine how someone could love Yuki more than I did, but I knew Emi had to. I wanted to say, 'Your mother is waiting for us in a coffee shop near the station,' but I didn't.

When Yuki's fine hair was wet it separated and revealed her scalp in places. Suddenly I wished she had thicker hair, more protection to counter the elements. All of us – not just Naoki and Yoshimura-san, not just Akemi, but also Emi, and also I – were elements in the atmosphere around Yuki. We all had the potential to rain on her, to burn her, to freeze her solid. I kissed her cheek with a loud smack. 'Let's get you dressed and dry your hair.'

The coffee shop was designed for ladies – apparently for nineteenth-century American ladies – with blue gingham tablecloths and prints of needlework samplers on the walls. Each table had a vase of dried flowers, and the menus were covered in flowered fabric and trimmed in eyelet lace. Emi was sitting at a table against the left wall, two-thirds of the way back, reading a magazine. I chose a table in the middle of the restaurant and seated Yuki facing the wall so that Emi could look diagonally at her. Sitting with my back to the door I could look diagonally at Emi. I felt the triangle of sight lines as if I'd drawn them with a fat pen and a ruler.

I ordered hot chocolate, and took a drawing tablet and a box of crayons out of my shoulder bag. I pulled a piece of paper off the tablet for each of us, and started drawing lines and patterns, nothing in particular. I stole glances at Emi. Sometimes she was looking at Yuki, but sometimes she was looking at her magazine again. I remember being astonished by the lack of expression on her face. Her forehead was placid; her hand turned the pages slowly. I'm a little disappointed in my young self for not understanding that to get through the moment she had to be sure there would be no vent allowing her emotions to the surface. I recognise now that when she was looking down at that magazine, she wasn't seeing it at all.

There was usually a lot of activity, many changes of crayon, when Yuki drew, but when I looked over I saw that she had used only royal blue, and had done a very straight line across the middle of the paper. That in itself was very impressive. Under the line was a long oval on its side, with two stick legs and two stick arms. I'd never seen her draw that type of figure anywhere but standing in the middle of the page. And it had never been determinedly oval before, only roundish.

'Ooh,' I said in true amazement. 'Who is that?'

'*Yuki-chan*,' she said. '*Pooru de.*'

'In the pool? That's Yuki swimming?'

She nodded.

'Wow!'

She was so proud of herself she swung her legs under the chair and reached out for another piece of paper. She wanted to make me say wow again. I slid her drawing to my side of the table and tore off another piece of paper for her. She did exactly the same drawing one more time before our hot chocolate arrived. I said wow.

Later, when we got up and put our coats back on, I only picked up one of the drawings Yuki had done, leaving Emi the original.

13

I didn't know what it meant that Akemi still hadn't moved in entirely, even a month after she knew she was pregnant. I hoped that the decision to do so would be put off indefinitely, but it did seem that she'd eventually be part of the household. Although she still wasn't spending every night with Naoki, she was sometimes at his house even when he wasn't.

I found myself alone in the kitchen with her one night after putting Yuki to bed. Akemi had helped get the meal ready, and eating together had been pleasant, but when I came down from bathing and reading to Yuki, the dishes were still in the sink and Akemi was looking at a magazine. I hurried to finish cleaning up the kitchen in time for the TV show – the sort of soap opera they called a 'trendy drama' – I liked watching. To my surprise Akemi wanted to watch with me. I would have preferred some alone time, but I decided it was a good thing, as I wanted to feel more comfortable with her. Watching with her would also mean I could ask her if I needed to understand something. I couldn't sit in my usual place, though. The only television in the house was a small one on top of a free-standing cabinet between the dining table and the kitchen counter, and in order for us both to see it easily we had to bring two chairs away from the table and into the kitchen area. We ended up sitting stiffly side by side with our hands in our laps.

The romantic leads were beautiful. The young man was unusually tall, with a long, straight nose. The young woman was as pretty as the rest of them, but stood out for her lovely pixie haircut. As far as I could tell, the whole drama revolved around how hard it was for them to spend time together, and how often they misunderstood why the other hadn't shown up. Akemi told me that I was sort of right about that, but there was also an issue with the young man's boss's expectations of him at work. Near the end of the episode, the woman had dressed up to meet the man, and was waiting by the phone for his call. She reapplied her lipstick and checked her hair. Eventually she fell asleep in her clothes, and the camera panned to the notepaper on her vanity table. In the middle of the paper she'd written just one word: *aitai*. I asked Akemi what it meant.

'I want to meet,' she said.

'But we knew that already,' I said.

Akemi laughed. 'These shows are very obvious.'

'They're good for my Japanese, though. The characters don't make long speeches like they do in American soap operas.'

She nodded. As we moved our chairs back to the table she said, 'I'm always disappointed, though. The women don't know how to go for what they want.'

'Not like you,' I said without thinking. I didn't mean the comment as a criticism, but I realised that my tone was questionable. She narrowed her eyes at me as if she was nearsighted and wanted to see me for who I really was. 'I meant that in a good way!' I blurted. She relaxed her eyes a little and nodded, but not in the down-up-down motion that means 'I accept your qualification', but rather in the up-down-up way that means 'Sure you did'. We didn't say anything after that. I went upstairs to bed, and after a while she did too.

The next day she asked me to pick up the dry cleaning. It was something Naoki usually did on his way home from work, and I was pretty sure she knew that, so I wondered if she was punishing me for that awkward moment. Testing me, even. Even if I hadn't offended her, I might have told her that it was Naoki's job, but I wanted to regain some footing. I didn't know yet that the way to get respect from assertive people was to match their assertiveness, or to top it. I only hesitated a little, and then said, 'Sure.' I included the errand in the morning's excursion.

It rained gently while Yuki and I were having breakfast, but the sky started clearing as we got ready to go out. The thermometer outside the kitchen window said 8°C, which I knew was forty something. I stuffed a hand towel into my shoulder bag because we were going to do a neighbour-hood tour: playground first, where the chilly slide and swings would be wet; apartment block where there was sometimes a cat in the window; Fashion Cleaner Paris; home for lunch.

We had a great time. I taught Yuki to stand up on a swing, the cat was in the window, and when I asked her what colour the line along the street was she said 'White' with-out hesitating. We were really in a good groove those days. I felt like there'd been a shift in our relationship. We weren't getting used to each other any more. We were just us, and we were in sync, strolling along the road, our road, and stopping at our dry cleaner's.

I'd been in before, to drop clothes off, but it was the first time I'd taken Yuki with me. We couldn't walk side by side through the door because of a pile of cardboard boxes, so I let Yuki go in first and stood behind her. She wasn't tall enough to see over the edge of the counter, so she looked around at the things at her level. I handed the ticket over to the middle-aged lady in an apron. She looked like she'd never seen the sun, and she had scoliosis at the top of her back that gave her a witchy air. We greeted each other and she couldn't take her eyes off my face. '*Ohana ga takai ne*,' she said. Your honourable nose is so high.

Naoki had told me that this was what Japanese people sometimes said about Caucasian noses. I had thought it was the tip of the nose they found so extraordinary, but when I didn't say anything the lady pressed a finger to the bridge of her nose, to make sure I understood what impressed her so much. Except that hers wasn't a bridge; it was a valley. I'd never consciously taken in the dramatic structural difference before. I felt refreshed to have been spoken to so frankly, and to have been educated. While she climbed up on a stool to find our dry cleaning, I thought about how if she lay on her left side to cry, the tears would slide unimpeded from her right eye over her left eye and down onto her pillow, not pooling against her nose at all.

Walking back home I held the shirts out in front of us. A cream silk blouse of Akemi's faced us as if it were the boss, with Naoki's cotton shirts lined up behind it. Even through the dry cleaner's bag I could see how heavy and fine the silk was in the lay of the gentle folds. Pearl buttons dotted the neck and wrists. I decided that I'd slide my hand in the bag and feel it when I was putting it away.

In Naoki's house, I was supposed to look in the wardrobes. I was supposed to open the drawers, take things out, put things in. Even so, I still felt like I was snooping. For some reason he and Akemi got ready for work in the morning without opening the brown metal window covers that slid into housings outside the glass. They switched the light on when the alarm went off and just continued from there. So when I went into their dark room to get the laundry or return their clean clothes, even after they'd left the house, I felt like they were still sleeping and I should tiptoe. It was hard to turn on the light because I worried that I would disturb them. Their impressions were still in the pillows. I knew that people didn't take their whole selves to work, anyway. There were parts of themselves that only existed in their bedrooms. Every day I forced myself to turn on the light, and I opened the sliding window and sent the window covers clattering into the housing before closing the window again. Once I'd done that and turned the light back off, I finally felt like I was alone in their room.

On the day I picked up Akemi's silk blouse I slid Naoki's shirts in between his slacks and the shirts already hanging in his wardrobe and hung Akemi's blouse up in the next wardrobe, where his suits had been shoved over to make room for her clothes. Then I slid my hand up from the bottom of the bag. The blouse was made of that type of silk you aren't sure you are actually feeling even when you see your fingers touching it. It was the most sensual fabric I'd ever touched, and I wondered what it would be like to be

125

the sort of woman who bought such a blouse for herself and wore it without a second thought. A sexy woman.

I glanced at the open bedroom door but couldn't be bothered to go and close it. Yuki was in her room with a doll and a tiny hairbrush. I raised the dry cleaning bag up over the shoulders of the hanger as if I were unveiling a bride. Now we were on our honeymoon and my heart was in my mouth as I undid the pearl buttons at the neck and the little white ones that went all the way down inside the covered placket. Before I took the blouse off the shoulders of the hanger I pulled my turtleneck off and threw it on the bed. I lifted the blouse gently off the hanger and slid my right hand into the right sleeve. The feeling was so lovely I shuddered. I folded my left arm up behind me to get my hand in the other sleeve, and when I extended my arm I ended up with the sleeves tight around my forearms and no way to finish the movement. I couldn't even get the shoulders of the blouse onto my own shoulders without the threat of ripping a seam. I'd thought I had a chance with that blouse because it was so, well, blousy. That was crazy thinking, though. Despite her firm handshake, Akemi was so petite I could have broken her arm.

Yuki asked from the doorway if the blouse was mine.

I was startled, but I'd been taking care of her too long to feel like I had to answer every question directly. 'It's too small, isn't it?' I said in my *Sesame Street* voice. I laughed, and Yuki laughed with me. 'Too small,' I sang. 'Too small! Too small!' I did a careful little dance, then I took the blouse off and wrapped it back around the hanger. I put my turtleneck back on, by which time Yuki was next to me between the bed and the wardrobe. 'That's better!' I said.

'Zat's bedduh.'

'Let's count the buttons,' I said, hoisting her up onto the bed. I started at the top, and we counted our way down to the eighteenth one at the bottom as I did them all back up. I pulled the bag back down over the blouse. Now it was a shroud. Our marriage had begun and faltered and died. I felt really stupid, and I couldn't get the plastic to look untouched.

We were all having dinner at home that night, so I took a couple of pizza bases out of the fridge. I knew that Naoki might criticise me for not serving fresh food, but I was hoping he'd be distracted by the fact that Yuki was helping to make the meal. We prepared the bases with tomato sauce and mozzarella, and when he came home he found her standing on a chair next to me at the kitchen counter, carefully arranging mushroom slices on top. We were going to make another one with tuna and shredded dried seaweed.

Naoki kissed Yuki's head and asked her what she had done today. She wanted to be able to please him with an answer, but she couldn't remember so she looked up at me. 'Did we go to the playground?' I asked her.

'Yes!' she said.

'Did you stand up on the swings?'

'Yes!' she said again, and again when I asked her if we saw a cat. Then she told him that Akemi's shirt had tons of buttons, with that gesture children use to mean lots and lots, raising her arms over her head and spreading them wide.

Naoki looked at me.

'We picked up the dry cleaning,' I said, breathing shallowly.

He nodded and turned back to Yuki, asking her how many buttons there were. Yuki looked at me, and I whispered the answer in her ear.

'Eighteen!' she told him.

'Wah!' he said. 'Amazing!'

Relieved that Naoki now had an answer if Akemi showed him her blouse and asked him if the plastic looked rumpled, I slid the finished pizza away from Yuki and replaced it with the one without toppings. As I opened the packet of nori I said, 'Yuki's doing really well with her counting.'

Clever girl, she obviously understood me and wanted to show off, so she started reciting, 'I one my faza, I two my faza . . .' I had learned this little rhyme as 'I one my mother,' but had remembered to change the gender before passing it on to her. We were still working on 'th'. 'I sree my faza, I foh my faza, I fie my faza . . .' She forgot if six or seven came next, so I joined her.

'I six my father, I seven my father, I *eight* my father!'

Yuki looked at me with twinkling eyes and I said what she was expecting: 'You ate your *father*?' She laughed, and then we both turned to look as she was drowned out by Naoki, who thought it was so funny he had to pull out a chair and sit down. I could see tears in his eyes.

14

Only a few cars came down the little road under my window at night, and they always drove slowly. Sometimes a bicycle went by, swishing after rain, whizzing when it was dry. I woke up at 7.50 every day when an old lady in Michiko's building raised the screeching covers that protected her sliding glass balcony doors and tore the lid off my night. She slipped her feet into outdoor slippers to step outside and hang out pyjamas, bath mats, pale narrow slips with padded brassieres, light pink girdles, dish towels and her husband's beige sweaters. Every day I thought, *Those clothes can't possibly have been dirty*. Children twittered on their way to school when they weren't too cold to talk. In the streets of our neighbourhood, activities were predictable, functioning like healthy machinery.

Inside Naoki's house, though, there was a wrench in the works, and her name was Akemi.

One morning near the beginning of February, Naoki was already downstairs when I got to the kitchen, sitting at the table with a cup of coffee. Or maybe Akemi had made it for him, and had retreated upstairs. I asked him if Akemi was awake.

'She is, but she's not feeling well,' he said.

'Oh, poor thing.'

'Can you bring her a cup of tea, please?'

I put tea leaves in the fine mesh sieve inside a one-serving teapot and poured hot water carefully over them. I knew she liked green tea, lightly steeped. I must have looked like a good girl to him, but I was thinking, *I'm not her maid and this situation is insane.*

Akemi and Naoki were going to get married. I didn't know whether the wedding was going to be before or after the baby was born, as Naoki had only told me about the engagement ceremony they were planning. He said he and Akemi were happy just to make the decision, and he bought her a big diamond solitaire set in white gold, or maybe platinum, but his mother was insisting on a traditional engagement ceremony, where the two sets of parents would meet and share a meal.

I poured the tea into a Japanese teacup on a small tray. If it had been a mug I could have just carried it up by the handle, but after six months in Japan, green tea looked all wrong in a mug to me. It still does.

I knocked on the bedroom door. There was no answer, and I didn't know what to do. I didn't want to go downstairs and then come back up again if Naoki got frustrated with me, so I turned the handle and opened the door wide enough to peek in at Akemi. She was awake, unblinking, lying on her side facing the window with both her hands flat under her cheek. I went in.

'Oh,' she said, disappointed that I was the one who had seen her thinking, possibly worrying, rather than Naoki. I wasn't the one who was supposed to ask her about how she was. I wanted to, though. I wanted to know if she was glad about the baby. I wanted to know how much, or how little, she liked Yuki. I wanted to know how she thought things should be rearranged when the baby came.

She turned and sat up against her pillow as I transferred the tea to her bedside table, and when she spoke I had the beginning of an answer to my rearrangement question. She said, 'Thank you. Has Naoki talked to you about the *hoikuen* visit?'

She was referring to a daycare centre.

'No,' I told her.

'Oh, well, he was supposed to. He has an appointment there this morning, and I don't feel like I can go. But I don't want to postpone the appointment. We were wondering if you would go with him.'

'Isn't it a little soon to be visiting a *hoikuen*?'

'Why?'

'Well, your baby isn't born yet. And they don't take newborns, do they?'

It was clear how stupid she thought I was when she answered. 'We're visiting for Yuki, not for the baby.'

After a beat I said, 'Oh, right. I'll talk to him,' and then I retreated, closing the door behind me.

I stood dumbly in the short hallway, face burning, and then took a few steps to listen at the door of Yuki's room, wishing she were awake. I could have woken her up, but then again I didn't want to have the daycare conversation in front of her. I went back downstairs alone.

Naoki was reading a newspaper. I sat down. 'You have an appointment at a *hoikuen*?'

'Oh, yes,' the coward said, as if he had just recalled the fact instead of having sent me upstairs to hear the news from Akemi. 'Can you come?'

'What about Yuki?'

'She can go to my mother's.'

I nodded. 'OK. But why do you need me to come?'

'You need to know where it is.'

That was silly. I knew that if Yuki went to daycare I'd no doubt be the one to drop her off in the mornings, but it wasn't a sure thing yet, and I could have figured out where it was on my own any time. But then it occurred to me that maybe Akemi actually wanted my opinion. Maybe she didn't trust Naoki to ask the right questions, or to take in what she wanted him to see. Maybe she cared more about Yuki than I imagined. The thought cooled me off a little bit.

'What time do we need to be there?' I asked.

'Nine thirty,' he said, and looked at his Patek Philippe.

I'm not the sort of person who could recognise a Patek Philippe watch at five paces, or any brand of watch – I doubt many people from Patuxet could – but by that time I had picked up and studied every trinket or accessory in Naoki's house.

'I'll get Yuki up.'

'It's less than ten minutes from here,' Naoki said as we turned left at the bottom of the steps, away from the playground and the dry cleaner's and the subway. We walked along between brown buildings, grey buildings, tan buildings, then Naoki said, '*Hoikuen* are run by the government.'

'Oh. So, are they open to anybody?'

'If you work only, or maybe you are sick, or something. You have to have a reason.'

'But I can take care of Yuki,' I said, finally seeing my chance to protest.

Naoki put his hand out to stop me from crossing against a light.

'We'd like you to help with the baby,' he said flatly. 'And with Akemi, like you did with Emi.'

'You hired me to take care of Yuki.'

'You will still take care of Yuki,' he said. 'When she is at home.'

'I can take care of both children,' I insisted, as the crossing light turned green and we started walking again. 'Yuki doesn't need to go to daycare.'

If I hadn't been so upset I don't think I would have said that. I didn't want to take care of Akemi's child at all. I didn't want to be wearing surgical gloves to handle a healthy infant, I didn't want to be at Akemi's beck and call, and, above all, I didn't want Naoki to take Yuki away from me.

The ball was in Naoki's court, so I waited for him to respond, but all he said was, 'We are here.'

Naoki went in first and I slid the glass door shut behind us. A wooden shoe rack on our left had enough cubbyholes for at least sixty small pairs of shoes, and most of them were full. In front of us a glass cabinet displayed a series of miniature meals. A middle-aged woman in a pale yellow skirt suit and slippers came out of an office to greet us. She and Naoki went through their bowing and greetings, and Naoki introduced me in Japanese; I bowed, and they continued in Japanese. Her name was Ogawa-san.

Ogawa-san showed us the bright, cot-lined room for the youngest children. In the middle of the square carpet two women in aprons were helping the babies crawl up and over

133

a ramp and up and over a short set of steps. There were two other rooms on the ground floor, but those children were in the playground behind the building, playing with balls and hula hoops and sit-on cars. Upstairs were the older kids, being led in the motions that went with a song by a teacher in an apron and headscarf. Naoki and Ogawa-san talked. I thought my own unwelcome thoughts about how very much Yuki would like to play with these children. I could see that everything about the place would be good for Yuki.

Maybe Naoki had known that I'd feel that way when I saw what Japanese daycare was like. Maybe that was why he didn't say anything after I told him I could take care of both his children on my own. I didn't think he was that smart, though. I was pretty sure he was just doing what Akemi told him to do. She really seemed to call the shots. As we walked back home I found myself wondering if Akemi's demands reminded Naoki of his mother in a way his psyche found impossible to resist. I wondered if Emi had failed because she hadn't ever considered sulking, and shaming, and leaving him out in the cold.

15

Michiko called one sunny Thursday in the middle of the month to suggest a picnic. 'Maybe the trees are beginning to bloom,' she said. 'Maybe it will be sort of warm at lunchtime.'

That was good enough for me. The weather had been very cold and dry since the beginning of the year, and seldom wet. I had expected some snow, but so far there hadn't been any. The last two days had been a little bit warmer, though, and drizzly. I understood Michiko's desire to grab at the sunshine and get out of the neighbourhood.

I made a plastic box full of little grilled cheese sandwiches that I had cut into stars with a cookie-cutter, the way I'd seen in one of Michiko's magazines, and wrapped sliced ham around peeled cucumber spears, cutting them into bite-sized pieces. I cored and sliced two apples, putting them back together and securing them in little plastic bags so they wouldn't go brown, and made a thermos of green tea. I was excited to see what Michiko would bring – it was always so tasty – and also to show her that although I was still making picnic food with American-style ingredients, I was working on my Japanese-style presentation.

'Isn't it early for blossoms?' I asked Michiko on the subway.

'Yes, a little bit.'

'I thought they bloomed in March.'

'The cherry blossoms, yes. This park has plum blossoms too. Maybe they will be starting.'

I scrutinised the trees lining the path we took inside the park, and they were keeping their buds a tight secret.

'These are cherry trees,' Michiko told me. The little map we received with our tickets showed that the plum grove was on the opposite corner of the park. The path took us past a pond designed as a miniature reproduction of a Chinese lake complete with rock islands, a bridge whose reflection created a perfect circle, and a field of dormant irises. When we found the plum trees, the buds clustered along the naked grey branches were open enough to reveal which would have pale pink flowers and which would be dark, but it was too early for them to be romantic clouds of colour.

'Let's come back next week,' I said.

A low fence of half-circle strips of bamboo tied with black twine, like the trail of a bouncing ball, protected all the crisp beige grass. The park was exclusively for strolling. 'Oh,' Michiko said, looking at the ground. 'I thought we could eat here.' We strolled some more, and came to a Chinese-style red-lacquered bridge. I suggested playing a game of rolling a ball over it to each other, to entertain the kids, but Michiko said that wouldn't be accepted. 'This is historical,' she said.

'How old is it?'

'It is Edo period, so, I think, four hundred years?'

'Oh! God. Yes. No. No playing.' After a moment I said, 'Four *hundred* years?'

'Yes.'

Yuki started kicking at the gravel of the path, and Atsushi joined in, but of course that sort of game wasn't allowed either, so it was a relief when we'd walked some more to come to a series of round stepping stones across a shallow stream, and no fence. Yuki and I stepped onto them first, and when we got to the end of the stones we turned around and started back, which meant finding a way to pass Michiko and Atsushi without putting a foot in the water. That was entertaining for a good four minutes. Then we had to decide what to do about lunch, which ended up meaning putting the kids into the strollers for the walk back towards the subway until we came to the Kanda River, and a bench, and laid our picnic blankets on the ground.

'These are cherry trees too,' Michiko said, looking up. 'This path is so crowded when it is viewing time. As bad as a train.'

Michiko took Atsushi's shoes off before letting him sit on her blanket, so I did the same for Yuki, and then followed Michiko's lead in keeping our shoes on but keeping our feet off the blankets. That made it difficult to move around the way I wanted to, and seemed like a real trade-off to me. I could have my inconvenience now, the Japanese way, or later, when I washed the blanket, the American way. Alone, I might have chosen the American way.

We put the food on the bench to keep the kids out of it, and started handing them morsels. Michiko had shaped rice into fat rounded blossoms, and had cut teriyaki chicken into perfect cubes. As we were starting to eat, a pair of bandy legs in khaki pants appeared at the edge of our blanket. An old man in a quilted jacket and a hat Frank Sinatra might have been proud of bowed and smiled, and without speaking pulled something out of his pocket and revealed it on the cushion of his well-fed palm: a spinning top of wood, striped with black, red and bright blue paint. He raised his bushy eyebrows at Michiko and at me, and then gestured with the top to the kids, and we understood that he was offering to show them.

'Is he going to want us to buy it?' I asked Michiko.

'No,' she said, nodding at him. 'He just wants to enjoy.'

The old man crouched. The path looked too rough for a top, but he only needed it there for a moment before he transferred the top to the end of an index finger and then to the back of a hand, jostling it gently as he turned his hand and brought it to spin on his flexed palm and then back again. The kids watched him silently, poker-backed and rapt. Once the top had come to a stop, he pointed at Yuki and bobbed his eyebrows at her, and it was clearly her turn. He got the top going and transferred it to an index finger, and then reached for her hand, smoothing it open with his thumb and holding her hand steady as he shifted the top from his finger to her little palm. Her shoulders rose up at the experience.

'*Kusugutaiiiii!*' she called out, and the man laughed.

'What does that mean?' I asked Michiko.

'She says it tickles.'

Atsushi scooched closer to the old man and patted his arm, and the old man did the same little routine for him, still never saying a word, speaking with his eyebrows and his smile. Once the top was spinning on Atsushi's palm, his

138

tiny hand supported by the old man's large one, Yuki asked Atsushi if it was ticklish, but he was concentrating too hard to answer her.

Atsushi's turn finished, the old man stood up decisively, wound the string around the top again, reached into his jacket pocket and pulled out a second top. I thought he was going to show us double-decker top-spinning, but instead he handed one to each of the children. Michiko and I said 'Oh!' in unison, and then she spoke to him in Japanese, and he waved his friendly hands to say 'No, no, it's fine', and we bowed our heads to him from the blanket, and made the kids bow and thank him too, and he walked off swinging his arms.

'I wonder how long he has been walking around looking for children to entertain,' I said. 'Do you think he's lonely?'

Michiko said, 'I think he's retired, and his wife told him to get out of the house.'

We laughed, and finished our meal. It was such a nice day out together. When we stood on the subway platform waiting for the train, Yuki wanted to be carried rather than stay in the stroller. Atsushi was already asleep in his. Normally I would have negotiated with her to get her to stay put, but I was so happy I found I wanted to hold her. Once she was on my hip I felt enveloped in a delicious little buzz of satisfaction and fatigue. 'Is the train coming?' I asked her when I began to hear it, and we watched for the bright headlights. Just before it came to a stop I stepped to the edge of the platform. Everything felt a little slowed down. I thought we both might nod off for a bit on the way home. The door began to slide open, and as I moved forward Yuki reached out her right hand and put it on the glass of the door, as if to help it along into its housing. The door carried her hand along until it was wedged between the rubber around the edge of the glass and the exterior wall of the train. She just looked at it, and I tugged her arm gently but the hand didn't budge. I was halfway into the carriage, halfway out, and started to shout because if the train doors closed her skin might have caught, her little bones might have broken. Poor Michiko didn't want to let go of Atsushi's stroller. A woman tore off down the platform towards the front of the train, shouting for a conductor. Other people on the platform shouted and gesticulated. Yuki still hadn't made a sound, maybe because I was talking non-stop into her ear, saying, 'Don't worry don't worry don't worry,' but Atsushi had woken up and started to cry, and then suddenly a small, round-headed man took hold of the train door with both of his labourer's hands and pulled it towards him. A young man in black joined him, and when they pulled the door together Yuki was free, and it began to be over. I stepped away from the train, and Michiko followed me out. At first glance Yuki's hand looked OK so before really investigating it I bowed deeply to the people on the train, tipping Yuki down with me, my heart flooded with gratitude and embarrassment and relief and guilt, and I was crying when I stood up again.

Michiko took over. She asked Yuki if her hand hurt while I tried to assess the damage through my tears. There were little red dents between the first and second joints of three fingers. Yuki said that it didn't hurt, and then a station attendant appeared and asked us to come with him. Halfway up the stairs Yuki said, '*Itai*.' It was hurting. The blood must have started flowing back into the dented spaces. By the time we made it to the little office by the ticket gate, I could see that her fingers would swell up.

The attendant showed us into the office, and I said 'Ice' to him. Michiko translated my request, and he seemed to say there wasn't any. 'Cold drink,' I said urgently, and he must have understood because he disappeared. The senior attendant inside gave me a chair. He and Michiko talked about what had happened, and then the first attendant came back with a small red can of cherry drink from a cold drinks machine, and crouched down and put Yuki's hand on it. I took it from him with thanks, turning her hand over so the back of her fingers was against the can. 'It's so cold, isn't it? Brrrrr!' I said as cheerfully as I could. Yuki was still just looking at her hand, but then Atsushi made the *brrrrr* sound too, and Yuki seemed to wake up. Michiko and the attendants looked relieved, and we all decided that it would be OK to go back home.

Both Naoki and Akemi were at home when we arrived, and Yuki gave them a garbled account of the day, starting, of course, with the train-door incident. Naoki took her hand in his and studied it. It didn't look too bad, the little bruises hadn't really shown up yet, but he looked up at me sharply. 'How did this happen?'

'She put her hand on the door as it was opening.'

'You were standing too close to the door.'

'Yes, I was.'

'Yes, you were.'

'I'm very, very sorry.'

'I pay you to *protect* her,' he said, and looked back down at Yuki's hand, shaking his head.

'Yes.'

Akemi said, 'Maybe she should start going to the *hoikuen* sooner than we thought.'

All the saliva drained out of my mouth, and I looked at Naoki to see if he agreed. He seemed as shocked as I was by the acid in Akemi's voice, and didn't form a reply. Looking at his stunned face, I now wondered if maybe he had been so quiet on our visit to the *hoikuen* because of his *own* worries about being separated from Yuki, rather than because of mine. Maybe the whole thing was being driven by Akemi. Yuki tried to continue her story about the day, but Naoki wasn't listening, just standing with his hands on his hips, looking at the floor. Yuki went over to where Akemi was sitting and told her about the old man with the top. I could tell by the way she was gesticulating. I took it out of my shoulder bag, and gave it to her to show around, but still Naoki didn't see her, and Akemi was watching Naoki.

16

On the morning of Friday, 21 February I told Yuki that it was my birthday, in Japanese, and she said what was always said – '*Omedetou*', meaning 'Congratulations'. I loved that. Congratulations on having survived another year. I thanked Yuki warmly, and enjoyed thinking about my birthday as an accomplishment.

We were dressing dolls and making them speak English when the doorbell rang.

It took a while to get to the front door because I was wearing the furry moccasins my mother had sent me for Christmas. I had to take those off, pull some shoes out of the shoe cabinet and slip those on, walk the ten feet of stone hallway and then open the door. If it had been earlier in my experience I might have gone to the door without changing my footwear, because no one was looking, but by that February I was as strict as any Yoshimura about keeping outdoor shoes for outdoors. My parents had given themselves a new bedspread for Christmas, and had sent me a photo of my grinning father reclining on it, but I hadn't pinned it alongside Porter's postcards on the corkboard by my desk because the sight of Dad's shoes touching the fabric gave me the willies.

Shoes on, I unlocked the door and pulled it open to reveal Porter.

I hadn't opened the door to a non-Japanese in six months, and the shock first articulated itself as a flash of 'What's Wrong With This Picture?' The answer: *Light brown hair.* Then I said, 'Oh my God,' into the hand covering my mouth. 'Come in!' I reached out and pulled him by his jacket out of the cold. Still holding his jacket I closed the door. He had his hands down by his sides and his eyebrows way up, and I knew they were asking me if it was OK to hug, and I put my arms around his neck. His cold cheek on my warm one was unfamiliar – we had never hugged in cold weather before – but I felt his long arms go around my back in a way that felt years old, and his long fingers held my ribs, like hinges on curved doors.

'I took the subway,' he said, with his lips on my neck, as if it were an endearment, and I laughed and was about to ask him how the hell he'd managed when he said, 'Oh! Hello!', and I turned my head to see Yuki standing in the doorway to the kitchen-dining area. Seeing us hugging made her uncertain, and she didn't say hello back.

'Yuki,' I said, leading Porter to the shoe cabinet, 'this is my good friend, Porter. Say hello!'

'Harro.'

'Harro,' said Porter.

'Don't do that,' I said. 'Take your shoes off.' I was so excited and nervous and giddy it made me bossy. I was grasping his jacket again as we stepped up together onto the wooden floor of the hallway, and I used him to steady myself when I put my feet back into my slippers. Yuki put her arms up to me and I picked her up, and she and Porter looked at each other. Porter stuck his tongue out at her to make her smile. 'Wow,' he said, and looked at me. 'What a great face.'

'I know. She's the cutest.'

'I totally get why you prefer her to me.'

'I do? I mean, you do?'

Porter laughed, and started to look around. I put Yuki down, and pulled on the back of Porter's jacket so that he'd shrug out of it.

'Let's show Porter our dollies,' I said to Yuki, and she marched into the tatami room. Porter followed me there, and stood with his hands on his hips taking it in. I remembered seeing it for the first time the previous August, thinking the *tokonoma* – the recessed area with the hanging scroll and the vase – was an inefficient use of space. Now I valued the quiet corner it represented, the insistence that one stand back from it in respect, to contemplate the painting. At the beginning of autumn, Yoshimura-san had replaced the dragonflies with a painting of a blue and orange bird among a splash of maple leaves. When the weather grew cold, she replaced that with a painting of a gnarled pine branch. Instead of a flower in a vase, there was a large, smooth stone, shaped like a gently sloping hill, on a low wooden stand made especially for it.

Yuki tried to get Porter's attention by making her doll say, 'How are you?'

'How am I?' Porter asked the doll as he folded himself down to kneel on the tatami. 'I'm fine. How are *you*?'

'I'm fine,' Yuki said, tipping the doll from side to side to show that it was the one talking.

'Would you like tea?' I asked him.

'I'd love tea.'

I got up to put the hot water on, and while I waited for it to boil I returned to the edge of the tatami room. Porter had picked up a doll, and was making it shake hands with Yuki's.

'You took the subway?' I asked him.

'The Narita Express from the airport, then the subway.'

'That's amazing.'

'It was very hard work.'

'I don't think I would have found it possible on my first day.'

'Clever me. Let's dance around, Dolly. Actually, I landed late last night. It's taken me this long to get to your house.'

'Really?'

'No. Ha. Gotcha. I stayed in a youth hostel.'

'And when are you going back?'

'Sunday evening. Let's look out the window. Come on.'

He wasn't talking to me any more. His doll led the way, Yuki and her doll followed in delight, and I went back to the kitchen to pour the water into the teapot, experiencing the thrill of knowing that he'd kept the secret of the trip, that he'd made arrangements for somewhere to stay, that he'd had kept the birthday gift of himself until the very day I turned twenty-five. I put the teapot and teacups on a tray and brought it to the dining table, imagining him lying on a narrow bed in a featureless hostel, blinking in the dark, too excited and too jet-lagged to sleep.

'Did you have any trouble sleeping last night?' I called over to him.

'Nope. It was great.'

'Oh.'

He got up and asked Yuki to come with him to the table, and she reached up to take his hand.

'Tonight will be much worse, I'm sure,' he said. 'High chair?'

I nodded, and he lifted Yuki into her place. 'This is my,' she told him, holding up the Hello Kitty cup of water I had put in front of her.

'Awesome!' he told her.

The teacups I had brought for us were Japanese, handle-less, and mismatched, one blue with large white dots, one white with a repeating pattern of pale pink leaves.

I remembered the first time Michiko had made tea for me. Both cups had been painted with cherry blossoms, but one was bigger, with a black background; the smaller one had a red background. She picked up the black one and began to turn it slowly around and around in her palms, warming it for me. I'd never seen anyone do something like that. I reached over and took the red cup into my hands to warm it as Michiko poured green tea into the black cup for me. She looked a little embarrassed, as well as pleased. 'The big cup is Hiro's,' she said.

'They look like a set.'

She nodded. 'They are often given when couples get married.'

'And the man's cup is bigger than the woman's.'

'Yes.'

'They're made like that.'

'Yes.'

'Even if the man is the same size as the woman.'

Michiko laughed. 'Yes.'

147

I told Porter that story, turning the blue cup in my palms for him.

'You're warming the blue one for me now?'

'Yes.'

'That's so lovely. But the story kind of makes me want to drink out of the pink one, on principle.'

'Nice,' I said, 'but the tea will be too strong if we wait longer. Can I give you the pink one next time?'

'OK.'

I poured for him, and I poured a splash into Yuki's water to please her, and I poured for myself, and we all dropped our faces to the liquid, and it was better than flaming candles and champagne.

Yuki and I took Porter to visit the massive, eerily quiet Meiji Shrine – the most beautiful place in the city, to my mind – and en route I chattered to him in a way I seldom chatter. I praised the vending machines that offered hot drinks as well as cold in winter; I pointed out how tidily the people who slept in boxes in the subway station lived, their shoes lined up so poignantly outside their cardboard spaces; I showed him the symbol of Tokyo, the fan-shaped ginkgo leaf, and we all competed to find examples painted on the side of garbage trucks, screwed to the front of buses, bent into the fence between the sidewalk and the road, moulded into manhole covers.

Porter piggybacked Yuki while I pushed the empty stroller down the long, wide expanse of gravel that led to the shrine, and Porter tried to get Yuki to pronounce his name correctly.

'Porter.'

'Pohtah.'

'Porter.'

'Pohtah.'

Every time she got it wrong he galloped like a horse and bounced her around, and she was weak from laughing by the time we reached the shrine courtyard. We watched a procession of five priests file by in their creamy robes and bulbous lacquered black clogs, their voluminous sleeves billowing, three of them in tall black hats that extended out behind their heads ('Like cassowaries,' Porter said), two of them in small black hats with a bouncing arc of fabric attached to the back ('Like great-tailed grackles'). If Yuki had asked me if I was her mother at the moment we arrived at the shrine, smiling, out of breath, and completely charmed by the company and the surroundings, I think I would have been tempted to say yes.

At lunchtime we sat with Yuki between us in the revolving sushi bar I'd been to with Emi. Yuki wasn't adept with chopsticks yet, but it's fine to eat sushi with your hands in any case, so Porter used his hands too. 'It's so much easier to turn the sushi over and dip the fish in the soy sauce this way!' he said. 'This needs to be a headline in the newspaper. EXTRA! EXTRA! HANDS FINE FOR SUSHI!'

I laughed.

'Subtitle,' he continued, 'Nervous People on Dates No Longer Need to Worry about Splashing Selves with Soy.'

We continued eating, and I realised Porter might have been talking about himself.

'Are you nervous, Porter?'

He'd been about to put a morsel in his mouth, and he

149

lowered his hand and looked straight at me over Yuki's head. 'I'm so nervous I'm surprised I can keep my food down. Aren't you nervous?'

'Yes.'

'Do you want to puke?'

'No, I don't want to puke.'

He sat up tall and looked around us. 'Why am I so nervous?'

'Jet lag can make you nauseous,' I offered.

'Nope. I'm nervous,' he said. Then he shrugged. 'It's kind of fun.' He picked his food up again and popped it in his mouth.

'*Omizu*,' Yuki said.

'Water, please?' I instructed her, and she parroted me. I raised my hand to get the attention of the waitress, and when she came I had Yuki ask for water herself.

'It's a nice job you have,' Porter said once Yuki had her water. 'You're good at it.'

'Thank you. Doesn't feel like a job.'

'That's the ideal.'

'Usually. But ideal jobs are hard to walk away from.'

Porter nodded. He looked like he was about to say something, but I spoke first. I asked him if he'd found his ideal job.

'It's not far off,' he said. 'But part of that is the location. So great.'

I nodded, and pictured him back in Hawaii in time for work on Monday. He was leaving on an evening flight on Sunday.

Leaving. Being the one left is so different from being the one leaving. Once he was gone, we'd be even. Then what?

150

I did want to puke.

'What shall we do tomorrow, then?' Porter said in bright contrast to the quiet, heads-down eaters around us.

'Tomorrow's Yuki's swimming lesson.'

'Excellent!'

'It should be easy to get to from your hostel. I'll draw you a map when we get home.'

I remembered how Naoki had torn a piece of paper off the roll in the fax machine to write the name of the train station near the sports complex for me in kanji and English, and the way the ink of his fountain pen went immediately from black to slate grey on the smooth absorbent paper, looking old rather than new. Once he'd done that he realised he couldn't help me any more than that and had to call his mother to come over and draw me a map, because she had been taking Yuki to her swimming lessons. Naoki had never been. I remembered how terrified I was of getting us lost, and how I had found it through the kindness of several patient people along the way.

The waitress came and tallied our sushi plates, and Porter snatched the bill from her and held it away from my reaching hands.

'But you paid for a plane ticket,' I said.

'But it's your birthday,' he said, getting up off his stool and striding to the counter. I'd forgotten.

I zipped Yuki back into her coat and retrieved the stroller from the corner by the door.

Outside, the day remained bright and invigorating. Porter took Yuki up onto his back again. 'I feel like I'm under water,' he said.

'Let's walk fast so you stay awake.'

We strode the length of Omotesando, and I pointed a few things out to him, but he didn't say much. By the time we arrived at the entrance to the subway station, Yuki was asleep with her head between his shoulder blades, and while Porter's cheeks were pink and glowing, the skin under his eyes seemed to have sagged. We put Yuki in the stroller and carried her down the stairs in it together. Porter's head lolled on my shoulder as we sat in the overheated train, and when we emerged from the station stairs onto the sidewalk at our stop I bought him a little hot can of coffee for the walk home.

'I've lost the will to live,' he whispered when we were taking our shoes off.

'You can take a nap on my bed,' I whispered back.

'But it's your birthday. I need to stay awake.'

'No you don't.'

He thought for a second, swaying on his feet. Or he tried to think. I doubt he succeeded. 'OK,' he said.

While it was always possible to move Yuki around in the night without waking her up, I'd never succeeded in keeping her asleep when I took her out of the stroller at nap time, so I left her by the shoe cabinet and led Porter upstairs. He didn't stop to take in the details of my bedroom before the need for sleep felled him, and suddenly I was the only one awake in the house. I listened to the quiet, and until I began to worry that Yuki would wake up and think she was alone, I didn't move a muscle. I tried to stop time, and it felt like I had. No car went past. No crow crowed. My breath sat quietly in my lungs. I had no difficult decisions to make that moment, that day.

*

'We can't go out for dinner, can we?' Porter asked thickly when I'd dragged him out of a deep sleep two hours later and sat him in front of a cup of coffee at the table.

'I don't think so. It's too short notice to ask Yoshimura-san to take care of Yuki for the evening. And I'd be nervous about doing that even with a long lead time.'

'What about Naoki?'

'I don't know when he'll be home, actually.'

Porter sipped his coffee several times. Eventually he asked, 'Could you call him and ask him?'

'If I were his wife rather than his employee, maybe. Even then I'm not so sure.'

'Dang.'

'It's OK. We'll be able to go out tomorrow night. And if Naoki comes home while you're here, you can meet him.'

'Whoopdeedo.'

Yuki's head snapped up from her modelling clay at the funny word. 'Whoopdeedo?'

Porter sat up a bit straighter. 'Yes,' he answered her. 'And thingamajig.'

'Singa—'

'Whoopdeedo, thingamajig, joegrabasixpack, doohickey.'

Yuki's giggles seemed to clear Porter's head more than the coffee.

'You must know doohickey. You don't know *doohickey*? Want me to make you one?' Yuki looked at him, dark eyes open wide and sparkling, relishing without understanding. Encouraged, Porter continued. 'I'll make you one. Gimme some clay.'

While they played, I took a packet of salmon out of the

freezer and sat it in a pan of room-temperature water to thaw. I hoped Naoki would come home, and that he'd have Akemi with him as well, so Porter could have as much of the picture as possible. We were on our own with Yuki all late afternoon and evening, though, only getting as far as three or four sentences into a lot of interesting conversations before Yuki's half-entertaining, half-irritating interruptions made us give up the effort and offer her our undivided attention.

Getting Yuki ready for bed, I imagined sitting back down at the dining table with Porter, reaching out for his hand and squeezing it as we talked, seeing how that felt. I looked forward to the rest of the evening, my heart quickening just a little as I started back down the stairs, but the shock of seeing Porter standing in shadow at the bottom of them made me stop on the second one, mouth suddenly dry, as threatened as if he'd loomed out of the darkness of an alley. I couldn't make myself take another step.

'How long have you been there?'

'Feels like forever,' he said.

I didn't know what to say.

'I'm getting kind of light-headed from standing, to be honest,' he continued. 'But it was nice to listen to your voices.'

He put his hands in his pockets and rocked on his heels, and that was a relief because I could see that he was nervous rather than predatory. It's strange, now, to think I ever worried that he might be, but once bitten, twice shy. Four times bitten, forever shy? Possibly. Stopping on those stairs had nothing to do with Porter's character, only with his gender. The nicest man in the world is still a man, and once you're taught that men are circling sharks, you're on the lookout for fins.

He kept smiling up at me, though. He looked so friendly and hopeful that I continued down the stairs and put my hands out to him when I was on the bottom one. It made my heart clang in my chest, but I did it anyway. His hands flew out of his pockets to meet mine and he stepped forward so that we were face to face, and then even closer so that our mouths met, and we both exhaled through our noses. I disentangled my fingers and put my hands on his face. His hands went to the top of my tail-bone, which wasn't what I thought I wanted, but when he pulled me closer and I felt his penis pressing me where I'd been pressed on the subway, it wasn't as much like being pressed on the subway as I'd worried it would be. I laughed, and he didn't ask why. Instead he said, 'Your heart.'

'You can feel it?'

'It's like it's banging on the door of my chest.'

That was a much better image than the one I was experiencing, in which I had two hearts – one that wanted me to take off my clothes immediately, and one that wanted me never to take off my clothes – and they were beating each other up.

I pushed him back a little so I could step down onto the floor, and put my cheek against his chest to see if I could feel his heart.

'Naoki could walk in at any time, couldn't he?' Porter said over my head.

'Yes.'

'I guess it's parlour games for us tonight, then.'

155

He lifted my face and kissed me again, and I thanked the risk of Naoki for buying me some more time.

We talked at the dining table about all the memorable things that had happened during his trip across the US that hadn't made it onto his postcards to me, and he left after eleven, without meeting anyone.

17

Yuki and I were up and out the next morning before Naoki had emerged (or Naoki and Akemi – I didn't know how many people were behind his closed bedroom door). We had agreed to meet Porter at the train station near the sports complex early enough for a meal before the swimming lesson, and there he was, looking around at the top of the stairs. The weather had turned nasty and a very cold breeze was playing with his forelock and with the map in his hand. 'Can we have soba?' he said, after kissing each of us on the cheek. 'Come back into the station, then,' I said, and we retreated into the relative warmth. I wouldn't have been able to manage eating at the stand-up soba restaurant near the bottom of the stairs on my own with Yuki, given the lack of chairs, but Porter was so keen, and Yuki so happy to be picked up by him, that we were able to have a satisfying lunch by taking turns holding Yuki in front of us at table height while the other one ate and fed Yuki too.

'How was your night?' I asked.

'What night?'

'Ooh. That bad?'

'I'll just muscle on through. Probably better not to try to adjust.'

'Don't be surprised if your memories are blurry.'

'I'll remember this soba,' he said.

'Oh yeah? It's not great.'

'Yes it is. It's amazing.'

'Pohtah turn!' Yuki said, and I transferred her to his arms so she and I could eat some noodles.

Before we arrived at the sports complex I called Naoki from a payphone to ask him his plans for the day, so I could find out when I could leave Yuki with him before going out again.

'You're not staying home tonight?' he said.

'I've got a friend in town, so I want to have dinner out,' I told him.

'Oh, OK. Well, I'm going out this afternoon. You can leave her with my mother.'

'OK, sounds good. See you later.'

I told Porter, 'I wonder if you'll meet Naoki at all. He's going out today.'

'I'll have to meet him next time,' he said as we pushed through the glass doors into the steamy warmth of the sports complex.

'You're coming back?' I asked as I folded up the stroller.

'Depends on how long you're staying. Might have to.'

'Wait here. I'll be less than ten minutes,' I said. I parked the stroller in the designated area and took Yuki into the locker room.

When I got back to reception Porter said, 'How long *are* you staying, actually?'

'Can we talk about that after swimming?'

'OK.'

'Let's go up to watch Yuki. She'll be looking for us.' I led him through the staircase door, hearing the twitters of the last few mothers as they left the staircase on the second floor.

'We can't talk about it up there?'

'It depends if Emi's there or not.'

'Oh, right.' His voice echoed in the damp cold of the stairwell.

'We won't sit with her, OK?' I said. 'I won't introduce you.'

'OK. I might smile at her, though, if she looks at me. It's in my nature.'

'Fair enough.'

She was in her usual place at the far end of the second bench from the front, sitting ramrod straight in a sweater of muted autumn colours. She looked over when she heard me say 'How about there?' to Porter, pointing to a space at the near end of the third bench, and she did a comical little double-take. I'd told her about Porter during one of our teas, so when her eyebrows twitched me the question I winked back the answer, and sat down. A few of the other mothers turned around to have a look at us, and when my eyes met theirs they gave me a little bow, keeping their eyes up as they did so to look at Porter a little longer.

'Hello, ladies,' he said, and they turned uncertainly back around.

'I'll let you find Yuki yourself,' I told him, and he was surprisingly swift at it.

It was even stranger than usual to leave Emi behind in the sports complex that day. If she hadn't been there I would likely have continued on in the bubble of contentment I felt surrounding me when Porter and I were on our own with Yuki. But I caught our smiling reflection in the glass as we walked back outside, and I was sure Emi's reflection wouldn't look so light-hearted when she passed that window on her own way out.

It took four stops on the circular, above-ground Yamanote Line and nine stops on the subway to get to the Edo-Tokyo Museum, a place I'd been to once on my own and had wanted to return to with Yuki. The walk from the station took us past the National Sumo Arena. 'Ooh, cool,' Porter said. 'Can we go in?'

'We could, yeah. I think there's a museum inside. Not so interesting for Yuki, though. Do you mind if we just do one activity today?'

'Sure.'

'Also, women aren't allowed to touch the ring they wrestle in.'

'Why not?'

'They're impure.'

'Oh yeah. Of course. I forgot.'

His bitter joke made us thoughtful as we approached the huge square in front of the Edo-Tokyo Museum. I shifted my focus to Yuki, who was showing signs of falling asleep. I wanted her to see the enchanting miniatures of seventeenth- and eighteenth-century life in the museum, so I stopped to take her out of the stroller. 'I know what to do,' I said, taking Yuki by the hand. 'Run!' Yuki and I took off across the bleak grey square towards the elevated, hyper-modern building. It looked as if it had stopped lumbering through the city and was deciding where to go next. Porter jogged after us with the stroller, and we were all laughing.

*

Grey in the face again after the museum, Porter went back to his hostel for a nap and I took the already sleeping Yuki home. The look Yoshimura-san gave me when I brought Yuki to her front door was a new one, and I couldn't read it. Normally she smiled quite sweetly, if not entirely naturally, or she looked distracted. This time, if it had been more normal for us to converse, I might have asked her if everything was OK, because I felt some anger around her eyes. Her mouth was no tighter than usual, though. Maybe it wasn't a good time for her to have Yuki. But she knew that I had Saturday evenings off. I told myself the inconvenience was something for her to take up with Naoki, not me.

Porter had said that he couldn't leave Tokyo without eating sukiyaki, because of the Kyu Sakamoto song, which was perfect, as it's a winter dish. The whole meal was perfect. The restaurant had a main seating area with tables, and a row of small, private tatami rooms along one side. We had one of those rooms to ourselves, attended by a very young, perfectly round-faced woman in a mauve-grey kimono. We submerged thinly sliced marbled beef, fluffy tofu, fat scallions, Chinese cabbage, chrysanthemum leaves and devil's tongue noodles in the soup bubbling in the cast-iron pot between us, and we drank Kirin Ichiban beer. Every time the waitress came to check on us and pulled the bottom of her kimono into the perfect position for kneeling by our table we loved her more.

'I want to be able to do that with my life,' Porter said, just a tiny bit cross-eyed, after she'd refilled our glasses.

'What?'

'Give it a little tug so that it fits just right for the position I want to take.'

I laughed. 'What position is that?'

'Oh. I don't know. I'm speaking generally. But while we're on the subject . . .'

'I just wear comfortable clothing. Then any position's fine.'

That seemed to derail him. I ladled some more greens into our bowls. 'Yeah, but,' he said, 'what about your life? How long are you going to stay here?'

I chewed on a tangle of chrysanthemum leaves. When I swallowed, the giddiness in my chest fell to my stomach too. 'I wish I knew,' I said.

'Do you really?'

'Yes I really.'

'Can you just, maybe, decide?'

'Like, choose a date, and tell them when I'm going?'

'Exactly. Wait. Woah. You look so sad. Don't think about it! I'm sorry I said anything! Stop thinking about it!'

'No, no, you're right. I have to. I can't stay for ever.'

'Well, you could.'

I feel like I'll remember the look he gave me when he said those three words as long as I live, because it was the look of love. Not the 'I can hardly wait to hold you' look of love, but the 'I'll wait to hold you; I'm here to help' look. He wasn't jumping on the fact that I'd said I couldn't stay. He wasn't pushing me to decide, to calm his own anxieties. I shook my head. 'Someone could, maybe,' I said, 'but not me.'

Porter failed to disguise his relief behind the rice bowl he held up to his face.

I continued. 'We haven't heard whether Yuki will be able to get a place in daycare yet, so I'm not sure exactly what my job is going to become, but either way, the house is getting crowded.'

'How about my birthday?' Porter said through a big wad of rice.

'How about your birthday what?'

'How about you leave on my birthday?'

'June the um, wait . . . June the second?'

'Yes. Akemi's baby is due in August, right?'

'You've calculated her due date?'

He ignored the question. 'So she'll probably start maternity leave in early July or something, so if you say you're going to leave in June, she and Naoki will have to get started thinking about who will take care of the kids, and they'll make sure someone is in place, and then it will all be fine.'

June sounded very soon to me, but I didn't want to say that.

'I'll think about it,' I told him, and our waitress came back and tugged her kimono perfectly, and knelt down to turn the fire off under our hotpot because the soup was reducing and the remaining noodles were starting to stick to the sides. 'Let's finish up,' I said.

Back out on the street I looked up at the sky and was surprised to find the weather had changed completely and the light of a fat full moon glowed on my face.

'The Japanese don't see a man in the moon, you know,' I told Porter, and we started walking.

'No?'

'They see a rabbit.'

'Oh!' He stopped walking and looked up. 'Can you see a rabbit?'

'I've tried.'

'Let me try.'

I waited.

'Is the rabbit they see really lumpy?'

'I don't know.'

'If it is, I've seen it.'

I took his arm and we kept walking. A wave of happiness made me clamp his arm against my chest and press my head hard against his shoulder.

Porter put his lips against the top of my head. 'If I weren't staying in a narrow bunk bed with the possibility of one, two or even three room-mates tonight, would you come back with me?'

'Yep,' I said, and I believed it.

The light was on in the kitchen when I got home, which wasn't unusual, but Naoki was sitting sideways at the table with his arm over the back of the chair, looking down the hallway at me. He didn't appear to have been reading a newspaper or a book, and the house was silent, so he hadn't been watching television. I hung up my coat and put my shoes in the cabinet and stepped up onto the wooden floor, and Naoki said, 'You had a man here in this house?'

'Yesterday, yes.'

'What man?'

'My friend who is visiting from the US.'

'He played with Yuki?'

'Yes,' I said, smiling at the memory. Doohickey. I could feel that Naoki was upset in some way. His voice was hard, but the beer hadn't worn off enough on the way back home for me to really pick up his signals. 'They had fun.'

'You let a man play with my Yuki without you?' His voice was building in intensity.

'What? I was here.'

'He was alone with Yuki. My mother saw him.'

'No, he was . . . Oh, wait.'

'You see! She was alone with a man!'

'No!'

Yoshimura-san must have been in her tatami room when Porter was on the floor with Yuki and I was making tea. From her tatami room she would have been able to see Porter at the window with Yuki, but not me talking to him from the dining area. When Porter and Yuki got up and left the tatami room, she wouldn't have known where they'd gone.

'You do *not* leave Yuki alone with anyone without telling me, and you *never* leave her alone with a man.'

I was still standing in front of him and he still sat there, like a parent who was angry about having had to wait up so long. But not like a father. Like a mother. He had his narrow legs crossed, and his pinched voice was rising.

'I *didn't*, Naoki,' I squeaked, feeling ten years younger, embarrassed and guilty, before I caught myself. I had to clear my throat to bring my voice back down. 'Naoki, I didn't leave her alone. I was here. I was making tea. Your mother couldn't see me.'

'Why should I believe you?'

Still slow on the uptake, I stalled for time. 'Well,' I said, hoping I'd come up with a reason, until finally I realised that I shouldn't have to give one. 'Why should you *not* believe me?' I asked him a bit more forcefully.

I don't think he had anticipated this question, and he changed tack. 'And where were you today?'

165

'At swimming.'

'Was he there?'

'Yes.'

Now Naoki stood up, exploding out of his chair towards me so that I had to wheel my arms to keep my balance in my socks. 'You took a man to watch Yuki in her *swimsuit*?' he shouted, spraying my face with spit. His face was red now, but it hadn't been when I came in, and his breath didn't smell strongly of alcohol. This wasn't drunkenness speaking. He was truly angry. These were his true feelings screeching at me, and I thought of Emi and how she had just wanted to leave to make it stop. I actually might have left too, if I had thought he'd let me come back, but I knew he wouldn't, and I had to stay with Yuki.

I sobered up. 'Naoki,' I said. 'You don't have to worry about Porter.'

'Yes I do,' he hissed, and stalked over to the kitchen. 'I have to worry about everything, and I gave you this job so that I can be peaceful. I am very busy.'

'You can be peaceful. Yuki will never see Porter again.'

He crossed his arms and glared at me. 'Or any other man.'

I nodded. 'Or any other man.'

After some thought he said, 'OK.'

'Please tell your mother. You have nothing to worry about. She has nothing to worry about.'

He didn't say anything to that, just walked past me out of the room and up the stairs, leaving me to turn out the light.

I didn't want to go upstairs, not until Naoki had finished his bath and there was no chance of seeing him, so I sat down at the table. I pictured myself in Hawaii, swimming with Porter. When I thought about Naoki shouting at me, June the second felt much too long to wait. If I gave him three months' notice, I could leave in May. Twelve weeks. Still an eternity at such close quarters with someone so erratic. But when I thought about Yuki, it still felt too soon. I didn't want to leave before I felt sure a new nanny would love her.

I went to bed when Naoki had finished bathing and I'd heard the closing of his bedroom door. Lying in the dark I thought about helping Naoki to interview candidates for my position. I imagined candidates coming to the house to meet us, and every time I opened the door, the woman outside looked like me.

18

Porter's youth hostel had a small, cold lobby with a cheap faux-leather couch and armchairs and a coffee table covered in manga comics. I was supposed to meet him there at nine but I arrived well before eight thirty and sat waiting on the edge of a chair, knees bobbing with adrenalin. He needed to be at Narita Airport by about five, which meant getting a Narita Express train at about four. That gave us seven hours together, a luxuriously long time if we just sat and talked, but painfully short if Porter wanted to go out and do things. I was worried that he would, and that time would fly. More than that I worried that my mood would ruin the day, because I still felt fragile and confused after Naoki's explosion the night before. I worried that Porter would be angry at Naoki and that I'd have to manage two angry men rather than one. I worried that Porter would want to find a place to have sex when I was no longer in the mood. I worried that I had more than one decision I didn't know how to make.

A couple of the manga on the table were in English, but most of them were Japanese. I picked up *Sailor Moon* to distract myself by trying to read the dialogue, but there were too many kanji. I could pronounce the sound effects, and I did that for a while, skipping to the scenes where Sailor Moon was fighting and exclaiming, but that didn't help me understand the story, and then I became fascinated by the way her gigantic eyes were drawn. In so many of the drawings her irises and pupils looked like the variable shapes inside a lava lamp – bright blobs in a dark liquid, or in space. That made sense, since her job was to save the solar system from destruction. In one big drawing, though, there were straighter lines, more like the road to the end of a tunnel. Maybe she'd made a decision. Maybe she knew what to do. Her tiny fists were clenched, the feet at the end of her long skinny boots planted. I envied her resolve, and put the manga down.

My fingers felt dirty after turning its pages, so I asked if there was a bathroom I could use. When I returned, Porter was standing by the coffee table with his back to me, looking out the window, bobbing on the balls of his feet. It was still before nine; he was anxious to see me too. It occurred to me to walk up behind him and put my arms around him, but I hesitated, standing at the corner of the registration desk for a moment, not wanting to begin the beginning of the end. There were so many ways the day could go, and I wanted them all to remain possibilities for one more moment. Then I took a few steps towards him and said his name. When he wheeled around and took me in he said, 'Woah, where did you come from? Did you stay here last night too?'

'No,' I said, laughing. 'Toilet.'

He clonked his shin against the coffee table when he passed it to get to me, wincing briefly but throwing the wince away before wrapping me in a hug and kissing me so loudly on the cheek that it hurt my ear.

'Ow!' I said.

'Oh no, sorry, sorry. Are you OK?'

'Yes, I'm OK now. Are you OK?'

'I think so, but let's look.'

He took me by the hand and we sat down on the couch with our backs to the registration desk, and he pulled up the left leg of his jeans to inspect the damage to his skin. 'Why isn't there more skin covering our shin bones?' he asked.

'I wonder.'

'I think everyone has hurt themselves in a way that exposes the white of the bone.'

'I've certainly done it shaving.'

'Horrible.'

'Think you'll survive?'

He pulled his trouser leg back down and sat up. 'Yes. The bonk to the shin, yes. Not so sure about the long goodbye that is the day ahead of us.'

I nodded, looked out the window, bit my lip.

'I'll need distracting,' he continued. 'Where shall we eat? Where shall we go?'

'I need to tell you something first.'

'Oh no.'

'No, it's not about you, Porter.' I took his cold hand. 'It's not about us.'

I told him about how Naoki had behaved the night before. As I talked, the sun rose above the buildings opposite the hostel, its light coming in like a tide across the coffee table so that by the time I had finished the story we both had our jackets off and didn't look at all like two people preparing for a day of sightseeing.

Porter had made a few confused and then outraged noises while I talked, but when I stopped he was quiet for a while. He looked down at the floor to think, and then looked back at me. 'Does that help you make a decision about leaving?'

'I thought it did.'

'Oh.'

'I don't think I can leave without making sure that whoever's taking care of Yuki is good for Yuki.'

'What about Akemi?'

'She won't be taking care of Yuki.'

'Maybe she will. Maybe having a baby will make her rethink her career or something.'

'Maybe. Anything's possible. I can't leave based on maybe, though. And she's not connecting with Yuki at all.'

He thought again. 'Devil's advocate?' he said.

'OK.'

'Was Yuki fine before you arrived?'

I felt my heart sink at the question, because the answer was yes.

'She was, wasn't she?'

I had to nod.

'So can you be so sure she won't be fine if you leave?'

'No, but a lot has changed. Akemi takes up Naoki's time. And Naoki's so strange, anyway.'

'Naoki's a nut. But he's her dad. Not the first strange dad in the world. People do OK with strange dads all the time.'

I crossed my arms and uncrossed my legs, trying to stabil-ise my position. 'I just don't feel right. And she's attached to me. I don't want her to feel abandoned.'

'Of course.'

We both looked out the window. Nobody walked by.

'Would you feel better if Yuki lived with her mother?' Porter asked.

'I think so.'

'But that's not going to happen, right?'

'Doesn't seem like it.'

Porter gently untied my arms and took my hands in his now warm ones. 'It looks like it boils down to this, Diana. One, you're worried about leaving Yuki with her nutty family. And two, if you don't mind my saying, you're worried that leaving Yuki might break your heart.'

He'd set off sparklers in my throat and he knew it. He put his arms around me and slid me across the slippery faux leather so that I was right up against him as the tears welled up and spilled over. Six months of tension that I avoided acknowledging felt like a tight ball of prickly twine in the centre of my chest. Crying made it roll, as if the tears were the twine and I was pulling it out through my eyes. I needed to cry until it had unrolled completely, but it hurt. To stop myself from making any noise I put my arms around Porter's back, grabbing his flannel shirt in my fists and pressing my forehead and eyes against his bony chest, closing out the light, squashing my nose against a button, shaking with waves of silent sobs, feeling confused, feeling unequal to the challenge, feeling appreciative that he didn't try to shush me when sounds escaped my efforts to subdue them, feeling amazed that I knew it was absolutely fine to hold him so hard. After a while my whole face was liquid, and I tried to sit up again but he held me close.

'But snot,' I said.

'It's OK,' he said, pressing my head against his chest again.

'Drool,' I said into his shirt.

'Also OK.'

That made me cry-laugh, and cry some more, but the pressure in my chest started to settle, and I turned my head so my cheek was against him. I opened my eyes and was dazzled by the sunshine.

'I need a tissue so badly but I don't want to let go.'

Porter shifted to look over his shoulder at the woman behind the registration desk and asked for a tissue. I heard her come towards us and saw Porter's arm reach back to receive the tissues, but I didn't move until he held the packet in front of my face. It took five of them to feel I'd cleaned up.

A tall young man with spiky blond hair came out of the elevator and clomped past us in denim everything and heavy army boots, singing, and opened the door so heartily that it clattered against the wall before returning slowly to close itself. He passed in front of the window, his mouth still moving in song, and the woman behind the registration desk muttered and tutted, obviously frustrated but sounding like a courting pigeon. I sat my pile of used tissues next to me on the couch and leaned back against Porter with a sigh, and he put his arm back around me. I think that was the moment when I realised that I might actually be safe with Porter, that being around him was both exciting and calming, not alternately but at the very same time.

I expected him to say something funny, but he didn't. He seemed to be waiting, and then he sighed deeply too, and we both slouched down so that we could rest our heads against the back of the couch like a couple in a movie theatre. Now that the sun had reached all the way across us, I could stop being so painfully aware of the passing of time again.

'I could fall asleep right here,' I said.

'Want to?'

'I'm starving, though.'

'Yeah?' he said. 'Thank God.'

I wanted to take Porter to an area called Kagurazaka. Michiko had recommended it to me, as it was like a mini-Kyoto, with several temples, and small streets of old, traditional restaurants, and even some geisha, but I hadn't made the effort to get there yet. I thought that taking Porter somewhere neither of us had been before would feel as if we were on a trip together, a pair of tourists visiting somewhere new to both of us.

'Somewhere to eat between here and the subway?' Porter asked as he closed the hostel door with exaggerated care and smiled through the window to the woman behind the counter.

'Probably,' I said. 'There usually is,' but the only place open in that neighbourhood at mid-morning on a Sunday was a bright yellow and black Doutor coffee shop.

'How's the coffee here?'

'I find it bitter, actually, but this place is popular.'

'Will I find it bitter, do you think?'

I had to stop to think.

'Did we drink coffee together in Boston?'

'Espresso,' he answered without having to think. 'In the North End. With those cannoli we couldn't finish.'

The memory made me smile. Summertime in the North End. Fat Italian guys in sunglasses sitting outside little restaurants, checking out the foot traffic. 'This coffee isn't like that. This coffee shop isn't like that. I don't know if you'll like it.'

'Can we try, even though you don't like it? Then you'll know if I like it.'

'Is that important?'

'I know *you* don't like it, but you don't know if *I* do, so that's not fair.'

'If you say so,' I said, laughing, pulling the door open and stepping inside.

He stopped me inside the door and turned me to face him. 'Am I overwhelming?' he said.

'Not yet.'

'How about stupid?'

'Not at all.'

'We don't have to have coffee here.'

'I know. But I'm starving. Look at all the individually wrapped cookies there are to choose from.' We looked at the display under the counter. 'And I want to know if you like their coffee.'

In the end we walked to Kagurazaka, holding hands inside Porter's jacket pocket, keeping to the sunny side of the street. Porter hadn't brought a hat, so his ears were bright red. The weather and the walking kept us hungry as well as cold, and we ducked into two restaurants along the way, eating sushi in a busy shopping district and then matcha green tea cake in a nondescript neighbourhood about half an hour later. Just when we were starting to talk about food again we found the Buddhist temple that Michiko had described to me. Porter asked me what it was called, but I didn't remember what she had said. It was so hard to remember Japanese place names because they didn't sound like anything I already knew. Unless they were repeated to me regularly, my brain couldn't hold on to them.

'Imagine a church daring to paint itself this colour orange,' Porter said as we stood at the bottom of the broad stone steps.

'Or installing tiger sculptures,' I said.

A pair of hulking stone cats, chiselled with faint stripes, watched us from either side of the stairs, heads down low between their shoulders, mouths grinning or growling, tails like snakes winding up their backs.

'It's not very Zen, is it?' Porter said.

'No?'

'Isn't Zen peaceful? Orange isn't peaceful.'

'Maybe the people are. I don't know about the buildings. Plus, maybe this isn't a Zen temple.'

A woman and what looked to be her mother climbed the stairs and stood inside the open black doors at the top. A man on his own went up as well.

'Hey,' said Porter, who had turned all the way around. 'Cobblestones.'

'Where?'

We walked back out to the sidewalk and crossed the street to a narrow alley that we entered and followed past walls protecting buildings topped with the same sort of handsome, curved, dark grey roof tiles on Naoki's parents' house. The further in we went, the more discreet the frontage, the fewer the people, and the more powerful the sense of travelling backwards in time.

'This is what Michiko must have meant,' I said.

'Is this what Kyoto is like?'

'I don't know, but it's not what Tokyo is like.'

'What are these places?'

'Restaurants, I think. Fine restaurants. See that lantern? That's a restaurant sign.'

We turned right at one corner and walked along in reverent silence. After a few more corners we suddenly stopped, by unspoken consent. To our left was a wall of wide horizontal planks of black-painted wood, to our right a wall of what looked like clay, painted ochre. Ahead of us, where the alley turned, was a low wall of flat grey stones topped with a fence of upright bamboo lashed together with black twine. The curves of cobblestones at our feet lapped towards us like an incoming sea.

'I have no idea what's going on here,' Porter said.

'Neither do I.'

'It's all texture. The only thing I can interpret is the texture.'

'Exactly,' I said.

'I've never seen anywhere so intensely private in my life.'

I shuddered involuntarily at the atmosphere of secrecy, but Porter didn't feel it. I think he would have said something if he had, but instead he turned towards me and looked intensely into my eyes. We'd been together for over three hours, but so far we hadn't looked into each other's eyes like that. Until then we'd had so much to talk about, or cry about, or eat, or look at, and we'd never been alone. Porter smiled and put his palms on my cheeks and his fingers on my hat, and I thought he was going to kiss me, but instead he closed his eyes and tipped back his head.

I waited.

After about fifteen seconds I said, 'What are you trying to heal?'

He looked back down at me, but kept his hands on my face.

'Nothing.'

'I've never seen anyone other than a faith healer do what you're doing.'

'I'm not healing,' he said. 'I'm absorbing. I'm inhaling this moment. I want to get you inside my body so I can take you back to Hawaii.' He tipped his head back again, closing his eyes, smiling.

Of course he was kidding. I knew it was the only thing he could think of to do in that place, at that moment, to mark how he felt and show me the extent of it. But when he tipped his head back the second time he did actually inhale, and I thought of Naoki inhaling Yuki when he was drunk and she was sleeping. Poor Porter. I was supposed to be enjoying his expression of passionate affection rather than remembering Naoki's. I put my arms around his neck and went up on tiptoes to hug him so that his hands came off my face.

'I wasn't done,' he said.

I relaxed a little into the hug. 'Like on *Star Trek*, when they don't get beamed up?'

'Yeah.' He sounded sad.

Neither of us let go when we heard an approaching *calip-calop* sound, and from over Porter's shoulder I watched a middle-aged woman in a rich brown velvet coat over a burgundy kimono pass us. She dipped her head as she did, an apology for intruding on our privacy, although we both felt we were probably intruding on hers. I came back down onto my heels and told Porter to look, and together we watched the immaculate French twist in her hair, the square bump where the back of her coat covered the tie of her wide *obi* sash, the bright white socks on her feet slapping against her dark laquered thong sandals, her sandals *calip-calopping* against the cobblestones.

'She bowed to us,' I whispered after she had disappeared beyond the turn in the alley.

'What a lovely country,' Porter whispered back.

A few seconds later he said, 'Let's leave this place before anything else happens to change the memory,' and we turned around and found a way back out to the street.

We ate sushi one more time that afternoon, and hurried to the bridge in Harajuku so Porter could see the dressed-up kids, and bought snacks for the plane in two different convenience stores, and drank hot sweet coffee from a vending machine to stay warm, and when we couldn't find a way to squeeze more time into the day we took the train that would deliver us back to his hostel. I wished we could sit down on the couch again for a minute – I felt like it was *our* couch – but we'd cut it so fine that once Porter had retrieved his backpack from behind the registration desk we had to hurry back to the train. I was going with him to Tokyo Station, where he'd get the Narita Express to the airport.

When I'd left Porter in Boston in August, I hadn't known when I would see him again, and that had been OK with me. Now he was leaving me, and I didn't know when I would see him again, and it wasn't OK. The train was crowded and we stood close together, exhausted and silent, and I thought about how all I had to do was choose when to leave. That was all. And that was too much. I was pretty cagey with my parents, and all my cheerful letters to them had been about what I was learning about Japan as opposed to what I was learning about my employer, or myself, so I didn't feel I could call them up for advice.

'How do I choose?' I asked Porter.

He looked all over my face for a moment, and then he said, 'You don't have to.'

'Yes I do.'

'OK, yes you do, but not today. And not tomorrow. Just wait a little longer, and see how you feel.'

I put my forehead against his shoulder.

'Are you glad I came?' he asked.

I looked up again so he could hear me over the clattering train.

'So glad.'

'But if I hadn't come, Naoki wouldn't have gotten angry at you, and you wouldn't be wondering about whether or not to leave.'

'Naoki is the reason Naoki got angry, not you. And I was already wondering.'

'OK,' he said, and we were quiet again, and watched a seated girl with long purple hair draw a line of very cute ants on the back of her hand.

'Is this "See you later?"' Porter asked me as we stood next to the Narita Express entrance in the soulless belly of Tokyo Station.

'Yes,' I said, and then reached up to his face, my heart clanging painfully in my chest again about the three words I was about to dare to say.

I tapped him on the nose.

'We're. Not. Done.'

He kissed me one more time and I could feel his teeth because he was smiling so broadly. Then he disappeared from the feet up as he faced me on the escalator down to the platform, raising his hand so that after the top of his head had descended I still saw his arm and finally just his waggling fingers. I waited for another thirty seconds or so, just in case he came back up the up escalator. You never know. And then I had to turn around and face the fact that working for Naoki was now more perplexing than pleasurable, and the adventure had paled. I was going to miss Porter. The tables had turned, and suddenly, strangely, loving him seemed like the safer option.

19

The engagement dinner was set for Thursday, 3 March, at the New Otani Hotel. On the Monday of that week, Yoshimura-san insisted that Akemi visit the Suitengu Shrine to pray for an easy birth. I don't know how she decided on that day as the one for the excursion. Akemi had to take the morning off work. Maybe the trip to the shrine was some sort of prerequisite in her mind. Maybe it was a hoop Yoshimura-san had set up for Akemi to jump through on the road to marrying her son, a way to impose a bit of tradition on an untraditional situation, to feel a bit better about Akemi. Or about Naoki.

Naoki insisted that Yuki and I go along with them, and that I'd enjoy it, although he didn't smile when he said so.

Akemi, Yuki and I were ready by just after nine, and stepped out of the front door in time to see Yoshimura-san in a dusty-rose kimono, bowing to her departing husband from their front door. When she stood back up, she acknowledged that we were there but showed no signs of hurrying as she went back inside. Akemi and I looked at each other, and in a rare moment of complicity we both smiled and rolled our eyes and decided to go back inside rather than wait on the step. I'd been with the family long enough to know that staying there, showing that we were waiting, would have meant a loss of face for Yoshimura-san. She was the boss, and we were meant to serve. Back inside we went, taking off our shoes and milling awkwardly around the kitchen. Yuki wanted to play in the tatami room, but I didn't let her, which meant finding something else to do. I'd forgotten to pack a snack, so I brought her to the kitchen and lifted her up to get a small box of chocolate-filled koala-shaped cookies from the cupboard, then tucked it in my bag. Akemi looked nice. She had bought a maternity raincoat – pinky-beige, with a broad collar, big shiny buttons and a belt that tied above her bump. It looked stylish between her dark hair and black leggings.

'That's a great coat,' I told her.

'Thank you.' She looked down at herself, cinched the belt a little. 'Nothing like this here. I got it in Paris.'

'Ooh,' I said, and that was the end of the conversation.

Akemi had decided we had given Yoshimura-san enough time to get her handbag, and slipped back into her patent black flats. I put on my yellow Aerosoles. I had bought them to cheer myself up, to celebrate spring, and when I was on my own I felt great in them. Walking along the street to get a taxi, though, sandwiched with Yuki between Akemi as Audrey Hepburn and Yoshimura-san as immaculate Japanese matriarch, I felt like a duck.

Dense fog had moved in by the time we arrived at the temple, and the pale, nondescript buildings around it lost their definition against the soft white of the sky. Only the dark red of the temple pillars and balustrades stood out, like the arteries of a heart. A patinated copper roof curved above the broad central portico, and we stood under it so that Akemi could pray. She rang the bell that was supposed to get her some heavenly attention, and clapped before bowing her head against her praying hands. Yuki imitated her and Yoshimura-san stared straight ahead through the temple windows. She had her fingers hooked through the short curved strap of her little handbag, her toes turned slightly inward as was customary for women in kimono. When Akemi finished praying, or looking like she was praying, we all gave Yuki some coins to toss through the slats of the wooden donation box and went back down the stairs, stopping at the bottom to rub the heads of the bronze statue of a mother dog and her puppy. The top of the puppy's round head was so shiny from rubbing it looked tonsured. 'Is this a special dog?' I asked Akemi, and she asked Yoshimura-san, who told us that people prayed to have a birth like a dog, because dog births were considered easy. Yoshimura-san bought Akemi a red and gold embroidered amulet on a white cord to further protect her during delivery, and we were done. All the boxes had been ticked, and nothing bad had happened to Yuki.

That evening I was in the kitchen with the television on low. I'd put Yuki to bed in the tatami room because Naoki would be home late. Akemi was staying at her parents' until the engagement dinner.

The only shows on were slapstick humiliation extravaganzas. I usually enjoyed them because the contestants were so stoic, so willing to dive head first into mud or have their privates whacked by miniature catapults. But it seemed to me that the shows were more about the facial expressions than they were about the sadomasochism. I was amazed by how much punishment the participants could take, sure, but I sort of already knew about that. What surprised me more was the tremendous range of emotional grimacing. One show I'd seen a few times featured two groups of five men wearing team kimonos. Attached to a wall at head height was a big rubber band. Hanging from the ceiling, several feet in front of the wall, were five marshmallows on strings. Each man had to put the rubber band around his face, under his nose, and strain forward in an effort to catch a marshmallow in his mouth. The harder he pushed against the rubber band, the more distorted his face became – the more like a fish, the more like a mask, the more like that photo of the Vietcong being shot in the head. Normally I was fascinated, but on that night I was just irritated. I wanted to be upstairs in bed, and the show wasn't cheering me up.

At 11.45 I dared to defy Naoki. I pulled the covers off Yuki and lifted her into a carrying position with her head on my shoulder, amazed as always by how children just trust that you're doing the right thing, and don't startle awake. Once she was in her own bed I went back downstairs and put the futon away so that Naoki would know we were upstairs. I didn't want him coming home drunk and thinking she'd been kidnapped. It felt great to leave a light on over the dining table and go upstairs to my room like a normal person. I changed for bed and read a few paragraphs of *The Book of Tea* by Okakura Kakuzo, a vintage book I'd bought in Jimbocho. I only dipped into it now and again, and I was up to the chapter on the significance of flowers in the tea ceremony: 'Where better than in a flower, sweet in its unconsciousness, fragrant because of its silence, can we image the unfolding of a virgin soul?'

I didn't hear Naoki come home.

The old lady in Michiko's building woke me up at 7.50 as usual with the opening of her window covers. I fell asleep again for a while. When I finally got up, Naoki's bedroom door was open and in the light from the hallway window I could see his bed was untidily made. He wasn't in the kitchen. He wasn't in the downstairs toilet. I checked the shoe cabinet for his work shoes, and they were gone. I started cooking the miso soup. Not a peep from Yuki. I finished preparing the miso soup. I wondered if she was sick, as it was after 9.30.

I went upstairs and opened her bedroom door. The light extended across to her bed and I saw it glint in her eyes. She blinked. I smelled pee. She often but not always peed into her pull-up diaper in the night, but I couldn't usually smell it so strongly. 'Hello, sweetie,' I said, and went to the window to open the window covers rather than turn on the unpleasant fluorescent overhead light. I left the window open and went back to kneel by the bed. Yuki hadn't sat up yet, which was strange. 'Are you OK, honey?' She nodded, and I pulled her covers down. The bottom sheet was damp all around her. So was her nightie. I tried to remember getting her ready for bed. Had I forgotten to put her pull-up on? I didn't think so. I always got her nightclothes and a pull-up out and put them on her bed when I was running her bath. I was sure I had done that. 'Up you get,' I said, and she climbed off the bed and stood next to me, reeking. I pulled all the bedclothes off, and when I did I found her

187

diaper, bone dry, down between the bed and the wall. Before I could ask her if she'd taken it off, she said, '*Shi-shi.*'

'Yes,' I said. 'Lots of *shi-shi.*'

'I want to *shi-shi*,' she said.

'Oh, OK, let's go.'

I picked up the wet bedclothes and dropped them on the hallway floor on our way to the toilet. I wondered how old Yuki would have to be not to need a boost onto the seat. When we were out I had to lift her, but at home we had a plastic step for her in both the upstairs and downstairs toilets. I reckoned that maybe she'd be tall enough to manage on her own when she was five. I pulled the nightie off over her head, and she stepped up onto Hello Kitty's face and straddled the toilet while I tossed her nightie onto the pile of sheets and blankets. I heard her pee hit the water. '*Itai*,' she said.

'*Itai*?'

'*Itai*,' she said again, eyes wide.

'Where does it hurt?'

I watched her think about the question and my thoughts flashed back to when a little girl I babysat in high school, who insisted on wiping her own bottom from a very early age, ended up with a urinary tract infection. Then her face relaxed, and she pulled at the toilet paper.

'Are you OK, Yuki?'

'Nn,' she said.

'Did you take your diaper off?'

She shrugged her little naked shoulders. I felt her forehead and her chest and her skin was cool. 'How about a shower?' I said.

While I washed her I considered various scenarios. A UTI might explain why her diaper was down the side of the

188

bed. Maybe she had felt pain, and had taken it off, and couldn't resist the urge to pee, and then was too ashamed to tell anyone. A UTI seemed unlikely, though, because I kept her so clean and well hydrated, but maybe I should have made her drink more during our recent outings. I figured that I'd know soon enough if it was an infection, as it would hurt again next time she peed, or she'd produce a fever. I'd force fluids. I preferred to avoid antibiotics, and I didn't think I could get cranberry extract in Tokyo – that was hard enough to find in Boston – but maybe one of the fancy supermarkets was selling blueberries. If it wasn't a UTI, maybe she'd had a cramp. Could lying in cold wet sheets give someone a cramp? Maybe. Maybe the wet sheets explained the cramp, but I still couldn't understand the wet sheets, and the dry diaper.

Naoki went out again that evening. He hadn't said anything about how Yuki hadn't been in the tatami room the night before, so I put her to bed in her own room again, making sure her diaper was on. Her forehead was still cool, and she hadn't complained of any pain during the day. We'd taken a bunch of yoghurt cups I'd saved to the playground to make a sandcastle, now that the sand wasn't so uncomfortably cold to handle. I showed her how to decorate the turrets with leaves for flags. 'Leaf' was difficult for her to pronounce. She taught me the Japanese word, *happa*, which was much easier, and sounded like the popping of a bud. We took some leaves home to trace and colour after nap time.

She woke up from her nap in an unusually bad mood, so I took her out into the garden before we started drawing.

Looking for birds and insects and more leaves helped the clouds to pass. On balance, it had been a really good day.

I had a dilemma when I went upstairs to bed. Normally I closed Yuki's door when she was asleep so she wouldn't be disturbed, and slept with mine closed as well, for everyone's privacy, but I wanted to know if she was uncomfortable in the night, and whether she'd wiggle out of her diaper again. I figured that keeping both our doors open would be strange enough to ensure that I slept lightly.

The closing of the bathroom door woke me. I fell asleep again to the sound of Naoki washing himself.

The closing of another door woke me again. I assumed it was Naoki's. He hadn't turned the hall light off, so I got up to do it, thinking, *Drunk again.* It was Yuki's bedroom door that was closed, though. Naoki's was still open. I checked that he wasn't in his bed, and glanced down the stairs to see if the downstairs lights were on. Darkness. The air in my lungs suddenly felt cold and thin as I turned Yuki's doorknob to reveal a familiar scene – Naoki bent over on his knees, embracing his sleeping daughter, nuzzling her neck, inhaling her like opium vapour – except that this time he was naked.

Whenever he came home drunk and nuzzled the sleeping Yuki in the tatami room, he'd let her go when I put a hand firmly on his shoulder. I did it more violently this time, digging my fingernails in and yanking him backwards, but he grasped Yuki tight against his chest and wouldn't let go, so I took him by both shoulders. He was surprised enough to let me turn him towards me. Between Yuki and his thighs, his erect penis peeked out into the blue glow of her elephant-shaped night light. I hiss-whispered his name and slid my hands in between Yuki's ribs and his, pulling her up into my arms. She was still wearing pyjamas and a pull-up, but Naoki had one of his hands under her pyjama top, against the skin of her back. 'No,' he said, 'please, I just want . . .' but he couldn't find the words and I took her and turned her so that she was heart to heart with me instead. Naoki rose unsteadily to his feet, penis now limp. I tried to look only at his face, at his look of abject sorrow, at the blue sheen on his slack lower lip. Yuki lifted her head from my shoulder and I put it back down, holding it there, rocking left and right, knowing that I'd take her back to bed with me but not wanting to leave her room before I knew where Naoki would be.

'Go to bed, Naoki,' I said. I expected an argument, but he hiccupped, and just like that the atmosphere changed around him. He put his hands on his hips and started nodding to himself. He even chuckled. 'Go to bed,' I repeated, moving over between him and the bed so I could shepherd him out into the hallway. He surprised me again by moving towards the door, but for a moment he stopped and held up a hand and talked to me over his shoulder. 'We will talk about this . . . We will talk about this . . . tomorrow,' he said, and then stepped into the yellow light of the hallway.

It was revolting to follow him to his room, seeing him into bed as if he were a selfish lonely child someone had left in my care. He threw an arm over his face and I pulled his door closed, resisting the urge to slam it. I turned off the hall light, went back to my bedroom and put Yuki in my bed, straining my back to lay her down close to the wall. There was no way to lock the door, so I slid my desk chair over to block it. It didn't occur to me to take advantage of Naoki's stupor to get away. I could have woken Michiko up. She would have taken us in, I'm sure. But then what? My brain didn't even go there. My only thought was to keep Yuki asleep, to keep her ignorant.

When I climbed back into bed she was staring at me. My heart jumped with fear, but I smiled. 'You're in *my* bed,' I told her, as if I'd just revealed an exciting secret, trusting that there was enough light from the street to show a twinkle in my eye. She didn't ask me why. She didn't even blink. I pulled the covers up over our shoulders, and exhaled contentedly before closing my eyes. I opened them again after as long a moment as I could stand, and she was still staring at me. 'Sleepy time,' I whispered, and closed my eyes again. When I next opened them, her eyelashes were back down on her cheeks.

20

I woke up because Yuki was patting my face. The memory of the blue-lit Naoki losing his erection had a dreamlike quality; accepting that it really happened gave me a feeling of vertigo. I disguised a full-body shudder by stretching and yawning. 'Hungry?' I said, and Yuki nodded and pushed the covers off. We both sat up. 'What shall we eat?'

'Flutes,' she said, and clambered to the edge of the bed to slide off.

'OK,' I said. 'We have apples. And maybe bananas. Let me put my clothes on first.'

Then it was time to move the chair away from the door. No choice but to do it. And to open the door. I opened it quietly, more slowly than usual, making an effort to look casual. Naoki's door was closed. I guessed he was still asleep, although I couldn't be sure. We stepped out into the hall, and I led Yuki straight to the toilet. I watched her carefully. It took longer than usual for her to relax and let the pee out, but she didn't say anything hurt. She took an age to decide what to put on over her ballet tights and leotard, but I didn't try to hurry her. I just sat on the floor of her room, listening for telltale sounds from Naoki. I felt like the stuffed fox that oversaw the kitchen. It was so big that I'd always imagined it to be male, but on that morning it turned female. The season was spring, and the vixen was protecting her kits. She never let her guard down; it was completely against her nature to take a night off. She was wired not to trust any sound she heard, so she stayed awake until she had to sleep, and she always slept hidden away with her litter.

Naoki wouldn't have let me sleep with Yuki, but I should have stayed up, I thought, every single time he was out. I should have waited for him to go to bed. I should have been sure he was asleep, every night, before I let myself close my eyes.

Yuki was still in her high chair and I was doing the breakfast dishes when she said, '*Ohayou papa!*' I nearly broke a bowl. When I turned around Naoki was rubbing Yuki's head, dressed for work.

'What did you give her?' he asked me.

'We had miso soup, and apple and banana.'

'Was there tofu in the miso soup?'

'No.'

'No?'

'Not today.'

'Why not?'

'I didn't think the tofu in the fridge was still fresh,' I lied.

'She needs protein.'

'There's protein in the miso.'

'Not enough.'

'Well . . .'

'Boil her an egg.'

I suddenly perceived Naoki as the wicked witch in the Hansel and Gretel story, insisting that I fatten Yuki up so he could eat her. I turned to the fridge to hide my disgust, and my discomfort that I had absolutely no idea what to say or do. I didn't want him to leave the house without bringing up the night before, though.

I took an egg out of the fridge, and the orange juice as well, pouring Naoki a small glass. 'Here,' I said. 'You must be thirsty.'

'Yes,' he said, taking it from me, seeming to appreciate my attentiveness.

What I wanted to say felt like a rock in my belly. I forced myself to speak. 'You were very drunk last night.'

He nodded as he drank. Then he said, 'I found my house, though. I found my bed.' He was pleased with himself.

Yuki piped up in Japanese, 'Yuki-chan Diana-chan bed.'

Naoki looked down into Yuki's smiling face to process the statement. Then he looked at me. 'She did?'

'For some of the night.'

'Why?'

'You don't remember why?'

'No.'

I believed him. 'Never mind, Naoki.'

'I was embarrassing?'

'More than embarrassing.'

'Oh.' He looked around. 'OK. Well. Thank you.'

I didn't know what to do with 'Thank you', and turned back to the stove to put the egg on to boil. Naoki left for work.

I was relieved, for the moment, but I hated knowing I'd have to bring the subject up again, soon.

Once I'd finished the breakfast dishes and Yuki was busy with something, I called Porter. I knew I had to call Emi, but I wouldn't really be able to talk to her about what to do unless Yuki was napping. I could have called Michiko. Maybe I should have called Michiko. We could have gone over to her apartment. I could have begun strategising. But the fact is I wanted to lean on Porter. I wanted to talk to him first, because it was so easy, and he'd understand every word I said.

I knew it was probably still too early to get him at home, but I tried anyway. He was gone. I waited for his recorded voice to ask me to leave a message and I told him it was me and I needed to talk, but I said *not* to call me back, I'd try again later if I could get some time alone. I hung up feeling like I was suffocating. I had to get out of the house. I couldn't think there. I told Yuki we'd go get some lunch on our way to ballet. We brushed our teeth, put jackets on and left.

When we came out of the station at the ballet stop we turned right rather than left and walked along the street of narrow restaurants and useful shops selling sturdy bras, woolly undies, cotton pyjamas, slippers, brooms and baskets. I had learned both the *hiragana* and the kanji for sushi, and scanned the signs along the road for them, not identifying any. It was mostly ramen along that street. A woman came out of the first restaurant we passed, and the odours that wafted out the door with her weren't inviting. The pork-based broth smelled old, the long onions bitter. We kept walking and I sniffed the air outside each restaurant to locate one that smelled sweeter. When I thought I'd found one, I lifted Yuki up to look in the window. A chef in a white apron and low white hat was dispensing fresh noodles straight into bowls of broth from a machine suspended above the counter. Neither of us had ever seen that before, so we went inside and I took the only seat available at the counter, sitting Yuki on my lap. We were going to share our food in any case, as we weren't very hungry.

I ordered one bowl, and took in more of the place, seeing things in Technicolor, as if I were living through my very last day on earth. Further along behind the counter, two more men in aprons and hats were mixing raw eggs with soy sauce and hot pepper powder and pouring the concoction over bowls of rice. I pulled apart some disposable chopsticks and checked them for splinters before letting Yuki have them. After a moment she started her chopstick-violin routine again. I could tell that she was singing, but it wasn't loud enough to hear over the slurping on either side of us, and the clicking of plastic spoons on porcelain bowls. I wrapped my arms around her ribs and kissed the crown of her head and wished we had somewhere else to go after ballet because I didn't want to go home. I distracted myself by watching the chef place slices of pork and boiled egg, small handfuls of seaweed and long onions on top of the noodles.

When our bowl arrived I took the chopsticks from Yuki and grabbed a few noodles, holding them above the bowl to let them cool before offering them to her. Then I took some for myself. A slice of steamed white fish paste floated on the broth. I had to force myself to eat. The whole time I did, I felt as if a hair was stuck in my throat.

Yuki said, 'Ziss,' pointing to the sliced pork.

'Please may I have this?' I instructed her, as I did every day, and I waited while she got all the words out before picking up a slice. She leaned forward and pulled it from the chopsticks with her teeth, pushing the whole brown-grey slice into her mouth with her fingers. 'Yuki!' I scolded, leaning to the side so I could look at her bulging cheeks.

She turned her face to me and laughed, muffled, showing me the cooked flesh in her mouth.

'That's too much,' I said. 'That's gross.' She could barely close her mouth to chew. I asked her if she wanted to spit it out, offering my cupped hand under her chin, but she shook her head and stubbornly persevered. I sat up straight again and waited for the chewing to end. I insisted that she drink some of the soup, and I made myself have some too. Then I had to get out of there.

I didn't realise it was Emi sitting on the bench by a little shrine on the hill that led to the ballet studio until she lowered the newspaper. She had come pretty regularly to Yuki's swimming lessons, but I'd discouraged her from attending ballet because we sat right in the studio to watch the children, and questions would have been asked. I'd seen her on the bench only once before. When I hadn't seen her again I'd figured she'd found the brief sighting – a minute or so on the way up and another on the way down – too frustrating. Her happy-sad eyes watched Yuki trudge along holding my hand.

We arrived at the studio before anyone else. That was fun for Yuki, because she could hang off the barre and make faces at herself in the mirror, which wasn't allowed during class. She had been quiet on the walk up the hill, and I was glad to see her being her usual self. The little girl who arrived next seemed to disapprove, but Yuki didn't care.

Two more little girls arrived and monkeyed around too. Finally the lanky teacher giraffed into the room and clapped her hands so that the girls lined up at the barre. Yuki stood out because I had forgotten to tie up her hair.

I'd been revisiting the night in scattered pieces since we left the house, but when the pianist started thumping out a rhythm for the barre exercises I relived the experience in full. Then I relived the previous night as well. *Had* I forgotten to put Yuki's pull-up diaper on? No, I couldn't have. If it had just come out of the bag it would have been pressed flat, and it wasn't. It had been worn. It *had* been taken off. By Yuki? It wasn't impossible. By Naoki? I had to imagine him going in to see her when he got home. Embracing her. But I couldn't imagine him taking her diaper off. Or I wouldn't. I shut the thought down and tried to take stock. I only really knew three things for sure: I *had* put Yuki's diaper on her after her bath; she *had* experienced pain when she was on the toilet in the morning; and Naoki had been sexually aroused by embracing her when I interrupted him the following night.

The little girls were standing perpendicular to the barre, with one hand on it and the other over their heads. From there they arched back as far as they could, exposing the delicate undersides of their jaws. Too delicate to bear. I stood up suddenly, receiving a frown from the teacher, and bowed repeatedly as I crossed in front of the mothers to leave the room. I stuffed my feet into my shoes and jogged down the street to the bench by the shrine where Emi was staring into space.

I told her everything.

And we started to plan.

21

I think that Thursday was probably as nice a day as any for Yuki, but it felt like a marathon to me. In the morning Naoki ate breakfast with Yuki and me, and read some of the newspaper before taking it with him to the toilet. I was normally impatient for him to leave the house so that Yuki could settle, but that morning I was practically shaking with it. He took for ever in the toilet, and his feet sounded unusually slow on the stairs. I put a cassette of English children's songs on, to change the atmosphere. I finished the dishes and called Yuki into the kitchen, where I stood her on a chair by the counter to help me make some modelling clay.

When Naoki came through to say goodbye he kissed the top of Yuki's head, sending a shock wave down my body. I wondered if his kiss had done the same to her. I couldn't tell. She didn't look up, and she didn't smile, but then again she was up to her wrists in dough, concentrating on squeezing it.

Seated at the table, we made a mama snake and a baby snake, and then a big turtle. I got a toothpick from the cutlery drawer and showed her how to give the mama snake some eyes. I needed to take a deep breath and exhale before

I did the smaller one. Yuki looked at me inquisitively, wondering if it was really such a big challenge. I gave her a smile and did the eyes on the baby snake before handing her the toothpick so she could do the turtle. She pushed it in very deeply both times, making the turtle look crazy and exhausted.

I made a ball out of the remaining clay and let Yuki work on pressing it as flat as she could. '*Kore?*' she asked, holding the toothpick over the flattened clay, meaning 'This?' She was asking permission to poke holes in it, so I said, 'Sure. Go ahead.' She was such a good girl. Looking at her I wondered if she was young enough to forget what might have just happened to her, and also to forget what would happen next. I could remember being three or four. I could remember playing with clay, and the snakes and turtles my mother had helped me make. I tried to remember my father from when I was three. In our family albums there were a lot of photos of me on his shoulders, but I couldn't recall being there. When I tried to bring it back, all I could think of was lifting the children I had babysat in high school onto my own shoulders, the sudden burn in my arms when they were heavier than I'd expected. I remembered Dad from when I was five, though, when Mom wasn't home and I told him I felt sick and immediately threw up on the living room carpet. Ever scientific, he said if I felt sick again could I please do it on the kitchen floor instead as it wasn't too far away. I remembered standing there looking at my vomit on the carpet, shocked that he'd got his timing all wrong. He was supposed to reassure me first, and assess my state, and find a way to make me comfortable, like Mom did. *Then* he could tell me where I should throw up next time and explain the difference between carpet and linoleum.

Naoki came home early from work with clothes fresh from the dry cleaner, and went straight upstairs to dress for the engagement dinner. I was doing quality control on how Yuki had set the table for our own dinner when he came back down and asked for my opinion on his outfit.

The expression on his face was so innocent and receptive that I was momentarily disarmed. I moved him to the centre of the dining area and walked slowly around him, fixing his suit jacket from behind, lifting the shoulders and setting them straight. Touching him revolted me again. I noted how the jacket vent lay flat against his buttocks, how his calves pressed against the inside of his trousers, and I imagined hamstringing him with bolt cutters. Snap, snap, snap, snap. I imagined snapping the tendons at the base of his skull as well. I didn't see any blood, or picture Naoki dead. I did see him on the floor, though: legs useless, head lolling, helpless as a newborn.

Back around the front I straightened his perfectly straight tie and checked his face for I didn't know what, a loose eyelash or something. I studied the skin around his eyes – he looked tired – and then I stared into them. It didn't matter how close I got, though, or how hard I looked. He didn't appear discomfited, and just stared simply back at me. I couldn't see what was in his heart, and he clearly couldn't feel what was in mine. Maybe he couldn't feel what was in anybody's. I gave up on playing with my power to intimidate, stepping back and telling him he looked very handsome. The smile he gave me was both as sweet as one of Yuki's and as complicated as any I'd ever seen. The effort required in smiling back tired me to the bone.

He turned to Yuki and said, '*Papa wa hansamu desu ka?*' She singsonged back to him that he was very handsome. I didn't make her say it in English, because *hansamu* was basically English already.

He rubbed her on the head, and then went down the hall-way to put his shoes on. At the door, he and Yuki went through their most recent parting routine. Yuki asked him if he'd be lonely without her. He replied that he'd be much too lonely. We all waved. He left, thinking I'd close the door and lock it for the evening, but I didn't. Yuki and I were going out too.

Emi had argued with me that going to the police in custody cases was fruitless, especially with no concrete evidence. It was her older sister, Junko, who had suggested that we try and get Yuki on video talking about the things that happened in the night, in case she was aware of them. The engagement dinner was the perfect opportunity to go out unnoticed.

Earlier in the day I had made a potato salad to go with cold cuts and green beans, so dinner took no time to prepare. I tried not to rush Yuki through eating it, although I could hardly swallow.

'What shall we do tonight, Yuki?' I asked her as if I had no idea myself.

'Mmmm, TV?'

'I know! Let's go see a friend!'

'Fren?'

'Who is it? A new friend.'

'I want TV,' she whined.

I felt a prickle of sweat above my lip and got up out of my chair. I lifted Yuki out of her high chair, saying, 'Great idea! Let's watch TV with a new friend!' I piled the dishes in the sink for later, and took Yuki down the hallway to get her jacket on. 'Maybe they'll have a nice video,' I told her.

I didn't feel like waiting the eternity it took for her to put her own shoes on, so I did it for her. 'Let's take the stroller,' I said, 'so we can go fast.' Once we were outside the house she became caught up in the spirit I was working so hard to create, and tried to get into the stroller while I was locking the door. 'Not yet, silly!' I said, and we laughed. At the bottom of the steps I strapped her in, and pushed her as fast as I could to the subway, running on legs I could barely feel.

Emi's sister was the director of a contemporary art museum. She'd told me on the phone that she was home by 7.30 every evening, while her husband never got home before ten. We were safe going to their house because Naoki had never visited it, so he wouldn't recognise the location if he saw the video. Junko didn't want to risk sending directions by fax, so she told me to call when we came up out of the subway. When I reached her on the squat green payphone at the top of the station stairs she told me to wait outside the FamilyMart convenience store I could see from where I was standing, and she'd meet us there in a few minutes. I took Yuki's hand and dragged the folded-up stroller with the other, and we scooted quickly into the FamilyMart for a box of koala biscuits. I gave the box to Yuki to take to the young man behind the counter. He was all in black, rocker-thin, with heavy chains dangling from his belt, and he had carefully styled his uneven hair over one eye, but when she handed him the box he received it with a neat bow that belied his rebellious look.

When Junko came around the corner and waved I said, 'Look! It's my friend!' She couldn't have been home from work long, and was still dressed mannishly for business in black trousers and a tailored shirt. When she bent forward to say hello to Yuki as if meeting her for the first time I hit an emotional wall. I had come to Japan in order to have an adventure, a great story people would have trouble believing, and now I didn't want to believe it myself. I wasn't ever going to want to tell it. My smile felt like a wince as I helped Yuki open the biscuit box. I wanted to stay right there, eating chocolate-filled biscuits. I wanted to pretend nothing at all had happened. Yuki seemed fine. Maybe she *was* fine. Junko said, 'Shall we go?' in Japanese, and Yuki started walking beside her. *Shall we go?* I had to ask myself. Junko, a supposed stranger, offered her hand to Yuki as they walked, and trusting little Yuki took it and walked away from me. That got me moving.

Emi was waiting for us in the far corner of Junko's spacious living room, wearing her large sunglasses. I appreciated that she still didn't think it best to be recognised. She looked tiny standing there with her arms folded, her hands gripping her slim biceps through her denim dress as if she herself were the flotsam that would keep her safe until she saw land. Junko introduced Emi as her little sister, and Emi dropped her arms and smiled sweetly, giving us a wave. Yuki pointed excitedly at the big TV screen. I asked Junko, 'Do you have any videos?'

'I have something better,' she said, and crossed the room to lean over a stack of LPs, picking up the top one to show us. 'Laserdisc. *Mary Poppins*.' Yuki stepped forward and took it in her hands, marvelling at the photo. There was Dick Van Dyke in his candy-stripe jacket and straw hat, and Julie Andrews in her froth of white lace, surrounded by cartoon animals. 'Waaaah!' Yuki said, taking it all in. Junko picked up a video camera from the coffee table.

'Hey, Yuki,' I said, 'my friend has a video camera. Why don't we make a video of you?'

She looked over her shoulder at me then back at the Laserdisc. 'Ziss,' she pleaded.

'Yes, I know, we'll watch that.' I stood behind her and took the Laserdisc out of her resisting hands. 'But first let's make a video.' I'd found that giving her a schedule with a sort of rhythm to it could move things forward. 'Video. Koala biscuit. *Mary Poppins*. OK? Video. Koala biscuit. *Mary Poppins*.'

Junko took over, inviting Yuki to have a look at how the video camera worked and then gesturing to me to go to a set of sliding paper doors decorated with a pale scene of mountains. I opened them to reveal the tatami room, where a light was already on. Other than a low square table pushed against the wall there was nothing at all in the room. Junko guided Yuki over, chattering away about how pretty she looked, placing her firmly in the unadorned corner. She then kneeled down in the middle of the room to start video-ing. I kneeled down behind her. Sometimes I wonder if we would have had more luck if I'd had the camera and Junko had followed my lead, but I'll never know. Junko seemed so sure of herself.

207

Yuki was uncomfortable. She leaned against the wall, put one foot on top of the other, pushed her tummy forward. Junko was still telling her how pretty she looked, and I heard Emi join in as well from behind us. Then Junko said, '*Anooo ne, Yuki-chan*,' and I knew she was gently changing the subject. She asked Yuki if there were things that woke her up at night-time.

Yuki said, 'Night-time?' in Japanese, and I couldn't tell whether she was stalling, or really hadn't understood the question.

Junko said yes, did anyone come into her room in the night?

Yuki looked around. 'Whose house is this?'

When Junko said we were at her house, Yuki asked her who she was. 'I'm your mother's sister,' Junko told her, and then looked at me in alarm, realising her mistake.

Yuki said, 'Mother?'

Junko turned off the camera and said sorry to Yuki, and that she was Diana's friend.

'Yes,' I said in Japanese, 'Junko is my friend.'

From behind us Emi asked Yuki if she would like to meet her mother. Both Junko and I whipped our heads around but it was impossible to tell if we'd made eye contact with Emi through her sunglasses. I turned back. Yuki was nodding.

Having put us in danger, Junko now came to the rescue by turning to me and asking if I'd like to meet my mother. I said I would.

She asked me if my mother was there. I said she wasn't.

'My mother isn't here either,' she said. 'I'd like to meet her, but she's not here.' She asked Emi if her mother was there.

'No,' Emi said to the tatami floor, 'she is not here. Of course she is not here.'

'So none of our mothers is here,' Junko said. 'Too bad!'

Emi asked Junko to try to video Yuki again. Junko looked concerned, but turned the camera back on and asked Yuki again if something had woken her in the night.

Yuki looked at the camera for a moment, and then said, 'Let's dance!' After a few seconds of indecision, Junko said, 'Let's dance!' from behind the camera. Before we could stop her Emi had climbed up onto the tatami and was holding her hands out for Yuki to take. Yuki had ballet in mind, though, and started to jump and turn, so Emi could only do the same. Junko kept the video running until the dancing wound down. I said, 'Koala biscuit!' and Yuki followed me back into the living room. Emi retreated into another part of the house, maybe the kitchen. Junko stayed long enough to put *Mary Poppins* on the Laserdisc player, then went to find her sister. I guessed they needed to develop a new plan, since producing a video hadn't worked and neither of them thought we could go to the police with only the testimony of a foreigner. Even with a video they doubted the police would feel inclined to get involved. 'They will call it a domestic dispute,' Emi had told me on the bench down the hill from ballet, slowing down to finish the sentence as if she'd been studying the words and was using them for the first time. 'They will confuse you. They will not help you.'

I found it very gratifying to watch Mary Poppins trying to teach Mr Banks how to be a good father. Yuki watched the movie, completely rapt, with a hand on my thigh. She didn't look like she understood much, though, not until they jumped into the chalk picture on the sidewalk. Then she got so excited she had to stand up to watch, and when Dick Van Dyke pulled down on his trousers and they became more of a penguin outfit she giggled. Emi must have heard us laughing, and came back into the living room in time to see Yuki gambolling around the coffee table with her leggings pulled down around her knees.

It was getting late, and when the first disk finished I knew I couldn't risk taking the time to let Yuki see the second one. She was too little to know that the movie wasn't over, though, so she didn't fuss.

I bumbled through my goodbyes and apologies at the front door. I didn't know exactly what to say, and whether to take any blame. All I could think of was, 'I'm sorry it didn't work,' and they both said, 'No, no.' Junko said, 'Not your fault,' and then, 'We will think of something else.'

22

Nothing happened on Friday. Emi didn't call.

On Saturday, Yuki and I went to the sports centre. Leaving the subway I could smell the rain that had fallen while we were underground. It was a spring rain. I saw Emi waiting at a discreet distance from the entrance in a yellow skirt and cotton sweater, again with the large sunglasses. I wondered if she was going to watch us walk by, as she had done at ballet, but when we were within earshot she said, '*Ah! Konnichiwa!*', as if our arrival was an unexpected surprise. We hadn't discussed meeting at swimming again, and certainly hadn't planned on talking there. I didn't think it was a great idea, but I couldn't pretend not to know her. I looked for recognition in Yuki's face, but saw none.

'It's my friend's sister,' I said, repeating it in Japanese, trying to sound happy. 'Say *konnichiwa*.'

Emi asked Yuki how she was, and Yuki said she was fine, and Emi looked at me and I affirmed that Yuki was indeed fine. Yuki piped up that she was going to the swimming pool. Emi said that was great, and she'd love to see Yuki swim. I worried that she'd gone a little crazy. Yuki told her to come and watch.

'I don't think so, Yuki,' I said quickly, and when I looked at Emi she had reappeared as her normal self, ready to be told she couldn't have what she wanted. Yuki started to whine, though, asking me why she couldn't come and watch, she wanted her to come and watch, and when I told her there would be too many people she started to cry, standing there in the street with her round face tipped up to the brightening sky. I had never seen Yuki so upset, and for a moment all I could do was stand and watch, drawing a complete blank as to how to behave. I said, 'I don't think there are enough seats.' It was completely lame, and Yuki knew it, and she raised her fist and thumped me on the thigh. Hitting me made her cry even more. She was so confused. I blocked out Emi's obvious discomfort and crouched down next to Yuki, wrapping my arms tightly around her. 'Hey there,' I said. 'Hey there.' Her wails became hiccupping sobs. She lifted her right shoulder and extricated her arm from my hug, pointing weakly at Emi without looking at her. I could feel her heart beating against my upper arm.

I would have known what to do if she'd been crying in front of a shelf of candy, or a Barbie. I'd have known what to do if she'd been pointing through a pet store window at a kitten. But she was pointing at her *mother*. Whoever Yuki thought Emi was, the fact remained that she wanted her mother to come and watch her swim, and I was telling her I wouldn't give up my seat to make that happen.

'OK, OK,' I said, kissing her wet face. 'My friend's sister can come and watch.' Emi was holding a tissue out for me, so I wiped Yuki's cheeks and nose, and came part of the way around to the idea that it should have been Emi comforting Yuki rather than me. I was the nanny. I was just the nanny.

I stood up and readjusted my shoulder bag and we continued towards the entrance. Yuki wasn't crying any more, but she was still recovering from the outburst, still hiccupping a little. After a moment, she took my left hand. A few steps later she took Emi's right hand. Emi dropped her head forward as if she were speaking silently to her own heart. In my memory now I think of us as being off to see the wizard. I don't think we were short on heart, or courage, or even brains, but I'd have been much obliged if he could have helped us find our ways home.

I tried to sleep in on Sunday, but I couldn't. I'd had no communication from Emi or Junko, and I still didn't know if they had a new plan. I was too restless to stay in bed, but I also didn't want to go downstairs. I sat at my desk and looked out the open window, waiting for the usual business of the day to begin. The old lady opened her window covers before Michiko did, but she didn't come out to hang the laundry right away. Maybe she was giving herself a little break, taking breakfast slowly. I heard the shriek of Michiko's rising window covers, but she didn't come right out either. About five minutes later, Michiko's husband appeared at street level, carrying a golf bag. He walked towards me down the driveway to the street and disappeared. I figured Michiko would be coming out onto her balcony soon, so I got dressed and went across the hallway to brush my teeth, stopping in Yuki's doorway to see how she was. Still sleeping. Naoki and Akemi's door was closed. Before I could distract myself I imagined them in the pitch dark, feeling them rather than seeing them. The coarse hair on their pillows. The soft skin on their peaceful foreheads and the stretched skin over their half-done baby. The dangerous damp warmth of their genitals. The sharp prongs around Akemi's diamond.

Michiko was out on her balcony when I walked into the driveway, and so was Atsushi, looking down at me through the bars. Michiko waved and her smile was warm and interested. When I was close enough I asked if I could come up for a minute. 'Of course,' she said.

Her kitchen smelled of instant coffee and toast, and also of the potato and cabbage simmering in a small pan on the stove. 'Cabbage for breakfast?' I said.

'*Hai!*' she said. 'Atsushi loves it. This cabbage is very sweet. And he likes to say "potato".'

Atsushi said potato, like a little parrot.

'Please come to the balcony,' Michiko said, and we all went back out into the sunshine so she could finish hanging up the clothes. I looked down on a two-level plant stand with half a dozen different types of bonsai trees on it, along the wall of the parking area to the right. The old lady's husband had come outside to tend to them, nipping at the tiny branches with a small pair of shears.

'In Japan we say it is a bad sign when your husband wants to grow bonsai,' Michiko said.

'Oh?'

'Yes. The marriage is over, we say.'

When I turned to look at her she was smiling.

'I think some people in the US say that about golf,' I told her.

'Oh really? Golf is OK.'

214

'It takes your husband away from you, though, right?'

'Yes. But when Atsushi is bigger, we can join him. I will never grow bonsai with him.'

'Why not? Isn't it just like gardening?'

'No. During gardening you can talk. Also during golf. But if they go outside to take care of their bonsai, they don't want to talk.'

She shook the wrinkles out of a small striped shirt and I smelled her laundry detergent. I thought about how fast Atsushi would grow, how quickly he'd need new clothes, and then more new clothes. I thought about how the bonsai trees wouldn't be allowed to grow. Quite a lot of things were like that in Japan. On one of my days off I had visited a market in the north part of Tokyo and had stopped in front of some short barrels of miso pickles. Although I knew they were sharp and delicious when rinsed and sliced, the full-grown cucumbers and daikon lying half submerged in the brown paste looked completely defeated, as if by quicksand. The baby eggplants seemed frozen in time, like a scientific experiment on display. Spooning against each other in the miso they looked too much like the fetal pigs in formaldehyde that we had had to dissect in high school. A vegetable had never made me sad before. I wondered how much growth Naoki would tolerate in Yuki. Would she still be 'pure good' to him if she began to rebel?

Done with the laundry, Michiko invited me back inside. She took the vegetables off the stove and cut them up on a plate so they would cool down for Atsushi. Then she got me to admit that I had left the house without breakfast, and made me some toast and instant coffee. I watched her cutting the toast on a diagonal and arranging it just so on a

215

plate, and I opened my mouth to tell Yuki's story, but I couldn't force the air through my voice box. I hesitated to make so much ugly noise in that peaceful space. I wanted to stretch the gentle moment out instead.

I also didn't want to be disappointed. I'd recently told her about the rape I'd seen depicted in the manga section of a women's magazine. I'd expected her to be frustrated, maybe embarrassed, but she just nodded. I waited a beat or two, and then had to ask the question outright. 'Why is there rape in a magazine for women?'

Michiko cocked her head. 'I think . . . Well, it's a kind of shock for us.'

She didn't say 'them', she said 'us'. It surprised me very much that she wasn't distancing herself from the women who read those manga.

'Is it a good shock?'

She sighed, and then she said, 'Our lives are boring,' with what I at first took to be a sad smile, but I didn't want to assume I knew what she was feeling. Maybe it was an apologetic smile? I didn't know.

As Michiko had been accepting of sexual abuse in manga as entertainment, I didn't want to hear her sigh sadly and accept it in the home as well. When she came to the table with our food I asked, 'Would you like me to babysit?'

'You mean, today?'

'Yes.'

Michiko sat down and watched Atsushi wrangling chunks of potato around his plate with a stubby fork.

'You could do something that's difficult to do with Atsushi along.'

216

'Like what?'

'I don't know, try on shoes, or something.'

She smiled. 'Yes, that is difficult, you are right. But . . . it's OK. I don't need to do that.'

I tried not to look disappointed at being denied the chance to feel helpful. I would have liked to have something concrete to do. But the fat white toast was delicious, and I left the apartment around ten with some relief from the sour stomach I'd been suffering since Wednesday morning. I walked to the subway station without a goal, but when the train came I went to Omotesando. In Kiddy Land, I bought Yuki a little yellow plastic carry case, about the size of a grapefruit, that opened up to reveal a miniature wonderland complete with stream and bridge, tree house and hidey-hole, slide and swing for a couple of sweet little monsters. I called Emi from a payphone but no one answered. I lingered over lunch. I strolled. I lingered over tea.

When I opened the front door at Naoki's it was to the sound of him shouting in English. 'Where are you?' he shouted, and then, 'No, tell me where you are!' I didn't stop to put my shoes away properly and hurried straight into the house. Akemi was sitting at the table and looked daggers at me when I came in. Naoki was on the phone, and didn't notice me right away. There were papers strewn on the table, and I stepped forward because some of them looked like my letters from Porter. Naoki saw me, and he lifted his red face and said, 'OK, she is here now.'

I asked who it was, and Naoki held out the phone to me, his hand shaking. 'It is your boyfriend. Tell him to come here.'

'What?'

'Tell him!' he screamed, so I took the phone.

'Hello?'

'Diana, get out of there. That man is crazy.'

'I know.'

'Get out.'

'I can't.'

'Why not?'

'Yuki,' I told him, and then my heart sank and I said, 'Wait.' I took the phone away from my ear and asked, 'Where is Yuki?'

'Tell him to come here, *now*,' Naoki said. He had moved around me to stand behind Akemi. Akemi said, 'She is next door.'

'He can't come here, Naoki,' I said. 'He is in Hawaii.'

This stopped Naoki for a moment, and I heard Porter's voice coming from the receiver.

'Sorry, Porter, what?'

'Find out what he's talking about, OK? Hang up, and find out, and I'll call again in ten minutes.'

'You called here?'

'Yes. You didn't call again. I was worried.'

'I told you not to.'

'You see!' Naoki shouted. 'You told him not to!'

'Ten minutes,' Porter said in my ear, and hung up.

I put the phone down on the table and looked at Naoki. Sickles of white outlined his nostrils. 'What's going on here?' I asked them both.

Naoki's lips and tongue sledgehammered the consonants in his answer. 'Your boyfriend abused my daughter.'

'I don't have a boyfriend here, Naoki.'

'No?' He stepped over to the table and picked up Porter's letters, shaking them in my face. 'Then what are these?'

'They're just letters, from a friend.'

'The man on the phone?'

'Yes.'

'Has he ever been here, to my house?'

'Yes. Your mother saw him. But he lives in Hawaii. That is why he writes me letters.' Naoki stared at the letters as if he couldn't believe they would betray him. Now I looked at Akemi. She had her forearms on the table and was watching her thumbs wrestle. 'Akemi,' I said, and she looked up slowly. 'Has Yuki been abused?'

She blinked quickly a few times, and I could see that she wished she hadn't. She steeled her eyes. One of her hands disengaged itself and touched a Japanese document. 'Emi's family lawyer delivered a letter.'

My face must have shown my surprise. I was at first confused as to why Emi hadn't told me a lawyer's letter was in the works, and then immediately angry. Surely getting the letter sorted out would have taken some time, during which Emi would have been able to warn me. I should have had time to prepare what I was going to say, but thanks to her I had arrived at the battle unarmed. That flash of fury brought questions about the rest of the plan – was Emi hiding anything else from me? Why would she? – but there wasn't time to think about them because the mention of the letter had pulled Naoki's pin out again. 'She's *mine!*' he suddenly shrieked, voice cracking, and he threw Porter's letters back onto the table and pointed at the front door. 'Get out of my house!'

I flinched, and took a step to obey him, but then I imagined Emi doing exactly the same thing, caving in, agreeing to leave, right there in that room.

I stepped back. 'No,' I said. 'Not yet.'

'Get out!'

'I *will* leave,' I said, shaking like a leaf but staring him in the eye, 'but not yet. I am going to wait for my friend to call back.' Naoki tried to argue but when I put up a hand he stopped. 'I will take the call,' I said, 'and I will tell him everything is OK. There has been a misunderstanding. Then I will go to my room, and I will stay there. If you want me to help with dinner, I will help with dinner. I will help with Yuki's bath if you want me to. Or I will just stay in my room. Tomorrow I will talk to the airlines about getting a ticket. *Then* I will leave.'

Naoki looked around the room in search of a response, but ended up putting his hands on his hips, sighing, staring at the floor. Then he seemed to have an idea. 'The problem is,' he said, like a disappointed father, 'I cannot trust you.'

'Cannot trust me to do what?'

Suddenly he looked as if I'd just put a simple equation to him and he couldn't resolve it. It looked like Akemi could, though. It looked like she had just incorporated a few new variables into her thinking, and was calculating like mad.

I sat down by the phone. Naoki sat down next to Akemi on the other side of the table and they talked to each other in low voices as we all waited for Porter to call back. It's strange to say that I felt like celebrating in the midst of such a wretched situation, but I was proud of how I had stood my ground and how I had laid out the next bit of the action. I wanted to talk to Emi, to tell her that she could have overcome Naoki if she had learned to plant her feet and stare him down.

When I answered the phone, Porter said, 'Are you alone?'

'No.'

'Yes or no questions only?'

'Great. Yup. Super.'

'OK. Are you in danger?'

'No.'

'Is the little girl in danger?'

'Maybe.'

'Yes or no only!'

'Yes.'

'Can you manage the situation?'

'Yes.'

'Do you need me to do anything?'

'No.'

'Is this conversation making that crazy man uncomfortable?'

I looked at Naoki. 'Yes,' I said, and then, 'Yes, there's been a misunderstanding.'

'Oh. No there hasn't, right?'

'Right.'

'OK. Do you promise to call me tomorrow?'

'Yes.'

'OK, let's wrap this up with something nice, simultaneously calming him down and freaking them out.'

I laughed.

'That's good. Now say how much you miss me.'

I laughed again and said, 'Well, I'll send you some soba noodles if you insist, but I'm pretty sure you can get them in Honolulu.'

'Stinker.'

'OK, then! Bye!'

'That was actually excellent, though.'

'Byeeee!'

I felt an unusual sense of power when I walked past Naoki and Akemi to the stairs. My mood darkened once I was in my room. I resented how Emi hadn't kept me in the loop. I needed her holding the corner of the safety net, and I wasn't convinced she was. I didn't feel safe at all. If she wasn't giving me the information I needed to make sure things worked out, what did that mean for Yuki? Was Emi selfish too?

I also regretted saying I wouldn't go out. I couldn't call anyone because there was no phone in my room, and I couldn't risk using the phone in Naoki's room as long as he was in the house. I imagined a plan for getting Michiko's attention by flapping a shirt out the window and tossing her a note asking her to call Emi for me, but decided against it. I could leave Naoki's, but Michiko had to stay in the neighbourhood, and Naoki was vindictive.

Now that I was involved in something risky, something important, I wanted it to move quickly towards its solution. I wanted to help devise the formula, but all I could do was lie on the bed and stare at the ceiling.

I woke up with a pounding heart to the sound of Yuki whispering, 'Diana-chan.' I blinked in the half-dark, but she wasn't there. The house was completely quiet. I turned on the lamp by the bed and my watch told me it was nearly 7 p.m. Maybe Naoki and Akemi had joined Yuki at his parents' house for dinner. Maybe he was showing them the letter from the lawyer. Maybe they were interrupting their own lawyer's Sunday evening for a consultation. Or maybe Naoki also hadn't decided what to do yet, so he wasn't talking, just eating. How was he looking at Yuki? How was Akemi looking at him? Was anybody *really* looking at anybody?

I went to Naoki's room and picked up the phone.

23

After talking with Emi I pulled my suitcase from under my bed and opened it out on the floor. I grabbed about half of the clothes from Yuki's drawers and laid them in the suitcase in colourful layers, adding a couple of pairs of shoes as well, and then I started packing my own clothes on top. I think I would have been crying if Yuki's clothes hadn't been in there with mine, but I was light-headed with purpose, covering them carefully, tucking mine in around the edges to keep them safely hidden.

I went over the altercation in the kitchen in my head and realised I hadn't needed to say that I'd check on flights out of Japan. Naoki had only ordered me to leave his house; he hadn't said anything about leaving the country. Even if he had, he couldn't have made me. I'd need a new sponsor for my visa, but I could teach English at a pinch, maybe to nurses, live in a hostel. I didn't think of that at the time, though, and when I tried to imagine it while I was packing, I couldn't. It wasn't what I wanted any more.

I slipped my reassembled collection of letters from Porter into the suitcase, along with a couple of things I'd been planning to send in my next letter – a pamphlet about sumo ('According to Japanese legend the very origin of the

Japanese race depended on the outcome of a sumo match') and a clipping about a company announcing a line of women's underwear imbued with shark-liver extract – as well as something I hadn't decided whether to send yet. It was part of a takeaway coffee cup. I had washed it and cut out the part with the writing. It said 'The Art of Hot', and under that, in much smaller letters, 'Side by side, I'll be yours for ever. Because please don't weep.'

I lay on my bed, looking at the beginning of a novel my mother had sent over, another John le Carré, *The Little Drummer Girl*. I looked at it, but didn't see it. I kept imagining myself reading it on an airplane. I needed to call my parents, but it was a good thing I didn't risk trying because I heard Naoki, Akemi and Yuki come in and take off their shoes. Yuki's voice was dominant. She sounded like she was in a good mood. I heard Naoki call her name sharply, but she had scrambled up the stairs before he could stop her. She ran across to my bed and climbed up on it, and we squeezed each other hard, and the hair that fell over my face smelled unpleasantly like room freshener. When she sat up I asked her if she had had a nice dinner.

'Yes,' she said, and looked around for the words she wanted to say, but she needed help.

'Did you have rice?' I asked her.

'Yes.'

'And did you have fish?'

'No.'

'Did you have beef?'

'Beehu.'

'Beef.'

'Beehu.'

Akemi appeared in the doorway with her mouth open to say something, but closed it again. I saw her notice my fat suitcase next to the desk. She looked back at us. When she still didn't speak, I looked at Yuki and said, 'So you had beef? And what else?' Akemi went away.

I did end up bathing and reading to Yuki at bedtime. I supposed the old habit of having me do it died hard for Naoki, even though he was enraged with me. Not that he actually said anything, and Akemi didn't represent them both by asking me to do it, but I'd learned a little bit about interpreting their silences. Yuki was with me. That was convenient. The evening should proceed as usual.

Lying on Yuki's bed, watching her descend into sleep, my adrenalin levels dropped, and my stomach started to rumble. I was starving. It had been eight hours since I'd eaten anything, so I had to go down to the kitchen. Naoki and Akemi's bedroom door was closed, and I didn't know who was in there. The bathroom door was open, and the light was on. I could hear the sound of the heater that warmed up the water for the next bather. I braced myself to interact with whoever might be downstairs.

No one. There was no sign of anyone either: nothing on the table, nothing on the counters. It was just the fox and me, on the lookout for danger.

We always had soba noodles and a bottle of sauce in the house, and that would have taken only a few minutes to prepare, but I found they took a long time for me to eat because I chewed them rather than inhaled them. If you didn't start swallowing your noodles whole as a baby it was tough to learn how to do it. We had some bread. The only thing I could find to put on it was some rubbery Camembert,

227

with lettuce. The adrenalin was back, and I didn't have enough saliva in my mouth to swallow easily. I drank two glasses of water, accepted that the meal would feel like a rock in my stomach for a while, washed my dishes and went back upstairs.

Naoki and Akemi's bedroom door was open now, and the room was empty. The bathroom door was closed. I'd never seen them go in the bathroom together, so it seemed only one of them was at home. I didn't want to talk to Naoki, but I decided that if it was Akemi in the bathroom, I'd give it a try. The door was visible from the end of my bed so I sat there and opened to page one of *The Little Drummer Girl* again: 'Sooner or later they say in the trade, a man will sign his name. The vexation lies in the waiting.'

I looked up at the sound of the door in time to see Akemi walk out of sight in a cotton robe. I jumped to my feet and arrived at her bedroom door as she was closing it. She stopped and looked up, leaving about eight inches of space for us to talk through. Her face was flushed from the bath, but it failed to make her look healthy and refreshed.

'Where's Naoki?' I asked her, trying to speak in a neutral tone.

'He went back to his parents' house.' Her voice was flat too.

I nodded, looked down, gave her a little silence to interpret.

'What are you going to do?' she asked me.

'I don't know.'

She nodded.

'Go back home?' It sounded like she was trying to suggest the best option. Maybe that was what she thought she would do in my position.

228

'I don't want to, really,' I told her. 'I like being abroad.'

She nodded again, and even smiled a little to show she understood. She had studied in the UK during college. She knew how interesting it was to be foreign.

'What are *you* going to do?' I asked in turn. Maybe it came across less gently, or maybe it sounded too complicit, and I shouldn't have said out loud that we both had a big decision to make. Whatever the reason, Akemi closed the door in my face.

She was putting her teacup in the sink when Yuki and I arrived in the kitchen the next morning. She looked pretty in her deep-red crepe maternity dress. Unlike most of the pregnant Japanese women I'd seen, she didn't dress her bump in childish clothing. She didn't go for bows or frills, and she always wore heels to the office.

I'd never seen her talk to Yuki as much in the morning as she did that day. She crouched down to ask her how she'd slept, and what she'd like for breakfast, even though I'd be the one making it for her. I could see down her dress. Her breasts were getting fuller, reminding me of the fantasy girls in the advertisements in the subway trains. She went back upstairs to brush her teeth and put on her lipstick, and left the house as the miso soup was heating up and I was frying eggs. I imagined her commute to the office. I imagined the women on the train admiring her, and the men finding her intimidating, admiring instead the man strong enough to take such a confident woman to bed.

I stopped myself. Maybe they didn't think any of the things I was imagining. And maybe Naoki wasn't actually strong enough for Akemi. Maybe her confidence intimidated him as well. Maybe she was actually one of the stones on the path that led that little boy shivering in the garden into his daughter's bedroom for a twisted sort of reassurance at night.

Naoki came downstairs with terrible bed head. His eyes were puffy and he'd done his shirt up wrong.

'Could I have one of those too?' he said, pointing to the egg I'd just put on the table for myself. He didn't wait for me to say yes before pulling out a chair and sitting.

He liked the yolk runnier than I did. I laid a plate over my egg, to keep it warm. Yuki already had hers, well done and cut into little pieces.

I employed a special sort of emotional Valium to subdue my revulsion and make the old routine possible under new circumstances. I remembered how to manufacture it from the days after my father touched my budding breasts, and again after my mother announced her affair. It was a deadening, a reliance on muscle memory. Back then my body knew how to move in order to get ready for school, and my face remembered its usual breakfast expression. Inside, my heart sat as heavy and cold as a ball bearing against my left lung, and in order to avoid talking about anything I didn't want to talk about, I asked my own questions.

'Tea?' I said to Naoki. 'Coffee?'

'Coffee.'

The time had to be made to pass, and making Naoki's breakfast was something to do. I turned my back and put a cup's worth of water in the kettle at the tap, looking out the window over the sink. A small triangle of sun had appeared on Michiko's driveway. I put the kettle on the

230

stove and turned the fire on high under it, then I turned the fire on low under the frying pan. While they heated up I got the instant coffee out of the cupboard and an egg out of the fridge. Yuki started singing. I cracked the egg into the still-oily pan, and I heard Naoki tell Yuki to eat. She kept singing, and I turned around to see her happily moving some egg around her plate. She had recently graduated from plastic plates to porcelain and I could hear the squeaks her fork made. Normally Naoki found this type of thing very cute, but when I turned back around to the stove he told her to stop singing and eat. I flipped the egg and the kettle's whistle began to build. Then I heard a slap. I turned around again, and Yuki looked shocked and scared, but then she took her cue from the kettle and they screamed together.

I could only turn one of them off. Even though I took Yuki out of her chair and held her on my hip, rocking her back and forth, she kept crying at the top of her lungs. I didn't know where Naoki had slapped her. Her face looked OK. It was red, but evenly red. Naoki stood up and started talking to me as if nothing had happened, except that he had to raise his voice. 'I am going to see my lawyer,' he said, and I nodded, and he went on, 'And Yuki will go to my mother's.'

'She can stay with me,' I told him, loud. I needed her to stay with me.

'You need to go out and buy a plane ticket,' he shouted back.

'So pay me,' I said.

He paused, then nodded. I was still rocking Yuki. She was still wailing.

'Get her ready,' he said to me, and once again he told Yuki to stop, pointing a finger in her face, before leaving the room.

I let her wail on. Her voice was a siren, expressing both her shock and my own that Naoki had slapped her. I wanted her to know she had every right to let that siren be heard. On and on she howled, and I hoped that hearing it made Naoki regret what he'd done, although I knew better than to expect contrition of him by now. I thought about whether Emi might ever hit Yuki. Remembering how upset she had been about Yuki gagging on the noodles, I chose to believe that she wouldn't. I had to believe that. It was the only way forward.

Once Naoki and Yuki were gone I made the mistake of standing still to think, and stood for too long. In the quiet, I felt barely there. I understood that I'd been superimposed on the kitchen, on the tatami room, on the stairs and in the bedrooms, and once I was gone the image of me would be taken right back off. I'd sent photos of Yuki and me to my parents, and to Porter, but there were none in Naoki's house. He'd probably take down the construction paper numbers I'd taped to the wall of the toilet to help Yuki learn them, and there would be no clear evidence of my having lived in the house at all, just as there was no evidence of Emi.

Except that I was going to take the heart out of it when I went.

I had thought I was going to be able to do so that morning, but with Yuki out of my hands I had to call Emi and tell her we needed to change the plan, that we'd have to wait until later.

'When?' she asked, and I didn't know. I didn't think I could stay at Naoki's more than one more night.

'When everyone's asleep?' I answered.

'Oh,' she said. 'It's very risky.'

'Yes.'

I waited while she thought. I was done thinking.

'All right,' she said. '*Shikata ga nai*.' No choice.

24

Before leaving the house I took a fresh set of underwear and socks out of my suitcase and hauled the suitcase downstairs. I left it by the shoe cabinets so that Naoki would see that things were moving forward when he got home. I also left a note on the dining table: 'I will be back late this evening, and will leave tomorrow.' I pictured him nodding, pleased, back in control.

I went over to Michiko's building and pressed her buzzer, and she let me in. Atsushi had a fever and was in the bedroom. The window covers were open, but Michiko hadn't folded the futons away, and Atsushi was asleep on one. My heart went out to Michiko as she looked down at his flushed face, his staccato breathing.

'I have a lot to tell you,' I said, and she put water on for tea. She offered me Lipton, but I asked for green. I knew where the teacups were now, and I took them down for us. They weren't cold, now that the weather was better, but I sat and turned the red one in my palms for her as I began the story. I wasn't asking for advice. I wasn't telling it because I didn't know what to do. I was telling her what was about to happen, and that I needed a favour.

Neither of us drank for a long time. The tea cooled as I talked, and Michiko listened. I saw intense concern on her face, and I saw sadness. She didn't look at me much; every once in a while she nodded. When I finished I let her think, and waited to see if she would ask me if I was sure we were doing the right thing, but she didn't. 'What can I do?' she said instead, so I asked if I could come back after I got my plane ticket, and could I possibly stay for dinner. She looked at the table, and she looked at Atsushi. Of course I could come back, she told me.

'Can I get you anything while I'm out?' I asked her. Now that we were back on normal ground, she looked at me.

'I need so many things,' she said, smiling and shaking her head, a mother with a dilemma.

'I can get them,' I insisted, but still she hesitated. 'Or I can babysit!' I said. 'I'll come back and you can go and do your shopping.' I didn't know who would have been doing whom the bigger favour if she accepted.

'I'm a nurse, remember,' I said, practically begging.

She smiled. 'OK,' she said.

'Great,' I said, standing up so quickly that the scraping of my chair startled Atsushi in his sleep. He did that dry sleep-crying you know you can ignore if you feel like it, but Michiko went to him, and I let myself out.

I bought two thousand-yen telephone cards at the nearest FamilyMart and slipped one into the payphone outside. It was late at night in Boston, but I dialled the number for my parents' apartment. My mother answered, and when she heard my voice the excitement in hers was so palpable that I immediately started to cry.

'Oh, Puss,' she said, 'what's happened?'

'I don't feel like I belong anywhere,' I told her, strangely able to say what I was feeling without my usual knee-jerk self-protection.

'Oh God,' she said right away, 'I know exactly what you mean.' I knew she meant it. 'It's a pisser,' she continued. 'Do you want to come home?'

'Ummm.'

'Not really?'

'Not really.'

'Yes. You're not done yet. I know some mothers would say come back home, but I really wonder if that's the answer.'

Not too long before, I probably would have felt this as further evidence that my family planet was a chilly one well outside the normal solar system. I didn't, though. I found it absolutely correct. My tears dried up, just like that, and as the red numbers on the phone counted my remaining money down, I gave my mother a quick outline of the situation. She made outraged noises, and at one point asked me if there would be an opportunity before I left to cut Naoki's balls off. We laughed together, and I was so grateful for it, and then she said, 'Diana,' in the voice that she had always used to talk to me about what she believed, no matter how young I had been. 'Live your life.'

Who knew what she actually meant, but I still found it encouraging.

'I've got to go,' I told her. 'I'll call again when I'm done here.'

'Call any time,' she said, and I was about to say goodbye when she said, 'Wait! Don't go yet. Listen to your father snoring.' I heard a soft rumble become louder, and imagined her holding the phone close to Dad's face. I pictured him with his mouth slack in total relaxation and I smiled, and relaxed. 'I don't know how I put up with it,' she said. 'I must love him.' Then my money ran out.

I stood outside the United Airlines office for a while before I opened the glass door. I'd already been through the street-level doors of the building, and in and out of the elevator doors. I needed to stop before I went through the last one. I checked that I had my ticket, my passport and my credit card with me, even though I'd already done that in the subway. What I was really doing was standing at the back of a springboard, wondering how the water was down below. It sparkled, but I didn't know the temperature. Or the depth. I wanted to feel it on my skin, though.

Once inside, I was faced with two identical women in United uniforms, red lipstick, and hair slicked back into buns. They looked up and smiled as I approached their long desk. The one on the left took pity on me for not knowing which of them I should speak to, and asked, 'How can I help you?' I gave an apologetic little bow to her twin, who gave me a bow of understanding and forgiveness back, and I sat in the chair in front of the left half of the desk.

'I need to change my ticket,' I told the agent. 'It's an open-ended ticket, to Boston via Seattle. I'd like to make a booking now, for tomorrow, but to Honolulu instead.' I handed her my ticket and put my hands on my bobbing knees, watching as she studied the details, interpreting the tiny blue print that had faded like an old tattoo after so many months in a drawer. Then she started to tap at her computer keyboard. She tapped and tapped and tapped, and it felt like she'd forgotten me and was writing a letter.

'OK,' she finally said, and I exhaled. 'There is one seat available at seven twenty-five p.m., and there are several seats available at ten fifty-five p.m.'

'Nothing in the morning?'

'No, there are only evening flights.'

'What time do they get in?'

She smiled. 'The seven twenty-five gets in twelve hours before take-off. The ten fifty-five gets in eleven and a half hours before take-off.'

'Ha!' I said, and she nodded.

'It is wonderful,' she said. 'You will need to pay more, though.'

'That's OK.'

Where would Porter be at 7.30 on a Tuesday morning, or at 11.30? I told myself it actually didn't matter. I chose the earlier flight, and handed over the price of a new adventure.

Michiko told me that Atsushi had eaten some soup while I was out. Asleep again, he looked a little less flushed. She put some subtle lipstick on before whispering her goodbye and going out for her shopping. With nothing to do I lay in a square of sunshine next to her little boy.

I woke up to the sound of the door and the rustle of plastic bags and when I opened my eyes I looked right into Atsushi's. How long had he been awake and staring at me? He didn't blink. It was awkward. I had wanted to be playing with him when Michiko got home, or at least reading at the table while he still slept. I pushed myself up onto one elbow, and when Michiko had put her shopping down and appeared at the door of the room, I was smiling at Atsushi. He had his back to her, so she couldn't see how unhappy he was. 'Is that Mama?' I whispered to his sixty per cent impassive, forty per cent scared face. She smiled and said, '*Tadaima!*', meaning 'I'm back!' Atsushi's head whipped around. It took just a second for everything finally to compute in his young brain, and he didn't like what it added up to. When he started to cry, Michiko picked him up and carried him into the kitchen making beautiful noises, and I followed, smoothing my hair, hoping there weren't sleep creases in my face. It occurred to me to be helpful and take the shopping out of its bags, but Atsushi was watching me while he cried on Michiko's shoulder, and I didn't want him to see me usurping her position any more. So I just pulled out a chair and sat at the table and accepted that I was not quite anywhere, and not quite anyone.

25

All the earthquakes I had experienced in Tokyo until that night had rumbled. They'd made the house shake like freight trains would, shouldering their way single-mindedly through the neighbourhood. During the bigger ones, it was as if the train carriages were unbalanced and some of them scraped against the house. The dishes chattered and complained. The hanging lamps swung a rhythmic 'No, no, no, no, no, no, no'.

Not on that night, though. On that night, enormous hands picked the house up and dropped it, *kaBAM*, and a dog barked, then everything was silent again. Yuki didn't stir. I waited for aftershocks – I knew that not feeling any didn't necessarily mean they weren't happening – and then the thunder started. The airquake. Everything under us and everything above us was moving. We were sandwiched in violence.

I waited some more, feeling as thin as a hair between the plate tectonics and the weather, and completely inconsequential on the very night when I was hoping to be of more consequence than ever.

Things went quiet again.

I had slept a little, around midnight I think, once we were all in bed, but it was just another nap. I didn't need my alarm. I had snapped awake, heart pounding, well before the earthquake, because I'd had a dream of taking Yuki to a doctor, and the doctor was about to examine her and I couldn't bear it. I was too frightened for her, and woke up with a painful pounding in my chest. Realising where I was didn't calm me down at all. I spent some time thinking through why I'd had that dream, and why I'd been taking her to a doctor rather than examining her myself. If I had had any suspicions of abuse on the morning I found Yuki with her diaper off, I would have known what sort of abrasions to look for. I could only conclude that I both wanted and didn't want to know what had happened to her, and the not wanting won.

At 2.45 I stood up, took off my nightshirt and folded it very small so it would fit into my backpack with yesterday's underwear, my book, my toiletries, and a sweatshirt and socks for when it got cold in the plane. I put on clean underwear and the jeans and long-sleeved T-shirt I'd taken off before bed.

You don't know how long fifteen minutes is until you have nothing left to do but wait to kidnap someone.

At 2.51 the rain started. I willed it to rain harder, to cover the noise I'd make carrying Yuki downstairs and opening and closing the front door, but it was an obstinate pitter-pat.

At 2.57 I put on my backpack and walked without breathing into Yuki's room. I inhaled, I exhaled, I peeled back her covers and slid my hands under her warm familiar form, lifting her floppy weight so her head was on my shoulder and I could grasp my own elbows under her bum. I walked back out, past Naoki's door, and took the stairs

242

slowly, deliberately, feeling the wood against my slightly sweaty feet. My ears felt like they'd tripled in size as I listened for danger. I turned left at the bottom and walked along the hallway. Because I knew no one would steal it, I'd put my suitcase outside the front door after Naoki was back home and in bed. I had told Emi I would. That way someone would be able to help me carry it without coming into the house. It would be a signal too: if the suitcase wasn't there, something had gone wrong.

I stepped into my shoes, crushing the backs down because I couldn't put them on properly without disturbing Yuki. I stood behind the door and listened to my own breathing. There was a flash of lightning and automatically I started counting, like I had been taught to as a kid, measuring the distance between the lightning and me by how many seconds it was before the thunder. Seven. The lightning was seven somethings away. With that much adrenalin in my system, I couldn't remember something as simple as that. Counting was calming, so I did it again. I did it so I wouldn't turn around and frighten myself that Naoki was coming down the stairs. One Mississipi, two Mississipi, three Mississipi, four Mississipi . . . I didn't know if it was 2.59, or 3.01. Nine Mississipi, ten Mississipi, eleven Mississipi, twelve Mississipi, thirteen Mississipi, fourteen Mississipi . . . I heard footsteps approaching the other side of the door. I released one of my hands, feeling nauseous, then grabbed the handle and opened the door.

A man I didn't know in a dark suit was walking down the steps away from me, hurrying to the open trunk of a black Mercedes. I quietly closed the door behind me and didn't lock it. I had left my key on my desk. Yuki didn't wake up as I went down the stairs, even with early spring rain falling on the back of her neck. I wondered if the man was Junko's husband. He was too young to be the women's father. He looked brawny, too, pressing down on the trunk to close it with a heavy click. He opened the back door of the car for me.

Yuki raised her heavy head and looked around as I was trying to get in. I lifted my legs quickly into the car. My backpack was soft enough to lean back on so I didn't try to take it off. I rearranged Yuki comfortably on my lap but I didn't say anything yet. No one did. The man closed my door.

Emi was next to me in the dark, wrapped in what looked like beige cashmere. She wasn't wearing sunglasses. Once the man was back in the driver's seat, Emi said, 'Quickly,' in Japanese, and we drove away. He had a thick neck, and glossy hair.

Yuki rubbed one eye, and asked where we were going.

'We're going to see your mama,' I told her.

'Mama?'

'Yes.'

'Mama?'

'Yes.'

Emi said, '*Okaasan.*'

'*Okaasan?*'

'Yes,' I said.

'Mama.'

'Yes.'

Yuki's head clunked forward onto my chest, and it could just have been that she was tired, but to me it also felt like the biggest nod, the most enormous yes ever. I reached over and took the corner of Emi's shawl (it *was* cashmere) and tugged at it. Emi leaned forward and helped me unravel Yuki a little so that I could pull a wing of it over her back.

In the dark comfort of the big back seat, watching the windscreen wipers waving at me, I began to feel the fatigue in my muscles. Emi laid a hand on the back of the driver's seat and said, 'This is Yoshi.' She left her hand on the back of the seat as if it were the man's own back. That was how I knew that Yoshi was her boyfriend. It was also how I knew for sure that Emi wasn't truly my friend, not in any of the ways that I understood friend to mean. Not only had she not told me about the lawyer's letter the day before, she also hadn't told me she'd started dating. And she hadn't told me her boyfriend would be the one coming to pick us up. I had thought that I was bringing Yuki to her mother, to help Yuki travel the line between our two points, but suddenly we were the three corners of a triangle: Emi, her boyfriend, and Yuki and me. When I left, would the three of them still be a triangle? How quickly would Yuki move over to be part of Emi's corner? How solid was the line between Emi and her boyfriend? How short was it?

I nodded at Emi, hoping that I looked supportive in the regular splashes of light thrown by the street lights.

'Are we still going to Junko's?' I asked her, just in case she hadn't told me about a change in plan. I was worried that the man had control now.

'Yes,' she said.

That was a relief, although going to Junko's really didn't seem like the safest bet to me. I'd suggested a hotel, but the sisters wanted us all to be together somewhere a little bit familiar when Yuki woke up. They didn't believe that Naoki would go to the police, given that he'd been accused of abuse, but I hadn't thought it was out of the question. Everything they'd told me led me to imagine that the police would take a kidnapping much more seriously than abuse. 'No,' Emi had said. 'He won't go to the police. His father will tell him not to, because it might get into the newspaper.' That finally made some sense, but it still seemed that Emi and Junko believed that all the love they were pouring into rescuing Yuki was some sort of guarantee of success. Naoki had never been to Junko's house, they reminded me, and didn't know where it was, and their parents had been sworn to secrecy in the event that he turned up on the doorstep demanding answers. They were convinced that we'd have enough time both to come up with the next step and to take it before he was on our trail.

I realised with a flip of the stomach that Naoki might think to contact the airport and stop me from leaving Japan. That's certainly what I would have done if my child had been taken. But then again, I hadn't taken her passport. In all my snooping, I'd never found where he kept it. That calmed me down. Naoki would know that I wouldn't be taking her with me when I flew, and maybe he wouldn't care if I left, only about finding Yuki.

In which case, he'd have to imagine that Emi was involved.

'We're nearly there,' Emi whispered.

I gave up. I thought of Naoki and Akemi, asleep. I thought of Naoki's sleeping parents. Lights off, window covers closed, completely in the dark.

When we arrived, the man, Yoshi, reached forward and popped the trunk. I opened my own door and pushed it wide with my foot. Now that I was feeling so tired it wasn't as easy to move. I heaved myself to my feet, and closed the door with my hip. Emi went up the steps to the house first, but Yoshi waited with my suitcase to let me go up before him. It was the first time I could really look at his face. He was handsome in the way a superior cut of beef could be handsome, and he reminded me of retired sumo wrestlers I'd seen on TV: still strong, still important, and not entirely comfortable in clothing.

Junko's husband was in bed, and it was clear from the size of Junko's eyes that she'd been sleeping too. Emi moved out of my way and let me follow Junko up onto the platform of the tatami room. She hadn't turned the light on in there, but the light from the living room showed me that there were two futons made up. I laid Yuki down on the one Junko indicated and pulled the unfamiliar covers up to her neck. When I stood up, Junko whispered, 'Emi can sleep here,' pointing to the other futon. 'I have made the couch for you.' I stepped back down into the living room with her to join Emi by the coffee table before saying no.

'Sorry?' Junko said politely. I glanced at Emi and she had an *I wondered if this might happen* expression on her face, so I nodded at her a little apologetically, *Yes, this is happening*, and said, 'Waking up in a strange place is enough, don't you think? She should see someone familiar when she opens her eyes.'

'But—' Junko said.

'Of course Emi can come in with us in the morning,' I continued. 'Or Yuki can go to her. But let's just see what happens.'

247

I suppose I was testing Emi's maternal instincts, as I figured that wanting to sleep next to Yuki right away merely showed maternal desire, rather than protection. But the test felt essential to me, given the emotional fallout that could follow.

Junko looked at Emi, and Emi nodded convincingly.

I swung my backpack off and asked for a glass of water. I realised that Emi's boyfriend had gone, and I gave him points for discretion. Emi sat on the raised edge of the tatami room, looking in at Yuki. I sat next to her and asked her if she was still living with her parents.

She nodded.

'And is that where Yuki and you will go?'

'I don't know yet. First, we must see what Naoki does.'

By this time I had decided that Naoki would call Emi's parents right away when he saw that Yuki was gone. He might even go to their house and rage at them, but they would be able to tell him truthfully that she wasn't there. If he barged in and rampaged through, he'd see that there was no sign of her. There would be a buffer of time before anything had to be decided. As long as their parents couldn't be bullied into giving us up, that is. I imagined that the lawyers would talk before Naoki and Emi did. Akemi would . . . I didn't know. I had no idea.

'We can go to Yoshi's place,' Emi said, and then Junko brought me the water. She also brought me a towel, and made sure that I knew where the light switches were. Emi got up and went to the bathroom, so I changed back into my nightshirt in the tatami room and put some toothpaste on my toothbrush. I took my turn in the bathroom, staring numbly at my eye bags in the unfriendly fluorescent light over the mirror, and when I returned to the living room Emi was already under the sheet and blanket on the couch, facing Yuki, but with her eyes closed, looking as tiny as a child herself. Maybe she was asleep; maybe she didn't want me to press her about Yoshi. I was sure she had felt me stiffen when she said they could go and live with him.

I turned out the light and slid my feet slowly over the floor until one of them met the step to the tatami room. I crawled to the futons on my hands and knees, releasing the smell of the mats. It was middle-aged tatami, neither young and smelling sharply of straw, nor old and faded. By the time I'd climbed under the covers, my eyes had adjusted to the dark. Yuki had a soft pillow, but mine was filled with buckwheat hulls. I lifted it and pressed it to work out a comfortable shape, but failed noisily. I would have shoved it off the futon to lie on my back without a pillow if I hadn't wanted to fall asleep facing Yuki in the hope that I'd still be facing her when she woke up.

When I heard Yuki whispering, 'Diana-chan,' I was afraid to open my eyes in case she wasn't actually there, but this time she really was, almost nose to my nose. There were no metal window covers on the big bay window of the living room, and the sun shone weakly through the elaborate net curtains. 'Good morning,' I whispered back, and Yuki said 'Good mohneen' loud and clear. I looked over at the couch and Emi was sitting up, watching us, so I sat up too. Yuki did the same.

'We're at my friend's house,' I said. 'Remember the big TV?'

Yuki located the TV and her eyes popped open wide. She looked at me. 'I want TV!' she said, and then, 'OK?' The way she cocked her head was so cute that Emi laughed.

Yuki looked at Emi, and then back at me. 'OK?' she said again, nodding to get me to nod.

I took a deep breath. 'You can ask your mama,' I told her.

'Mama?'

'Yes,' I said. 'My friend, that lady.' I pointed. 'She is your mama.'

Yuki stared. Emi smiled, and even from that far away I could see her lip trembling. Yuki looked at me again, and I nodded. Convinced, or at least obedient, Yuki looked back at Emi. 'TV OK?' she said quietly.

'How about breakfast?' Emi responded, in Japanese.

Yuki looked at me.

'Good idea!' I said. 'Breakfast, then TV.'

'Let's make a delicious breakfast,' Emi said, and Yuki got up.

'Careful,' I said, to be sure Yuki realised it was a step down from the tatami room to the living room.

'The kitchen is this way,' Emi told Yuki, crossing to the hallway that led to the back of the house.

I forced myself to stay where I was and leave them alone. I heard cabinets opening and closing, Emi's muted questions, Yuki's responses and exclamations. I saw my suitcase by the front door and went to get it, opening it out on the tatami room floor. I transferred my clothes to the lid so I could take Yuki's out, and arranged hers in a few neat piles against the wall of the room. I had only hidden five pull-up diapers in the suitcase. I put them in their own little pile.

We'll have to do some shopping today, I thought, and then corrected myself. *They'll have to do some shopping today.*

Suddenly I felt winded. I stared at Yuki's colourful clothes, many of which I'd bought at Naoki's command with Naoki's money, all of which I'd washed and folded, none of which I'd wash and fold again. The thought came to me that loving Yuki was forcing me to take a huge risk, and that that may have been the best thing that had ever happened to me. Then I felt sorry for myself that I couldn't say that I was the best thing that had ever happened to her, because I hoped that the best thing that had ever happened to her was happening right then in Junko's kitchen. I slid the tatami room doors closed and curled up on Yuki's futon with a fizz of tears in my throat.

I wasn't there long. I heard Junko and her husband come downstairs, and I heard their voices join Emi's and Yuki's in the kitchen. I stayed where I was, and realised that I'd regret letting Yuki catch me crying if she came to find me. I knew she'd want to make me feel better if she did, and today was not a day to get Yuki worried about me. I heard Junko and her husband leave the house, and forced myself to get up and get busy. I took my towel and went to the kitchen to ask Emi if it was OK to take a shower.

Yuki was taking a bite out of a piece of toast so fat that the jam was going up her nose, and it made me laugh. 'So big!' I said. Yuki laughed too, mouth wide open, food visible. Emi was sitting next to her with a boiled egg in an egg cup, poised with a teaspoon for when her daughter decided she wanted a mouthful. Yuki could manage on her own, but I didn't tell Emi that. She had still been feeding Yuki when she was forced to leave, so I imagined she'd want to start from there. She told me where the shower was, and I said, 'See you later, jammy nose,' before heading for the stairs.

All the doors to the rooms upstairs were closed and the hallway was dark and forbidding. I showered quickly to get back down to the now brightening living room, and I dressed in the outfit from the day before. I took a clean top from the suitcase and slid it into my backpack so I could freshen up on the plane before landing, and then I tidied up my suitcase, folding my nightshirt as carefully as I would have if I'd been watched by the mothers at the swimming pool. Now that Yuki's clothes were out of the suitcase, there was room for the things I had left behind and would never see again: my winter boots, an old sweater, my parka, three previous John le Carré novels. I did the webbing straps up over my clothes, pulled them tight, and closed the suitcase. The next time I would open it I would be where Porter was. I couldn't imagine looking at him. I could only see myself sitting next to him looking out of the window of his room, waiting for my soul to catch up with my body, hoping the Japanese white-eye would sing.

26

Emi put the second *Mary Poppins* disk in the machine and I stayed in the tatami room, folding up the sheets and futons and watching Yuki watch the movie. It was as entertaining to watch her face react to Dick Van Dyke as it was to watch Dick Van Dyke's face. Emi was enjoying Yuki's enjoyment too, and she didn't leave the couch once. I would have liked to get her alone to ask her a few questions about Yoshi, but I couldn't make it happen.

When the disk finished I went to the bathroom, and when I came back Emi was talking about going to a nearby supermarket before lunch and Yuki's nap. I didn't want to go with them. The plan was for me to withdraw, and I had to stick to the plan. I didn't need to get to the airport yet, but even so, it was time to leave.

'Hey, Yuki,' I said, crouching down by the couch, looking up into her face, 'isn't it nice to be with your mama?'

She gave me two definitive nods.

'Do you know where my mama is?'

She didn't seem to understand.

'Where's Diana-chan's mama?' I asked her, and Emi asked it in Japanese too.

Yuki lifted her hands and shrugged her shoulders. 'I doh know.'

'She's faaaaaaar away,' I said. 'So far I have to take an airplane.'

'Oh,' Yuki said.

'I want to see my mama,' I said. I supposed it was true, although I didn't know when I would.

Yuki asked me in Japanese if I was lonely.

Yes, I replied in Japanese. Yes, I am lonely. Then I switched back to English. 'Shall I go see my mama?'

Yuki nodded.

'Good idea?'

She nodded again.

'You can be with your mama and I can be with my mama!' I said, standing up, feeling giddy, just like the type of three-year-old I was imitating. 'Here's my suitcase,' I told her, walking over to the tatami room to get it. I set it down on the living room floor and put on my backpack, and when I announced that I was ready the words had to leapfrog the lump in my throat.

'We can leave at the same time,' Emi said, and then she asked Yuki to come with her to the toilet before we left.

'Wait, OK?' Yuki said to me, patting the air in front of her with her palm to keep me where I was. Then she took the hand Emi had offered to help her get down off the couch.

Outside, the air was fresh. The houses of the crowded neighbourhood had dried off, none the worse for the earthquake and the storm. I looked down at my feet, concentrating on carrying my cumbersome suitcase down the front steps without falling over, and Emi had her back to the street while she locked the door, so it was Yuki who saw Naoki first. '*Papa da!*' she said just before I heard a car door slam. When I looked up, he was coming around the front of his car and approaching the steps. I put my suitcase down in front of my legs, blocking his path, and glanced over my shoulder. Emi had taken Yuki up onto her hip. I didn't know why she hadn't gone back into the house. There was no time to say anything to her because Naoki was right in front of me saying, 'Give me my daughter.'

'She's Emi's daughter too.'

'I have custody.'

An elegant old lady in a Burberry scarf was walking past his car. She didn't actually pay any attention to us, but I pretended she was greeting me and I smiled at her, and bowed, and said, '*Konnichiwa.*' Naoki looked over his shoulder to see what was happening behind him, and I turned and told Emi to go inside. She came back to life and spun around to unlock the door.

'Yuki!' Naoki called out. 'Daddy's lonely!'

I heard the lock turn. Naoki tried to push by me, shouting up at the house as the front door closed, and I shoved him hard enough to make him take two steps backwards. Getting my hands on him and pushing him away brought my magma to the surface, boiling with old shame and regret and frustration and disgust, and I started shouting too. 'What are you going to *do*, Naoki? Make Yuki choose on the spot? Give her responsibility for taking care of *everyone's* feelings?'

'I have custody!' he screamed.

'Custody is a *privilege*!' I shouted back, barely a foot from his face. 'And you don't deserve it!'

'Get out of my way!'

I put my hands on his chest, ready to shove him harder than the first time, but when we leaned into each other I felt the bones under his insubstantial muscles and in a flash I knew that I could bar him from the house with force, because I was at least as ferocious about keeping him away from Yuki as he was about getting to her.

I didn't know how long he'd feel like struggling with me out in the street. I couldn't stay there for ever. He tried to get around me by putting both hands against my right side to shove me into the ivy by the steps. I quickly shifted my hands onto his shoulders and pushed him back to arm's length, shaking him the way you want to shake a child having a temper tantrum but aren't supposed to. 'Naoki,' I said firmly, and said it again to get him to look at me. When he complied it didn't occur to me to be amazed that he did, because I had been so sure that he would. I knew that he could be bullied. 'You are being a first-class *asshole*.'

He tried to push past me again, less harshly, and I was able to hang on to him. He was running out of steam. 'You can't go in there, Naoki. Think about it.'

'I have to get her.'

'Think! Yuki's old enough to remember your behaviour.'

I was about to add that she was old enough to remember *all* his behaviour, but his eyes teared up. 'My angel,' he said. A film of spit connected his parted lips and gleamed weakly in the sun.

I wasn't going to comfort this man. 'Get in the car,' I told him. 'Get in the car, go home, think about what's best for *Yuki*.'

He looked surprised. 'I'm best for Yuki.'

'Oh really?'

'Emi left Yuki.'

'You made her.'

'No, I didn't.'

'Whatever, Naoki. I found you in her bedroom at night.'

'So what?'

'Drunk, Naoki. *Naked*.'

He tipped his chin up, but I noticed the swallow. 'I am her father,' he said. 'We can be naked.'

'Erect,' I said, and the lump in my throat was back. The word was so hard to say, not only because the memory was so awful, but also because somehow, I don't know how, we learn not to want to say it, and not to want to hear it. The same goes for penis. I spat it out of me. 'Your *penis* was *erect*.'

A fraction of a second of unhappy surprise, and then the chin up again. 'So?'

'*So?* Oh my God, what is *wrong* with you?' I said, pushing him away from me.

For a few seconds we just stared at each other. When he didn't answer, I put my hands on my hips. 'I'm standing right here until you're gone.' I told him. 'Get in the car. Go home. Think about what's best for Yuki.'

He looked up at the house. 'I'll come back,' he said.

'Get in the car.'

I stayed where I was for several minutes after he left in case he only went around the block. I looked at the houses opposite. They sat shoulder to shoulder like people on the subway, squeezed in together but not talking. They watched me clomp back up the steps. Emi must also have watched

257

me from behind the curtains, because she unlocked the door to let me in when I got to the top. Inside, the second side of *Mary Poppins* was playing and Yuki was back on the couch. Emi and I stayed by the door. 'He says he'll come back,' I told her quietly.

She was wringing her beautiful little hands. 'Oh, no,' she said. 'How did he find us?'

I chose not to respond that she clearly came from parents who could be bullied as easily as she could. 'Emi,' I said instead, a little severely, 'is this going to work?'

Her eyes stopped darting around and her hands went quiet. 'Yes,' she said. 'It is going to work. I will call Yoshi.' She walked through the room to make the call from the kitchen, and I was left alone again with no role. Part of me had been pleased, coming back up the steps, because I had ordered Naoki away and he had gone. I hadn't let something happen. I had made something *not* happen. But how many more things were going to happen now? If I stood there behind that door for ever, could I make sure they were only good things? I was tempted to try. My brain calculated the cost of cancelling my ticket, finding a room in a hostel . . . and then all the stuffing went out of me. I lurched over to the couch to sit down next to Yuki.

'*Papa wa?*' she asked, with her eyes still on the TV.

'He went home,' I told her.

No reaction. Grown-ups moved fast, got in and out of cars, went away and came back when they felt like it. Little kids didn't often wonder why for very long.

Emi reappeared and motioned me to join her in the kitchen. We stood by the table, which hadn't been wiped of

jam and crumbs yet. 'Yoshi is taking us to Tokyo Disneyland,'
she said.

'For the day?'

'No. He will get us a room.'

'He will get you all a room?'

'What?'

'Who will stay in the room?'

'I will stay with Yuki.'

'Oh. Not Yoshi.'

'Not Yoshi.'

'OK.'

I knew I was being pushy, but Emi seemed to have taken
my questions at face value. 'I think it is good,' she said.

'Yes. Yuki will be amazed.'

After a short silence I went to the sink and got a wet
cloth to wipe the table with. 'How long will you stay?'

'I don't know. Three days, I think.'

'And then?' I shook the crumbs into the sink, rinsed off
the jam.

'Then, I hope, we will know what to do.'

I thought about who 'we' were. Emi had her parents,
who as far as I knew hadn't tortured her as a child. She had
a lawyer, who was finally willing to play a role now that
abuse appeared to have been involved. She had her strong
sister, and maybe her sister's husband was supportive as
well. She had Yoshi, whoever he was.

Suddenly we heard Yuki's voice calling 'Okaasan!' from
the living room. Emi's face lit up and she rushed out to her
daughter.

I had to convince myself that Yuki would be fine. I wasn't
sure that I would be fine, not without a child to care for.

What was it with me and children? My mind drew a blank, and then it filled with the answer like a footprint in sand near the water's edge. Bizarrely, Naoki had said it: children were pure good. With everyone else – absolutely everyone – you took your chances.

I hung the cloth over the kitchen tap, stretching it out so it would dry effectively, pulling the corners even. I held it like that for a while, and then I let go.

At the airport I pulled out my second telephone card and slid it into a payphone. It was shortly after 2 p.m. on Tuesday for me, so it was shortly after 7 p.m. on Monday for Porter. He could have been working late, he could have been out for dinner. I chewed the skin that was still peeling off my lower lip even though the cold dry winter was over, and he answered.

'Porter, it's Diana.'

'I already knew that.'

'How?'

'I told everyone not to call me until I had heard from you, so that if my phone rang it *had* to be you.'

'Oh. That's amazing.'

'It's only logical. Are you OK?'

'I'm sort of OK.'

'Where are you?'

'I'm at the airport.'

'And where are you going?'

'Honolulu.'

After a moment he said, 'I don't believe you.'

'What?'

'Only kidding. It's just . . . Well, it's amazing. When do you get here?'

'Seven thirty in the morning.'

'Tomorrow morning?'

'For you. This morning for me.'

'Ha!'

'I know!'

'I'll come get you.'

'Are you sure?'

'Of course!'

'Actually . . . I kind of like the idea of making my own way there. I've got your address.'

'OK. If you like.'

'Yeah, I think so.'

'How many minutes can we talk now?'

'Only about five more, I think.'

'OK, so I can tell you about the caves under Moiliili. They're limestone, and they're right under downtown, and I might see if I can get on a project to investigate how extensive they are, and how safe.'

'Oh no.'

'Why? It's cool!'

'I was looking forward to being on stable ground.'

Porter was silent, and then he quietly said, 'You know that Hawaii is basically a volcano, right?'

I answered him quietly. 'Yeah.' I had forgotten, though.

'We don't have to stay here.'

I didn't know what to say. He jumped back in. 'Wait, you've been living over a huge network of tunnels all this time. Tokyo's got like a gazillion subways, right?'

'Yeah, but—'

'Plus you've got earthquakes.'

'Porter—'

'And winter. You've got cold weather. You've been living with all those things and all we've got here is volcanoes.'

'Porter. I'm coming. I'm not trying to decide. You don't have to make a pitch for the place. I'm coming.'

He went quiet again, for a second. 'Maybe I actually don't believe you.'

'I'm getting on the plane in four and a half hours.'

'OK. OK.' He exhaled noisily. 'That's OK then.'

I looked at the red numbers. We were just under halfway through my money. My heart stuffed itself into my throat. I stared at the blank wall in front of me and said, 'I won't be living with you, Porter.'

'Why not?'

'Well. It's just . . . People are so shit.'

'Oh, yeah. People . . . You're right.'

I thought I might cry.

'You're also wrong,' he said.

I said, 'I hope so.'

'How about cats? Do you like cats?'

'Yes.'

'I could get a cat. Then you'd want to be at my place all the time. And the cat wouldn't be people.'

I laughed.

'I think I heard tears in that laugh.'

I sighed so he could hear that too. 'Really hard day. Week.'

'Gotcha. Anyway, OK, that's fine. I'll, um, I'll see about finding you a room.'

'You have a couch, until then?'

'Sure.'

'OK. Only a little time left.'

'Can't you get another card?'

'I can. Or I can save the money.'

'You're always doing math.'

'No, I'm not.'

'Dang. First attempt at showing off how well I know my beloved? Complete failure.'

I laughed again, and permitted my heart to flutter because it wanted to so much, and the red numbers clicked on.

'We're going to get cut off,' I told him.

'Only till tomorrow.'

'Only until earlier today.'

'Ha! Wait. Is the little girl OK?'

'I don't know.'

'Shit.'

'Yeah.'

I rushed to change the subject. The phone cut us off as I was saying, 'Please get a cat.'

27

When I can't sleep I fly high above the earth. I started doing it in Tokyo when I tried to imagine where Porter was. What I looked down on then appeared more like the Hawaii page of the atlas I grew up with than real islands. I've been living here for nine years now, so these days the view is more realistic. I float above the Oahu coast.

One of the first things Porter and I did once I'd arrived in Moiliili was take a scuba diving course. We held hands all through those dives, as newbie divers often do, and didn't let go once we'd become confident, using the connection to get each other's attention. Just a little pressure and we knew to look where the other was pointing (barracuda, puffer fish, turtle), no need for the effort of waving. We snorkelled with spinner dolphins once, and learned that they rest during the day in the shallow bays of west Oahu and spread out to hunt at night.

That was the night I let go of the idea of renting my own place and held hands with Porter on the trip from the couch into his bedroom. We kissed and hugged, and he could feel I was scared by the intimacy, but still I didn't want to go back to the couch. We held hands. I didn't feel contented and reassured – I felt stupid and insecure – but it was what I could do that night.

Porter fell asleep first. I woke up in the dark because he was up on his elbow, tapping me on the thigh. 'Are you going?' he was saying, sounding awake and bright even though his eyes weren't open. I waited. 'Are you going?' he asked again, starting to look unhappy when he didn't get an answer. 'Yes,' I ventured, and he gave the darkness a neat nod before turning over and pulling the sheet up over his shoulder. 'OK,' he said in a childlike voice I'd never heard him use. 'Have a good time.'

I stayed awake a long time over that. When I told him in the morning, he couldn't remember the dream at all. He decided that he must have been talking to someone he was merely friends with, and I agreed that had to be the case. Sometimes I think that he was expressing an ideal situation, though: a relationship where you can go exploring and wish each other a very good time at it, knowing that you'll be back in the same bay later. It's a metaphor for a lifetime of personal development, I suppose, but for me it's a better metaphor for how orgasm takes you away from each other. It's not the moment when you become one with your partner; it's the moment when you are furthest away from them, and from any self you recognise.

'Do you ever get used to the feeling?' I asked Porter after the first time we succeeded in getting me there.

He grinned. 'Nope!' But I decided that I'd have to try to take the edge off it somehow, so that it wouldn't always be so upsetting. The earthquakes of my young life continued to have aftershocks, and I hated leaving the bay.

When I can't sleep I sometimes imagine enough moonlight to watch the spinner dolphins from above as their pods break up to hunt, circle their meals, teach their calves, echo-locate. I feel myself relax when I imagine them coming back together, drawing in close with the dawn.

I don't just look down on Hawaii any more. I fly across the Pacific and the continental states to Patuxet, zooming in over our old house and down the roads that lead to the beach. I fly the length of the beach, then I ascend again so I can see the towns ours abutted, one a little richer, one a little poorer. I picture parents and kids, kids and kids, parents and parents, swirling in and out of the rings of each other's circuses. They juggle each other at times, and throw knives at each other, training each other not to flinch, daring each other not to quit the game.

A little further north I look down on the Back Bay apartment building my parents moved to when my dad retired. I'm usually wakeful around two in the morning, which is six hours behind Boston. At 8 a.m. my dad will be making toast and boiled eggs; Mom will be choosing what to wear to work. Over breakfast she won't be ashamed to tell Dad if she had a sexy dream about someone from the office, and Dad will have the rest of the day to decide what to do with the knowledge. I don't know what he does with what she says, but he absorbs it and breaks it down somehow, and it seems to work for him.

Sometimes I fly west rather than east. From high above, Japan is a seahorse with a spine of mountains. When I descend over the main island of Honshu in my mind I recalculate the time. Two a.m. for me is 9 p.m. on the same day for Yuki, so it's dark where she is too. She's twelve now. I look down on the house she shares with Emi and Yoshi and her five-year-old half-sister, Ai, whose name means love. I see the top of Yuki's head, bent over her books. I've never been to the house, but I've seen photos. It looks like the other houses on the street (two storeys, pale putty walls, dark grey roof) except for the juxtaposition of a tightly trimmed, perfectly rectangular front hedge with a jumble of scruffy potted plants on the steps. 'Those are Ai-chan's project,' Emi told me.

It was just last month. We were sitting on the brand-new sofa bed Porter and I bought before the family arrived for a weekend stopover on their way to Maui. We'd only recently been back in touch, thanks to the Internet, on Emi's initiative. I had been good about sending Christmas cards to her until after Hadley was born, and had had several New Year cards from her as well. I knew that she'd been able to keep Yuki. Exactly how wasn't clear to me, but I had the impression that they'd found a way to make the Yoshimuras feel a fight would have been bad for Naoki's father's reputation and business. I knew we'd got Yuki out just in time, since Akemi could legally have adopted Yuki after marrying Naoki without any need to consult Emi about it. I knew that Naoki and Akemi's baby was a boy. After Emi's cards dropped off, maybe after she had Ai, I forgot to send her a change of address card when we bought the house. Then I got an email from the alumni office at Boston College, telling me that Emi was trying to get in touch, and giving me her email address. I was impressed that she had remembered where I'd studied nursing, and had made the effort. We arranged the visit.

I became even more wakeful at night.

I ached to hug Yuki when I met the family at the airport, but I wasn't sure if she was a hugger. In any case, her suitcase

268

didn't have wheels and she was carrying it in front of her with both hands. I took it from her as a way to interact, and she looked at Emi for guidance as to whether it was rude to let me carry it. I asked her if she was well, in Japanese, and she said she was. Ai couldn't stop talking about the colour of the ocean she'd seen from the plane, and then of course she exclaimed about the heat as we left the terminal, and that dispelled the tension. Yoshi sat with me in the front of the car, and I tried not to stare at Yuki in the rear-view mirror as she looked out the window in the back.

When we pulled up to the house Porter and our kids came barrelling out the front door holding a big WELCOME sign. We must have surprised them, as they hadn't finished colouring in all the letters, but Hadley and PJ were excited to hold it up. It got them lots of appreciation from Emi and Yoshi, but Ai just stood in front of them and stared. She wasn't suddenly shy; you could tell by the set of her square face (she resembled her father) that it was a power play. Who would speak first? My kids stared back in wide-eyed expectation of some sort of interaction, and just when they looked as if they were getting uncomfortable, Ai walked past them. 'Princess Ai-chan,' Emi said, and we all bumped happily against each other as we made our way through the front door.

I didn't get to stare at Yuki until I showed her the guest room she'd have to herself. Ai-chan would be in with Hadley and PJ, unless she wanted to sleep with Emi and Yoshi on the sofa bed. I walked in to put Yuki's bag down and when I turned around she was still standing in the doorway with her feet together. They'd all taken off their shoes once we were inside the house, and her socks were dark green with strawberries on them. I felt relieved at that child's touch, since her tan trousers and checked blouse looked as if they might have been Burberry. Her hair was thicker now, and longer, but she still had bangs. I watched her eyes flit around and take the room in, and my heart was as nervous as if I'd been on a blind date. I felt awkward and inadequate standing alone in the middle of our rather plain guest room, and I wanted to measure up. Finally her eyes landed on me. '*Atsui ne,*' she said. It's hot. '*Kigaetara?*' I answered without having to think. How about changing clothes? 'Nn,' she said with a nod and a smile, and I saw her again. There she was. My heart exhaled.

We traded places as she came into the room to lift her suitcase onto the bed. I couldn't think of how to say what I wanted to in Japanese, so I told her, 'Come to Hadley and PJ's room when you're finished.' Yuki dug in her bag and then looked over at me with a bright pair of shorts in each hand. I watched her intelligence emerge through the polite veneer as her mind sifted through what I had just said. Finally she said, 'Excuse me?' in such a comically thick accent that I could tell she was making fun of both of us. I giggled as I mentally tipped my hat. 'Afterwards over here,' I said in Japanese, pointing in exaggerated dumb show in the direction of my kids' room, and she said, 'OK,' with a big cheesy thumbs-up. She looked back down at her shorts and when I left the room she was shifting from hip to hip in a little which-one-should-I-wear? dance. She was happy. I didn't know what she'd been through since I'd left her at Junko's house – what Emi had been able to protect her from, or any of what she'd felt – but at that moment, at our reunion in my house, she was happy.

270

At lunchtime our efforts to converse were like popcorn heating up in a pan. We started and stopped, started and stopped, and then suddenly everyone was talking. Porter tried to engage Yoshi on his work, and I wanted to listen, but Emi asked me if I was going to take up nursing again. Ai-chan started commenting on everything, even the bamboo-print wallpaper, so Emi interpreted what she was saying for me while PJ announced that he had mixed the pasta salad himself. Hadley asked Yuki if she played a musical instrument, and I wished I could say it in Japanese to help out, but I had to drag Emi's attention away from Ai-chan in order to get the question asked.

After a little while we settled into eating and passing things around the table, but now and then someone would pipe up with a comment that got everyone popping for a while, and then we'd settle again, wondering how to speak in a way that most people would comprehend. Porter asked everyone, slowly and deliberately, if they wanted to go to the beach in the afternoon, and I saw Yuki understand before Emi had interpreted it. Yuki asked in Japanese if the water would be cold, and I told her in Japanese that it wouldn't. Maybe I answered grammatically, maybe I didn't, I don't know, but no one corrected me, and Yuki understood. Porter flashed me a smile of congratulations; he knew what it meant to me to be in conversation with Yuki. Yoshi cleared his throat, and Emi looked over at him immediately, so I knew she had a sense for the different types of husbandly throat-clearing that is the cousin of the sense for the meaning of one's infant's cries. She seemed to have matured a lot in the years since I'd last seen her. She seemed steadier, both more confident and more generous. I looked at Yoshi as well. The kids' forks clicked against their bowls as they speared their penne and their slivers of ham. Yoshi held up his glass of beer and silence fell.

'We are very grateful,' he said in his sonorous, thickly accented voice, looking first at me, then at Porter. 'Thank you. *Domo arigatou gozaimasu.*'

Porter and I exhaled our 'You're very welcome', and our 'Thank *you* for coming', raising our glasses too and, I hope, drowning out the way Hadley was leaning over and whispering to me, 'What is beddy grateful?'

After lunch, Yoshi stayed in the kitchen to drink some more beer and help Porter with the dishes, and PJ and Ai-chan played with fat Lego bricks on the floor by the living room coffee table. Only a few hours into the visit and Hadley was already idolising Yuki, not only because Yuki was an older child but also because she had made a floppy origami frog out of Hadley's paper napkin. So Hadley was at the coffee table drawing Yuki a picture as a token of her devotion.

Yuki was walking slowly around the living room looking at every single thing in it, turning one of my Japanese wooden dolls in her hands, holding a large cowrie shell up to her ear. When she came to my favourite photo of Porter and the kids and me, taken during a visit from my parents, she exclaimed, 'I want to do this!' in Japanese. In the photo we're in the ocean. I have Hadley on my shoulders and Porter has PJ on his and we're in the middle of a game of chicken. Porter and I had actually had a disagreement about the right time to put sunscreen on the kids that morning – I didn't think he was taking the sun seriously enough, especially where the extra-vulnerable skin of our children was concerned – but all I have to do is look at that photo and I know that we really agree about taking care of them. Hadley and PJ are stretching their arms out towards each other, ostensibly to destabilise each other, but both Porter and I know that neither of them really likes toppling into the choppy turquoise water yet. We know that they're actually reaching out to each other for balance. So no matter how much Porter or I feel like winning the game, we only pretend to struggle, pretend that one child is stronger, and then the other, pretend to lose our balance, and then fall over slowly, dramatically enough to give them a thrill, but carefully enough to give them time to hold their noses before they go under.

Emi said, 'Good idea!'

As Emi and I were alone on the sofa bed, I took the opportunity to ask Emi a quiet question.

'May I show Yuki a photo of her and me?'

Emi said, 'Of course.'

'Oh good. I was wondering . . . I mean, I don't know how much she knows about what happened.' I still hate raising difficult subjects, so I hadn't asked about her memories in an email before their arrival. If I wanted to show Yuki a picture of us, though, I had to know.

'She doesn't remember the time with her father,' Emi said. 'Don't talk about that.'

'Of course.'

'But don't worry. You can show her the photo.'

She was about to say something else but I was suddenly emotional and stood up to go to the bookcase between the windows. I felt winded, disoriented by how breezily and yet so definitively she'd said that Yuki didn't remember the period when I was in Japan. Of course I knew that Yuki didn't feel about me the way she had nine years before, that was obvious, but I'd harboured the hope that something of our time together had stuck. I wanted a moment alone to come to terms with what Emi had said, but I told myself to carry on because there was more reason than ever to show her a photo of us. I pulled out my Japan album and leafed through it until I got to the photo Porter had taken of me with Yuki on my hip inside the Edo Tokyo Museum – one of only three photos I have of us together. Heart pounding, I brought it over to Yuki, turning the album towards her and pointing. I didn't say anything, just let her take the photo in. Emi joined us to look at it as well, and I waited until Yuki looked up at me. She looked down again, and then back at me. '*Kore, anata desu ka?*' she asked me. Is this you?

'*Hai*,' I said. '*Yuki-chan to.*' With Yuki-chan.

She nodded, studying the photo again.

'Do you remember me?' came out of my mouth.

Yuki looked at Emi, who asked the question in Japanese.

'No,' she said in English with a cheerful smile, which was confusing and awful, and then she said something else in Japanese.

Emi interpreted: 'Yuki says, "I don't remember you, but I know who you are."'

That was enough for me. More than enough. I felt a little dizzy and I needed to sit down. Yuki started turning the pages of my album, and then I understood her to say, 'What about our album?' to Emi.

'Wait a moment,' Emi said to me. I returned to the sofa bed. Emi laid her suitcase flat to unzip it and pulled out a

274

large photo album, which she brought to me. 'We made this for you,' she said, and I thanked her in astonishment. Emi sat down on my left and Yuki sat on the other side of Emi, but after I'd looked at a few pages of photos of Yuki growing up, she got up and came to sit on my right, leaning in closer to point to one of the upstairs windows of their house. Now we were shoulder to shoulder and thigh to thigh. 'This is my room,' she said, very deliberately, as if she'd been practising. Porter came into the living room drying his hands on a dishcloth, looking like he was about to say 'How's everybody doing?', but when his eyes found mine he closed his mouth and his bright smile softened. Emi pointed to the plants on the front steps of their house and said, 'Those are Ai-chan's project,' and I laughed, and blinked, and a pair of tears splashed onto the back of Emi's hand, startling her. 'Oh!' she said, and then she put her arm around me and I tried not to cry, but I felt Yuki patting my back and I couldn't help it. Yoshi asked Emi if I was OK from over by Porter, and I felt Emi nod. Ai-chan asked really loudly why I was sad. PJ was oblivious. Only Hadley was clearly worried and came to stand in front of me with her hands on my knees. There was crayon under her fingernails, which meant they needed trimming. I'd need to do that before we went to the beach. 'I'm happy, honey,' I said, and lifted my arms up and brought them down around her and Yuki, locking my hands together, crushing them to me, laughing-crying, sniffing and sighing into their hair.

ACKNOWLEDGEMENTS

I am indebted to Alan Hodges for having invited me to Japan 25 years ago; to my mother, who kept all my letters from my eight years there; and to Linda, who shared her experiences with me. The ever-patient prodding of Barney Karpfinger gave me the courage to open Diana up. Editors Eleanor Birne, Mark Richards and Becky Walsh provided guidance of many sizes and depths. Tat Small, Andrea Lee, Chris Huntington, Jane Massey, Valerie Lester, Maura Harvey and Junko Watanabe read various drafts and gave me invaluable advice and energy. Chris Wells was always available when I needed a Tokyo fact checked. Andrew Gurnett was, as ever, reader, sounding board, consoler, cajoler, sine qua non.

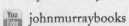
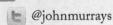
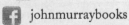